THE STUD

'I don't want to sound conceited, but imagine a taller Tony Curtis with a touch of Michael Caine and Kris Kristofferson.'

Handsome Tony Blake – regarded by the girls as a sexual athlete, host at the most famous discotheque in the world. Thanks to Mrs Fontaine Khaled wife of the famous billionaire. She collects men as other women collect jewels. Anyone looking for 'pot, booze, or birds' could apply to Tony – if they could get near him.

Then he met Fontaine's seventeen-year-old stepdaughter and realized that there was a lot more to life than his benefactor had to offer . . .

Also by Jackie Collins in *Star*

LOVEHEAD
THE WORLD IS FULL OF MARRIED MEN
THE WORLD IS FULL OF DIVORCED WOMEN

THE STUD

Jackie Collins

A STAR BOOK
published by
the Paperback Division of
W. H. ALLEN & Co. Ltd.

A Star Book
Published in 1977, reprinted 1978
by the Paperback Division of W. H. Allen & Co. Ltd.
A Howard and Wyndham Company
44 Hill Street, London W1X 8LB

First published in Great Britain by
W. H. Allen & Co. Ltd, 1969

Mayflower edition published 1970
Mayflower edition reprinted 1970 (twice), 1971, 1972, 1973, 1975

Copyright © Jackie Collins 1969

Printed in Great Britain by
Richard Clay (The Chaucer Press) Ltd
Bungay, Suffolk

ISBN 0 352 39562 1

For O.L.

ONE

TONY

There is something very exciting about the beginning of the evening—well, the beginning of my evening, usually about ten-thirty, eleven o'clock. Every night at 'Hobo' is like a party—a great party where everyone knows and likes everyone else.

They start coming in slowly. First the ones that want to be sure of a good table, then the watchers. Usually this whole group is stacked neatly out of the way on the wrong side of the room, or if they are really rough, in the back room. We've got a closed membership, but a few manage to find their way in. Then everyone sits around waiting for the swingers, and about twelve-thirty, one o'clock, they start arriving. Golden-haired girls in cowboy suits, Indian gear, boots, backless topless skirtless see-through dresses. The wilder the better. Their escorts varying from the long-haired mob of rock groups to the latest young actors. Elegant young debs in full evening dress, with chinless-wonder escorts. The older society group. The rich Greeks. The rich Arabs. An odd movie star—an odd M.P. or visiting senator. Anybody famous who's in town. Young writers, dress designers, photographers, models. They all come to look and be looked at, and to see their friends. It's like a building excitement—reaching a breathless climax at around two a.m. when the room is so jammed you couldn't get anyone else in except maybe Frank Sinatra, and Mick Jagger.

It seems ridiculous that six months ago they would hand me a couple of quid and wouldn't recognise me if we passed in the street. Now they couldn't wait to grab hold of me— 'Dahling'—kiss—kiss—kiss—'Who's here tonight?' Sly grab if the boy-friend or husband wasn't looking. 'Please don't give us a lousy table like last time'—affectionate squeeze and promising look. Then husband or boy-friend steps forward— firm handshake, few masculine chummy words, and I hand them over to Franco, swinging head-waiter supreme, who whisks them off to whatever table their position rates. The watchers on one side of the room, the doers on the other. All very neat, the squares with the bread tucked firmly away in the back room.

Yeah, I'm very popular now, everyone wants to know. Funny thing, isn't it? I'm the same guy, talk in the same voice, the clothes are a little more expensive but that's about the only difference. You wouldn't believe it though, the ladies practically fight to climb in the sack with me. You would think I was doing them a big favour, and listen, the way things have been going I think I am! I tell you it's a great life if you don't weaken.

I suppose you're wondering how this all came about, how a guy like me, Tony Shwartsburg from somewhere near the Elephant and Castle, turned into Tony Blake—man about town, friend of the stars, host at the most 'in' discothèque, 'Hobo'. I have exchanged confidences such as 'Where can we get some pot?' and 'Got any birds?' with some of the most famous in the land. 'Tony can arrange anything' is a well-known catch phrase around town.

Well, to begin with I had the same useless tough life as most of the kids in my neighbourhood—fighting in the back streets, watching in on the fights at home. My parents, Sadie and Sam, were a nice old Jewish couple who hated each other. Sam couldn't care less about me, but to Sadie the sun shone out of my left ear. 'Learn a trade like your cousin Leon,' she would say, 'let the family be proud of you.' I got laid at thirteen, just before I got barmitzvahed. If the family knew they'd sure as old harry be proud of me. It was all good clean fun. The girl, she was a few years older than me, gave me the crabs, and I spent about six months alternatively trying to get rid of them and passing them on to any girl who got lucky! Eventually I passed them on to the wrong girl and everyone found out. Sadie had hysterics and Sam patted me on the back and bought me some ointment.

At sixteen I got caught pinching petrol from a car. It was a good racket while it lasted. You hosed it out into a can, and sold it back to the garage where it had probably come from in the first place! Anyway, they shoved me on probation and that was the end of my criminal tendencies.

I got a variety of jobs, delivering papers, sweeping up in a factory, usher in the local cinema—I got fired from that when the manager found me making it with a bird in the back row of the stalls. It was his best usherette and he was screwing her at the same time, so he was a bit choked. Unfortunately I knocked her up and there was a family scandal, but seeing the manager wanted her back, as good usherettes were hard to

8

come by, he paid for her to get unknocked up and everything was all right.

By this time Sadie and Sam were getting a bit fed up with me, and who could blame them? Sam stopped screaming at Sadie and started on me. It was a good job someone thought of Uncle Bernie.

Uncle Bernie was the success of the family. He owned two delicatessens and had sort of cut himself off from the rest of his clan. Anyway Sadie felt that as she was his only sister he owed her a favour, and she dragged me down to his place in Great Portland Street and insisted he gave me a job. He wasn't too thrilled at the prospect, but knowing he wasn't going to get rid of Sadie any other way, he agreed. He had a daughter, Muriel, a big strapping girl with lots of thick black hair—everywhere—you name a place, Muriel had thick black hair there. She wasn't bad apart from that, a bit sexy looking. Big tits and a thin crooked nose. I suppose I shouldn't have, I mean she was my cousin and all, but one day the opportunity arose, and if the opportunity arises who am I to put it down? Of course Uncle Bernie found out and there ended my career in a delicatessen. It was all too much for Sadie, and even Sam wasn't too pleased about it all.

Life at the Elephant was becoming a drag anyway, and having got as far as Great Portland Street, I thought why not go a bit further. I got a job as a dishwasher at the Savoy, and a room in Camden Town. Life was great. I entered my twenties a happy man.

I met a girl, Evie, a pretty curly-haired blonde, she was a hostess at a clip joint. She fixed me up a job as a waiter and I discovered the world of tips. It was great, taught me a lot about people. Taught me the right way to milk a pound from a drunk whose intention was to leave nothing. I was making twenty quid a week. I branched out to striped Italian suits and pointed shoes, then dated girls with a bit more class, hairdressers, shop assistants and all that group. Not bad, I felt like a king! Visited the Elephant on Sundays, and handed Sadie a fiver. Of course she never took it, she always came out with a speech about how I should save my money, settle down, look for a nice Jewish girl and get married, be like cousin Leon—in my opinion a real schmuck.

I left the clip joint and started as a busboy in a high-class restaurant, not so much bread but a road to better things. And the better things were all around me. The birds that came into the place. Beautiful! Furs, jewellery, expensive smells.

From there I became a waiter in another high-class place and I became involved with Penny, daughter of the owner. Penny was something else. Red hair, she was very neat, small and compact. I suppose I fell in love with her. Couldn't make it, that was probably why. Looking back on it now, I reckon she was undersexed, but at the time it bothered me a lot. She was the first girl that I had wanted and couldn't have.

I don't want to sound conceited, but imagine a taller Tony Curtis with a touch of Michael Caine and Kris Kristofferson.

Anyway Penny and I wanted to get married. Her father of course was furious, but she got round him and since he didn't want his daughter marrying a waiter he opened a new place and put me in charge—sort of a de luxe head-waiter.

It all started there. That's where I first saw Fontaine.

Of course everyone's heard of Fontaine Khaled, she's sort of like a national institution, though not so old—around thirty-five I would say, even now I still don't know the truth.

Fontaine looks very haughty upper-class English. Beautiful, of course, with chiselled cut bones (by nature or cosmetic surgery no one knows), a fine parchment skin, an angular boney body which lends itself to fancy clothes, and long blonde hair worn pulled back.

When I first saw her I couldn't take my eyes off. Here was a lady. Sounds corny I know, but there was no mistaking the fact. She had been a world famous photographic model, and had retired to marry Benjamin Al Khaled, billionaire. She was always in the papers, jetting here there and everywhere, showing us around her house in Acapulco, her castle in Spain, her town house in London or penthouse in New York.

I read the columns a lot. In my business it's always good to know who's who, so as soon as she came in I knew it was her. She was with three men and two women all of the same social scene but not in the same class as her. I led them to their table personally, a thing I had stopped doing when I took over the place. I even referred to her by name just to let her know I was around. But she didn't give me a glance. So much for the instant impact of Tony Blake.

There was no Benjamin Al Khaled with her, and I didn't think she was anyone's date, very square the fellows with her, typical no balls types, with loud public school voices.

She was wearing what I thought was a rabbit coat, but later I discovered during a course of intensified education that it was chinchilla. I thought I was pretty hip then, but I didn't even know a Gucci handbag from a Marks & Sparks.

I hovered around the table a lot, but not so much as a look.

I eavesdropped, 'St Moritz is becoming a terrible bore'—'Did you know Jamie broke his leg in Tibet?'—'Do you *believe* St Laurent this year?'

Pretty dull snatches of conversation came my way.

The one that paid the bill left a nothing tip.

Two nights later she was back, this time with her husband. He was much older than her. They were with another old guy. She threw me a brief smile on her way in, which startled me, and after that they came in a lot, whenever they weren't flying round the world.

Penny was causing me problems. Since her father had promoted me, so to speak, I was having a fair amount of success. Customers liked me, I remembered their names, saw their food was just right, and became casually friendly with some of them. The place developed a good reputation, people were disappointed if I wasn't there. They liked to be greeted by name and made to feel important.

Penny's father realised I was good for the joint and I realised Penny was no good for me. It was not a good situation. She started to get very narky and jealous, accusing me of all sorts of things, which were true. Well, I don't know if she thought I was jerking off or what, but I certainly wasn't getting any action from her. I moved to a small one-roomed flat off the Edgware Road and she caught me there one day with a red-haired croupier—female of course!

What tears and scenes! She even offered me her virginity, but by that time, I didn't even fancy it. So we parted bad friends.

Needless to say it was a matter of time before her father and I also parted company. I had my eyes wide open for another job. By that time I had had the waiter bit, I wanted to move up in the world, progress. The ideal situation would be to get my own little place, but for that one needed bread, and who had any?

I cast my eyes around and one memorable night they met squarely with Fontaine's. It was one of those looks, her cool aquamarine eyes clashed straight on with my moody dark stare (many's the bird who's told me I've got a moody dark stare) and that was it. We both knew something had to give.

She went to the powder-room shortly after and I was waiting when she came out.

'Tony,' she said, she had a deep very English clipped accent, 'you're wasting yourself here—why don't you drop by and see me tomorrow, I have an idea that maybe you can help me with.' She handed me a small hand-engraved card with her address and added, 'About three o'clock will be fine.'

I nodded dumbly, to tell you the truth I was a bit knocked out by the whole thing.

I must have changed my outfit ten times the next day—was a casual look best or should I go for the slightly formal Italian gear? I finally settled for a pale lilac shirt with a stiff white collar, and a black silk suit.

I arrived half-an-hour early at this knockout pad she had in Belgravia. It was too much! I found out it was an ex-embassy. They even had a swimming pool.

A butler settled me down in what I suppose was the living-room, but it turned out to be a mere waiting-room. It was all expensive with crazy carved furniture and jazzy old pictures on the wall. Some of them were rather sexy—there was one with three birds and one guy that was a bit strong, but just when I was studying it a bit closer Fontaine came in. 'Are you interested in art, Tony?' she asked. She looked great in a long sort of silk robe and her hair all loose.

Man, I can still remember how nervous I was. This was class, this was real class.

'Let's go in the study,' she said. 'Would you care for a drink?'

I asked for a sherry, I figured it was the thing to have.

'You don't look like a sherry man to me,' she said, her eyes cool and amused.

I started to get excited there and then, and in the tight black trousers I was wearing, this was no joke. I approached her warily, she didn't back away, in fact she came towards me. I put my arms around her, she was tall, I could feel her bones through the thin robe. She fastened her arms about my neck and pulled my mouth on to hers.

It was some kiss, she was like a hungry animal pushing and probing with her tongue, biting and sighing. I think I can safely say I gave back as good as I got.

'Let's go upstairs,' she said at last, and added, 'It's all right, Benjamin is away.'

I followed her to a small elevator and we pressed closely together as it started up. She unzipped my trousers and rubbed me with her long fingers. Man, I was ready to shoot off there and then!

Suddenly the elevator stopped and she shrugged off her robe. I stared at her lean body. She had tiny breasts with pale extended nipples. 'Are we there?' I asked foolishly.

'No, but we soon could be,' she replied pulling at my trousers.

The elevator was small, gave you a touch of the claustrophobia, but she managed to get me down to my bare skin.

I must say in all my dealings with birds I've never had one behave like *this*.

'Tony, you come up to all my expectations,' she muttered. 'Sit down, I'll show you how to do it in a lift.'

Oh man! What an experience! Thinking back I didn't get a chance to do much because she did everything. Of course I rose to the occasion magnificently. Really I was out of my depth and knew it. I just let her have her way, I wasn't going to blow this set-up. She dug her nails deep into my back and twisted her long white legs around me. She didn't moan or cry out. She muttered, 'Screw me you bastard, keep it hard.'

Well, I'd never had any problem doing *that*.

Afterwards she was all calm and businesslike. She stood up and put her robe on. She waited for me to struggle into my clothes, then the elevator took us back to the study.

I was destroyed. I flopped into a chair. She rang a bell, and the butler appeared with tea.

She chatted away in her high-class tinkly voice and who would have thought that half-an-hour earlier she'd been frothing and raving about in the elevator.

'I want to open a discothèque,' she said, 'something different, something chic, somewhere to go that's fun—something mad and exclusive.'

'Yes?' I was all interest. Here came my big chance.

'You could manage something like that, couldn't you?'

She chatted on about how there was nowhere to go that was chic. 'All these places now are filled with scruffy little nothings —don't you think this town needs something different—somewhere for grown-ups like Paris has, or Rome?'

Her line of chat killed me. Somewhere for grown-ups yet! However I nodded seriously. I was looking for an out from the restaurant—this could be it.

'You start looking for premises, Tony,' she said, 'money's no problem. My husband will finance the whole thing. We'll pay

13

you fifty pounds a week and five per cent of the profits. How's that? Of course you'll be running the whole show, does it appeal to you?'

Did it appeal to me? Yes sir, it definitely appealed to me.

She stood up, smoothing her robe down. 'I have to get dressed now. Start looking and keep in touch.' She turned at the door. 'Oh, Tony, in the lift, that was nice, very nice, let's do it again soon.' Then in the same cool voice she added. 'The butler will show you out.'

It was all too much. This was a real cool lady and a raver to boot. I had a feeling I'd fallen in the right direction.

I set to work, started getting up early in the mornings and hanging around the estate agents, saw a lot of lousy joints. I had a feeling for what she wanted (ha ha) and I kept right on looking until I found it. It was a rooftop restaurant that had gone bust—bad neighbourhood everyone said, impossible to park—but baby, you get the right doorman and nowhere's impossible. To me, it was just right. Not too big, not too small. Different, because instead of creeping down to some cellar you went up and you had windows and a view. I called Fontaine right away, and she came gliding over with a chauffeur in a Silver Cloud Rolls. She loved it too. We were in business.

We had tea at Fortnums. I hadn't seen her since the day at her house. She was wearing a silver mink coat and hat, and everyone turned to take another look. She stared at me with those cool eyes and I knew the look. 'Benjamin's home,' she said, 'but I have another place.'

'Well, let's go,' I said, gulping down dainty tea sandwiches and feeling pretty good.

She dismissed the chauffeur and we took a cab to a small apartment building in Chelsea. It was one room luxury, a big bed covered in white fur, rugs, mirrors everywhere, louvred shutters to remove the daylight and red-tinged lights. A few erotic pictures on the wall, a lot of dirty books in a built-in bookcase next to the bed.

'This is my whore's room,' she said with a small tight smile. I didn't know what to say, I'd never met anyone like her before. She took off her clothes and stretched out on the bed. I fumbled with mine, I mean, well, I was embarrassed!

I finally got them off and started some action. She just lay there very stiff, smiling slightly. Very different from the last time. It was rather exciting really, took me off guard so to speak, I mean, I was expecting it to be like the last time. It didn't take me long before I was through—wowee! I rolled off her and studied our bodies in the mirrored ceiling.

She said very slowly, 'Tony—how would you like to learn to be a good lover?'

I sat up on one elbow and stared at her. Was she kidding? I mean I was all there you know, I'd never been lacking in *that* department.

As it happens, looking back on it now, I suppose she did teach me a lot. Little tricks she'd picked up in Beirut, Tangier, South America. You name it, she knew it. She was a great teacher, very detailed. I grew to look forward to our little classes more than anything. Of course I was knocking off another bird on the side. Fontaine didn't know about it, but it was useful, gave me a chance to do my homework so I'd be in good shape for Fontaine.

Lana was a stripper, a bit of a scrubber but a knockout when it came to practising my lessons. In fact, she added a few ideas of her own. She had the best pair of knockers around, a big full juicy bird. I mean Fontaine was very classy and all that jazz, but a bit lacking in the tits and ass department, a man likes his steak rare, but he needs his bread and potatoes too.

Life was really good. I left the restaurant and started organising the new place. Interior decorators, waiters to find, members' lists, ordering stock. There were a million and one things to do. Fontaine chose the name, 'Hobo'. It was good, although Benjamin offered the suggestion of calling it 'Fontaine's'. She said that would be tasteless and vulgar. She was right, she was usually right.

And so eventually we opened. Big party, lots of publicity, all the right people. They all came, they always turn out in bulk for anything free. Fontaine personally supervised the guest list and I think that's what started the whole thing off, her guest list. It was such a wild mixture—from rock groups to movie stars to high society to hookers (international ones of course!). It was great. It all just happened, and within a few weeks 'Hobo' was *the* place and all of a sudden I was *the* person to know. It's wild really, I still sort of expect the bubble to burst. But here I am, Tony Blake—ex-nothing, ex-waiter, now great host, lover and friend of the stars.

Great me!

TWO

FONTAINE

I have always enjoyed waking late and breakfasting in bed. Benjamin says it's because bed is my favourite place. He's right actually. He gets up at the unearthly hour of seven a.m., so I lie awake with my eyes closed and listen to him cough and belch and fart! Delightful! Benjamin Al Khaled in the mornings—I wonder what the society gossip columns would make of an exclusive like that! I've begged him for separate bedrooms but that's one thing he won't surrender to. He likes his nightly ashes hauled, and maybe in the middle of the night too if he feels like it. So the communal bedroom stays. It's worth it, he's very very rich. Even I don't know how many millions. He's sixty-one years old and randy as hell.

Bed is delicious. I can lie here and think and relax and not have to do anything. At eleven my maid wakes me. She brings breakfast and the papers, runs my bath and lays out the clothes I tell her to. I can have anything I want. Benjamin will give me anything except actual cash.

We have been married for five years and both of us were married before. His ex-wife is a bitch. Plain and dreary with two hulking great children by him— Alexandra and Ben junior. My ex-husband is somewhere in California now, basking in the sun on the money that Benjamin had to pay him to agree to a divorce. Paul was always lazy. When we were married he never did a stroke of work, just lived off my hard-earned modelling money. He was rather beautiful though, and very virile. It was a shame to have to divorce him, but I was bored with modelling, and one doesn't grow any younger, and there was Benjamin offering me a title and all that divine money. Well, really I had no choice.

Being married to Benjamin is rather like a part-time job. He works so hard and travels so much that I hardly ever see him. That's why he said I could do the discothèque, somewhere for me to go, 'a little interest' as he calls it. 'Little interest' indeed. It's making a fortune! Benjamin would have a fit if he knew, he hates me to have any money of my own. I think he thinks it would make me independent of him. Isn't that silly? As if I would be independent of three or four million.

Benjamin thinks I'm faithful to him. He told me. He thinks that if I'm well looked after at home I won't want any more. For a man of sixty-one he's really very naïve, especially since he's away half the time. As if I could be satisfied with that withered old thing!

Fortunately I have arranged my life rather well, and I have occasional exciting affairs. In London the current one is Tony. He's really rather divine. Very obvious looking, but tremendously sexual. Tall and strong, he has a body rippling with hidden muscles, and a black hairy chest which is *very* exciting. His face is an open invitation to bed. What an innocent he was when I got hold of him, and look at him now. Of course, basically he'll always be a head-waiter, but I think I've improved him beyond recognition.

The first time was a disaster. Of course he had an animal charm, a sexy walk, but that was about all. In bed he had a marvellous body, but he had no idea, no skill. For someone so well endowed it was a shame. I thought to myself, he is very attractive in a basic way. If he appeals to me he would probably appeal to lots of women. That's why I decided to use him in the discothèque. I needed someone, and as it turned out he's just the right person. Of course I know he's having an affair with everyone in sight now, including my best friend Vanessa. He thinks I don't suspect. Isn't that silly? I mean I don't mind a bit, but of course I must pretend not to know, pretend a little touch of jealousy, otherwise his manly pride would be hurt. Vanessa and I laugh about it, 'Tony the stud' we call him. It's great fun comparing notes. He thinks he's the best lover in the world. He's not bad, but if he wasn't so well endowed he would be disastrous. Poor conceited Tony.

I'll never forget the first time he came to see me at my house. The clothes he had on—unbelievable! A cheap black silk suit with trousers so tight his pecker shone through like a beacon! I decided I had to take a look. Benjamin was away, so I took him in my lift and enjoyed him there. Well, I mean to say there is nothing more dreary than always doing it on a bed. When I got his clothes off I thought 'not bad', but after it was all over I knew there was a lot to teach him.

The best lover I ever had was this great black zulu. I was doing a swimsuit lay-out for one of the glossies deep in the heart of nowhere—and we took a break for a cigarette and he grabbed me behind a tree and gave it to me quickly. Delicious!

17

I'll never forget it, his timing was perfect, he brought me to the most beautiful climax ever! Unfortunately he moved to a new location the next day and I never saw him again. I often think about him, usually when Benjamin is sprawled on top of me huffing and puffing.

Vanessa says Tony is awed by me! Can you imagine! I suppose it's being married to a billionaire and everything. Rather useful, brings people to their knees, lots of respect and all that. Fame, money and titles that's all people really care about.

I don't want children. What for? They ruin your figure, give you a lot of boring trouble, and then leave you. I don't need children, I don't have what I suppose is called the maternal instinct. Personally, I like being free. My God, my mother never gained any advantages by having me. A woman should be strong, I've seen too many marriages fail because the wife was weak. Vanessa has three children and she never sees them. They live with their nanny on the fourth floor and she never goes up there. They might as well be in Siberia. Isn't that silly? She doesn't look too bad, a bit saggy. Saved by that pretty pretty face. One day I'm going to tell Tony I know about him and Vanessa. He'll have a fit! He thinks he's being so clever. He's like a little boy, hates being found out. I don't care, as long as he's got enough left for me he can do what he likes. He's really an idiot, a sexy idiot stud! It's that lower class mentality of his, he'll never change. He's useful though, definitely worth keeping on the leash. And so eager to learn. Always asking me where my bag came from, and what perfume was I wearing, and who made my clothes.

Think I'll give him a call, pop in before the hairdresser ...

THREE

TONY

Tonight's going to be good. Two big parties in town and every-one will be coming along after. Fontaine nearly caught me today. Fast asleep in bed with this bird—Jànet something or other, and her ladyship phones. 'I'm coming over.' Charming! Wake up Janet, she complains, horrible whiney voice, long sloppy black hair, ugh! I must have been well stoned. She struggles complaining into a dress hardly long enough to cover her ass, nice ass. I shove her out the front door, five minutes later Fontaine comes wafting in. I hardly had time to hide the sheets!

Sometimes she's like a witch, very cold. 'I have to go to the hairdresser,' she announces, stepping out of her Rhavis skirt, Gucci shoes and Dior stockings. At times I hate her, I'm not a machine. She remains standing with her suit jacket still on, her hair hidden in a mink turban. She leans obscenely against the wall. She wants it standing up. I think of her husband. Poor guy, he's working his ass off while she's handing out the action. Never trust a woman that's what I always say. She looks like a high fashion model top half and a dirty photo-graph bottom half. The thought excites me and I manage to accommodate her. Oh man, I can imagine the scene if she'd caught me this morning!

She dresses briskly, her legs are getting thinner, she diets too much. 'I'll see you tonight,' she says zipping up her skirt, 'keep my table for seven—we have a French diplomat and his wife with us.' Then she was gone, leaving a cloud of Hermes 'Caleche'.

It was a good thing when it all started. The Fontaine Khaled and all that jazz. But she's kinky, she's definitely kinky and I don't want to be used the way she uses me. Her whore's room and her strange preferences. What about her old man? He must be a right idiot. Now I've got all the crumpet I want. High class crumpet galore. But she's got me by the balls. 'Hobo' is hers, if I want out of screwing her then I'm out, period. It's not really fair. I built the whole place up, worked my ass off until five every morning, and all I get is fifty lousy quid a week. Peanuts to what the joint is making—and I've yet to see my share of the profits. I have no contract, nothing. I just work for her. She's a pretty cool bitch—a pretty clever bitch.

'Franco, bring me a scotch.' Franco's a great head-waiter. Probably I could grab him if I left here and opened up somewhere else. But with what? I've got no bread. People have offered to back me in a new place—women—it would be the same scene all over again. What I was casting my eye around for was a guy to promote a new joint, one of the rich Greeks would do. Got one in mind, but I'll have to play it cool, make it seem like his idea.

'Hallo, Tony darling.' This bird threw her arms round me, I swear I'd never seen her before.

'How are you?' I said beaming with pleasure, winking. The well-known Blake charm churned forth.

'I'm fine, this is Chicky and this is Robin and this is Henry.' Three nonentities strained forward to give me greetings. The evening was starting.

There are certain regulars who always congregate at the top table. It's called the top table 'cos it's at the top of the room in the best position for seeing everything, and it's where I sit, when I sit, which is about twice a night. I always make sure it's available for any visiting celebrities in case there's nowhere else. The regulars can always be shuffled around. If I have a date she sits there. Oh, I'm allowed to have dates as long as it's not the same girl too often. After all, they just sit there by themselves all night.

The regulars are all guys, a varied selection, my friends. There's Sammy—small, wiry, dark-haired. A hat manufacturer —crumpet mad—always chatting up different birds. Likes them tall. I should really get him and Fontaine together, but she thinks he's revolting and he says she's a rich old bag. Any female over twenty is an old bag to him. Sammy's a sweet guy, but a lot of people don't understand him.

Then there's Franklin, quiet, young, good-looking and shy. Sits there drinking Coca-Cola all night. We all reckon he's a virgin.

Next Hal—an American promoter, constantly stoned, a wow with rich old widows. Fortyish, attractive if you like the Dean Martin type. He has a big heart, every bit of honest bread he makes he sends to his kid brother in New Jersey and that's the only thing he doesn't brag about.

Lastly, Massey, a singer. Good-looking in that special

way spades have. Great dancer.

When there's nothing better to do and if none of us have dates, we sit there and discuss the talent. 'I'd like to screw that!' is a constant cry from our table.

Fontaine hates them all. 'Why do you always have that motley group around?' she questions. But they pay, so there's nothing she can do. They all suspect about Fontaine and me, but no one actually knows. I like the regulars, they're a good group of guys.

Franklin came in first tonight. With a girl, surprise, surprise. His father is a big guy in the film business. The bird he was with was definitely too hot for him, probably thought he'd put in a good word with dad. She had those pouty lips and jaded eyes that all would-be movie stars have. Too much screwing and not enough fresh air! Franklin was treating her like a lady, all proper and polite. He's a nice kid, but a schmuck. Treat them rough if you want to lay them. She had lots of long thick reddish hair and she gave me the well-known come on look.

'Janine James—Tony Blake,' Franklin said, 'Janine's over here doing a film.'

'Hi,' she simpered. Ugh, American broads turn me off, that horrible nasal twang. I gave her my angry knowing stare, that usually gets them. She responded with what I took to be a sexy look. Poor Franklin, he didn't have a chance with this one.

The next of the regulars to bounce in was Sammy, friendly, Cockney, pussy-crazy Sammy. As luck would have it he had no date, and he immediately launched into a line of chat with Janine. Franklin sat silently, I could see it was going to be one of those nights.

Fontaine's usual table was next to ours. I had explained to her a hundred times that she couldn't have the top table because it was the only table that could be made easily available in an emergency. This bugged her, but she settled for the next best. After all, she certainly wasn't there every night. Maybe six nights in a row then not at all for two or three weeks while she was on her travels. The places she went made me dizzy. Benjamin had his own private jet which was useful. She never came in with less than five or six people. She had this girl-friend Vanessa, blonde, pretty, a bit plump, but with huge bouncy knockers. Married to the son of the owner of a very famous chain store. Worth a fortune. Got three kids. Vanessa was a mess. She idolised Fontaine and copied her faithfully. It was only fair that I should knock her off. She practically begged me. I went to her house one afternoon while hubby was at the office and the kids were out with nanny. I don't think she knows about me and Fontaine, anyway she promised she wouldn't tell anybody about us. I hope to God she doesn't. It's all very risky. Anyway she's a lousy lay, but these unbelievable tits! I could just stay playing with them for hours, they smother you, all big and soft, very mumsy. Vanessa is usually in Fontaine's group with or without hubby who isn't bad—a lot better than Benjamin. I hear he's got a girl tucked away in a neat little flat. In my business you get to hear most things.

Fontaine and party made the grand entrance about one-thirty. She was covered in white mink to the ground. Her hair was piled high and secured with the gleam of diamonds. Husband was by her side, shorter than her and fat. She looked fantastic. Who would have thought that in the morning she had been leaning against my bedroom wall with her pubics on show! I had an insane desire to shout out—'I've had that!' but instead I went into the whole greeting routing. All the kisses and nice to see you's and all that bull shit. Vanessa and hubby were naturally present. She looked her usual pretty mess. Whispy hair, boobies flopping in a chiffon dress. I gave her an unseen tweak on the nipple when I kissed her cheek. She blushed, I shook hands with hubby. 'How's Veronica?' I was tempted to say, Veronica was his girl-friend. They had this elderly French couple with them, another youngish man and this girl. She stood back from the others and was quite obviously embarrassed by all the loud greetings. She was plainly dressed in comparison, a simple wool dress slightly too long and a single strand of pearls. She had long shining auburn hair pulled straight back and secured with a plain pearl slide. Very little make-up, in fact she wasn't that pretty—but there was something about her that gave me a jolt I could feel right in the pit of my stomach. She had these wide brown very innocent eyes, they stared at me with slight contempt. She certainly wasn't some little ding-a-ling obsessed by who to lay next, or how short her skirt could get. She was quite young, about seventeen or eighteen. All in the space of seconds I knew that I had to have this one. This one was special.

They were all sitting down. Wasn't anyone going to introduce me? Fontaine was busy ordering champagne, her cool aquamarine eyes darting around to see who was in. She waved at a few people and then Vanessa's husband took her off to dance. If there's one thing Fontaine's lousy at, it's dancing. It's good to know there is at least one thing she can't do. She's got no rhythm, sort of jerks around like a skinny puppet.

I smiled at the guy with the auburn-haired girl and extended my hand, 'I'm Tony Blake,' I said, very friendly like. The girl didn't even glance at me, she stared off into the middle distance, looking bored. The guy was a creep. Square suit, short back and sides, a real nothing.

Benjamin joined in, 'Oh, Tony—don't you know Peter Lincoln Smith?' The name rang a bell. I had met his father several times. He owned half of London. 'And this is my daughter Alexandra,' Benjamin finished proudly, 'just arrived home from Switzerland today.'

His daughter Alexandra! My mouth must have hung open for at least five minutes. His daughter! She threw me a sulky 'How do you do.'

The French couple butted in then, and I had to chat to them. It seemed their daughter came in all the time and they had heard lots about me. I knew their daughter, ugly little blonde nympho who wore Paco Rabanne dresses and thought she was the knock-out of all times. I hadn't actually been there, but Sammy had, and his verdict was thumbs down.

Benjamin was now urging the creep to dance with Alexandra. She was blushing and saying she didn't want to dance. Peter Lincoln Smith was caught in the middle and didn't know what to do, to please Daddy or daughter. Daddy won, and a reluctant Alexandra was led off to the dance floor. There were hints of a great body. The dress wasn't showing off anything, but it was there, hidden underneath. I didn't know what to do, I was caught up with this girl, don't know why. I hadn't even spoken to her, she was probably a spoilt rich bitch. I fancied her like crazy, man, this was going to be tricky, dare I take the risk?

Fontaine came back to the table, breathless and slightly hot in all that white mink. The whole room had seen it, so she slipped it off, revealing a black body-moulding backless sheath. She certainly knew how to show herself off.

I took myself back to the regulars' table and ordered a stiff scotch. Massey had arrived with a thin angular model girl called Suki. Her hair was cropped close to her head, her skirt close to her ass and she wore a weird white make-up with huge clown-like eyes.

Massey was his usual cool self. 'Hey, man,' he said sitting down beside Sammy, 'what's the action tonight?'

23

'Same old action, everything's swinging,' I replied.

He was wearing a white suit, very smart. I thought I might get myself a white suit.

I spied Alexandra on the dance floor. Amongst all the movers she stood quietly holding her boy-friend at arms' length doing a sort of nothing shuffle.

I grabbed Suki and took her off to dance edging my way near to Alexandra. The only reaction she gave was a slightly incredulous look at Suki. Shit! What could I do to make the rich bitch notice me? Suki was a very stylised dancer, religiously studied every new step, and wouldn't be caught dead doing anything that was out. She and Massey made a great couple. Me—I did a sort of wild shake and that was it.

'I bet this is different from Switzerland,' I yelled above the din of the music, an inane grin on my face.

Alexandra just ignored me. Either that or she didn't hear me.

Suki said, 'What?'

'Nothing,' I muttered, dragging her back to the table.

An Italian actress, Carla Cassoni, was just making an entrance, surrounded by three attentive men.

'Wowee,' Sammy whistled through his teeth. 'How about that?!'

She was beautiful, black hair, olive skin, a body edging on being plump, but ending up merely voluptuous. Her new movie had just opened in town. Something about a peasant girl who gets raped by an army—I could understand the army!

I hurried over to give greetings, shaking hands warmly, meeting crystal-clear green eyes, a throaty accented voice. Ordinarily I would have become Charlie Charm, dancing attendance, but tonight my mind was elsewhere. I saw she got a good table, and left her with the three guys. Miss Rich Bitch was sitting at her table. Peter was being led off to dance by Fontaine. I nipped in quickly, Vanessa was dancing with her husband and Benjamin was talking to the French couple. I sat down next to Alexandra and we both stared off into space. She was drinking plain orange juice. 'How do you like it?' I asked.

'How do I like what?' her voice was soft and very precise.

'The club,' I waved an expansive arm around.

'Very nice,' she said, stifling a yawn. I noticed her nails were cut short and painted a buff colour, most of the girls or women I knew had either long red talons, or short chipped bitten ones.

'Would you like to dance?'

24

'No thank you.'

No thank you indeed! Most girls would give their false eyelashes to dance with me! We sat there with nothing else to say until Fontaine and Peter returned.

The club was filling to capacity. The music was getting louder and louder. Time to take off the records and put on the group. Time to circulate around some tables, give them the chat. Time to give the waiters a blast. I got up, silly little cow, she wasn't even that pretty, and man, like I could have the prettiest. I grabbed my scotch, gulped it down and wandered around the joint. People liked me to sit down at their table, it showed they were really 'in'. I tell you this is such a phoney business; maybe that's why I dug Alexandra sitting there so bored and unimpressed.

I joined the table of the Italian star. She was with her 'Producer'—fat—good-looking, didn't speak a word of English; a fag English actor, and his stunt-man boy-friend. Carla Cassoni was very lovely, with this incredibly throaty accent. The producer kept a firm hand on her thigh, but she winked at me and flirted, safe in the knowledge that he didn't understand one word.

'You are very attractive,' she purred, 'such a lovely body, but no money huh? It ees beeg shame,' she laughed a deep sexy chuckle. She was a smart cookie. I asked her to dance, she shook her head, ' 'Ee is veree jealous,' she indicated the producer, ' 'ee don't like me to dance with other man.' Nobody wanted to dance with me, it is just wasn't my night.

Suddenly Franco rushed over, stared bug-eyed at Carla and whispered something in my ear. It seemed some spade chick had come in featuring a topless dress, and what was he to do. Should he ask her to cover up, or what? He pointed her out, she had just sat down, and the top of her dress which was all fringe, parted as she moved, revealing firm dark brown breasts. It was tantalising, now you see them, now you don't. The guy she was with was old, suited, obviously out on a jaunt. She was a wild chick called Molly Mandy—part-time dress designer. What the hell, there was no law against topless dresses. I told Franco to leave her be. A few people had noticed and a lot of staring was going on; then she got up to dance and the staring really began. The old guy didn't care, he got up there with her, proud as punch. She started on a slow shake, titties hardly moving, then suddenly she started to go and the fringe swung and the titties swung, and baby she swung. Everyone stopped

25

dancing and made a hand-clapping circle round them. The guys all loved it, some of the birds looked a bit choked. I saw Fontaine rush over to the side of the dance floor with Vanessa to get a better look. It was a wild scene. Then the Greeks joined in, threw some glasses to start it off, then a couple of them shouldered the old guy out of the way and started dancing with Molly. One of their girl-friends, not to be outdone, ripped off her blouse, unhooked her bra and joined the scene. Everyone cheered. The time had come to stop it otherwise we'd get the police in. Charming! I pushed my way through the crowd just a little too late, one of the mad Greek shipowners had grabbed hold of a brown tit and the old guy attempted to punch him and ended up flat on his back. A lot of screaming started, but Franco had his waiters in there so fast, and the old guy was carried out, and the Greeks were persuaded back to their table, and Molly sat down at our table saying 'Shit, man, what's all the fuss?' It was action like this that made 'Hobo' the only place in town.

I glanced over to Fontaine's table, she was just sitting down, laughing. Alexandra and escort had gone, probably left during all the confusion. Just as well. 'Hey, Molly baby, don't come here like that again.'

She smiled at me, rows of white pearly teeth plus a few gold fillings. 'What's the matter, Tony sweetheart, don't you like my boobies?' She shook her shoulders and the fringe parted giving me an eyeful.

'You know I like them—but not in here, you'll cause a riot, come on, I'll take you back to find your boy-friend.'

She made a face, 'Man, that old fart's out cold, I feel like some fun tonight.'

I was getting irritated, what did she expect—to tag on to me? I didn't even fancy her—I looked to Sammy, but he was busy chatting up Janine.

I took a grip on her arm and led her to the reception area, the old guy was laid out in the office at the back. He was just coming to when we got there. 'I'll arrange a cab, you take him home,' I hissed at her.

She pouted, 'O.K., but maybe I'll come back, isn't it about time you and I had a scene?'

I gave her a shove towards the old trout and got out of there. I think it was the gold fillings that turned me off.

Fontaine summoned me with the imperial wave when I was back inside. I knew the gesture well—she raised one long thin arm high and sort of clicked her fingers at me. Charming! Sort of a—come here serf!

I went. After all she was the boss. 'Tell us about it,' she said, excitement gleaming in her eyes. The others all leaned forward too, anxious to hear the story. 'Who was that pathetic little man with her?' Fontaine went on, 'I mean, really, they made a ridiculous couple.'

She gave me a sharp kick under the table, her signal that she wanted me to ask her to dance. I obliged. I hated dancing with her, talk about looking ridiculous, is there anything more ridiculous than an elegant-looking lady jumping and squirming around like a seventeen-year-old? Especially when she's got no sense of rhythm. I gave my secret signal to Flowers— the disc jockey, to put on a slow record. He launched into a medley of Tony Bennett, making a face, he was strictly a Motown man.

Fontaine held me tight. 'Did you touch her?' she asked licking silver-coated lips.

'Did I touch who?'

'Oh, you know who, she looked straight out of the jungle!'

I ignored that. Fontaine had a poor opinion of anyone who wasn't in her set, she was also very bigoted, and was for ever trying to get me to get rid of the black waiters and Flowers. In bed one time she had gone on about how they made her feel uncomfortable, and then she had got very excited and given me a few scratches on my back I'll probably have for ever. I can't imagine anyone making Fontaine uncomfortable.

I would never get rid of Flowers, he's the best D.J. in town. A tall thin spade with freak out hair and pale blue eyes. Usually stoned out of his mind. But he can feel a room like I can feel a woman.

Fontaine was dancing very close. I glanced over at her husband. He was talking with the French couple.

'Hello, Tone,' a girl greeted me. She was dancing alongside us. I smiled at her.

Fontaine dug me in the ribs and said with an amused smile, 'You love it don't you, all these little dollies after you?'

I must admit I did love it.

Wouldn't you?

FOUR

FONTAINE

I arrived at Tony's shortly after phoning him. A horrible little scrubber with long black hair came yawning out of his apartment. I waited a few minutes before ringing the bell, it would never do to let him know that I knew all about his little 'affaires'. One would think he would show a degree of taste, but no, he would sleep with anything, studs usually do.

He greeted me with a kiss. What a sloppy habit, I have a great distaste for kissing, especially when his mouth has the lingering odour of someone else.

Immediately he started fumbling with my clothes, and getting my skirt off, he pinned me to the wall. I must admire him, he's never at a loss. He took me like that, quite exciting, though only momentarily of course.

The awful thing about Tony is that he's a terrible bore. He has nothing even remotely intelligent to say. After sex I really have to get away from him.

I dressed again and told him I was late for the hairdresser. Of course I wasn't, so I popped in to visit Vanessa.

Vanessa reminds me of a big blonde jersey cow. Placid, slow, always churning children forth. What on earth Tony can see in her I really can't imagine. Probably that big mother earth bosom.

In my position it's difficult to acquire friends, I mean it's got to be someone on the same social level, otherwise they're just absurdly jealous. All my friends from before became impossible after I married Benjamin. Each new mink coat or diamond ring was greeted with tight little smiles, they just couldn't stand it. Vanessa of course has no need to worry, I suppose her husband is nearly as rich as mine, although to look at her you would never guess.

I love having beautiful clothes and jewels and being envied and stared at. I suppose I always knew that I was destined for this kind of life.

I was a very plain child with a very plain mother and a bastard of a father who made mother's life a misery. Felicity Brown of Bournemouth. I grew up very quietly, went to the best girls' school, decided I would like to be a vet, and knew nothing about sex except what the other girls whispered. All nice little English girls want to be vets, it's a part of our tradition—well it was then anyway. At sixteen I was allowed on my first outing with a young man, none of this 'raped at thirteen' business in my past. He was nineteen, the local doctor's son and a nice quiet boy. We got along fine, held hands, had a few furtive kisses and decided to get married. I was a good chaste Bournemouth virgin engaged to be married, with a sweet marquesette ring, and stars in my dull little eyes. We decided, along with the help of our middle-class parents, that we would marry when he was twenty-one and I was eighteen. My future was cut out and planned. He went off to finish his medical studies and I enrolled in all sorts of activities, such as sewing and cookery classes. I really didn't know any other boys and I thought I loved Mark. What a situation! I had no idea what love was all about.

At cookery class I met a girl called Marcia. She was pregnant and unmarried and people whispered about her. My mother called her 'fast' and 'shocking', and my father said it was a disgrace she was allowed to join the cookery class. But join she did, and she was the first breath of fresh air I had encountered in all my nearly seventeen years.

We became friendly and I told her all about Mark and my plans.

'What's he like in bed?' she enquired. I looked at her blankly.

'Oh no,' she started to laugh, 'don't tell me you haven't?'

I had to admit that I hadn't, what's more I wasn't going to because it wasn't what nice girls did, was it?

This made her laugh even more, and then she got very serious and said, 'How on earth can you marry someone if you don't know if you like each other in bed. It's very important, you *must* do it.'

Of course she was no walking advertisement for sex, with her belly swollen out and no visible husband, but I did think she was right, I *should* try it.

I waited anxiously for Mark to come home on holiday, half excited, half terrified at what I planned to do.

He was allowed to borrow his father's car and we went to a film and he held my hand and afterwards we went to one of the big hotels for dinner.

It's very difficult when you're a nice quiet virgin suggesting that your equally nice quiet fiancé make love to you, especially

29

when he's never attempted anything along those lines.

I said, 'Let's drive down to the beach, it's such a lovely night.'

'Oh, Felicity, I'm tired.'

'Please, Mark.' I was quite determined to get the beastly deed done.

'All right,' he reluctantly agreed.

We parked somewhere along the front and sat there, he made no movement towards me.

After a few moments of silence, I said, 'Mark, if we're going to get married don't you think we should get to know each other?'

'What are you talking about, Felicity?' he replied crossly.

I moved closer to him, 'You know what I mean.'

He was genuinely shocked and pushed me away, 'If I want that type of girl there's plenty around.'

I was very excited by this time, the first time in my life I had been sexually excited, and Mark—the man in my life, was pushing me away. I was furious.

He drove me home in silence and I refused to ever see him again.

The next night, still determined to find out what sex was all about, I went to a local coffee bar, and there met a tall leather-jacketed boy called Ted. I had seen Ted before around town, and I decided that he would do to initiate me into the mysteries of life. We started to talk and when he invited me for a walk I accepted readily.

We strolled along making our way towards the beach, and then he grabbed me, kissed me, pushed his hands up my skirt, and we both fell down on the sand. I was ready for him without any preliminaries. He forced his way into me and the pain was exquisite and I clung to him and begged him for more, and as he was finished and went limp I wouldn't let him go. He was trying to get away and I was hanging on to him. It was wonderful. We fought silently and he called me a bitch and said I was hurting him! Me hurting him, that was a delightful statement.

A new Felicity Brown had emerged. I loved it! I tried everyone and everything. A whole new life had opened up for me and soon Bournemouth wasn't big enough and I left for London. My father by this time was pleased to see me go. My mother shed a few tears I think.

I arrived in London, tall, skinny, with mousy hair, but

plenty to offer. And by the time I was twenty-two I was Fontaine—top model. Beautiful—a few changes here and there, blonde, a girl with London at her feet.

I was making lots of money and lots of men, and then I met my first husband, Paul. He was very attractive. Lean and lazy with smoky green eyes and a beautiful body. He was a sometimes male model, sometimes actor, but mostly enjoyed living off some lady. He was divine in bed. His gymnastics nearly matched up to mine. He was the first man who really satisfied me and saw I stayed satisfied.

So one day we got married amidst a blaze of flashbulbs, and he sat back while I worked, and life went on. He gambled, drank, and was unfaithful, but we stayed together, because I suppose I must have loved him.

Everyone told me I was mad but there was still a little bit of Felicity Brown left in me somewhere, and I wanted my marriage to work.

At twenty-nine I looked in the mirror and took stock. I had been a top model for seven years and that's a long time to have been at the top in any profession. How much longer could it last? Paul used up all my money, soon I would be thirty, and how many more magazine covers lay ahead?

Also I was exhausted. Modelling is not an easy job as people seem to think, it's back-breaking work, a constant grind of hairdressers, make-ups, blinding hot lights, and anatomically impossible poses.

I certainly wasn't faithful to Paul any more, after six months of marriage we both agreed it was ridiculous to confine ourselves to each other. As a matter of fact, we had rather a lot of fun with 'group parties'. Very interesting.

I finally decided Paul was a luxury that would have to go and I cast my eyes around for someone more substantial to take his place.

I met Benjamin in St Moritz. I was doing a fur show there for one day and he was with his unbelievably dreary wife and two ghastly children. We met in a group and I knew who he was. We managed a few words alone, 'Can I see you in London?' he asked. He reached a little past my shoulder in height. I gave him my phone number.

It took exactly five weeks for him to offer to divorce his wife. I played my game very carefully, I gave him everything but, and I had him mad for it. There's a ghastly expression Tony uses—'I'm hot for you, baby,' and that just about sums up how Benjamin felt.

It was no problem getting rid of Paul. Benjamin paid, and he took. Benjamin's wife was also easy. She agreed to divorce him with no argument. Of course she got a fortune and also the children. We have never spoken, but I am obliged to see Ben Junior and Alexandra sometimes. They are really very dreary. Young Ben is twenty and an even shorter version of his father. Alexandra is just plain, no sparkle, like her mother I suppose.

So that's my story. Benjamin and I got married, once more in a blaze of flashbulbs and we honeymooned on a new yacht he bought for the occasion. He buys me whatever I want, and I have my occasional stud and I'm happy—I suppose.

Whatever happened to Felicity Brown?

Vanessa was not dressed when I arrived. Her big breasts were flopping about in a blue dressing-gown and she was eating toast and honey and reading a gossip column.

It's very important in our circle to see your name quite often in print. If Vanessa hadn't been very rich she would have been a real slut. I knew that Leonard, her husband, was keeping some little tramp in a flat, but I hadn't told Vanessa, what was the point?

We greeted each other warmly, and I ordered a champagne cocktail from their Filipino houseboy and sat down and relaxed.

'What's new darling?' Vanessa yawned.

I slipped off my jacket, 'Nothing much, just had a little session with the stud.'

We both laughed. 'Was he in good running form today?' Vanessa enquired.

I have a feeling she has a secret crush on Tony, offhand as she may try to be.

'Yes,' I replied, 'when is he ever not?'

Vanessa was a bit bored at that, she had to wait for Tony to approach her, *I* had a far different kind of relationship with him.

The houseboy brought my cocktail. It was cold and delicious. A good champagne cocktail really sets you up for the day.

'What are you wearing tonight?' I asked.

Vanessa shrugged, 'I haven't really thought.'

Hadn't really thought indeed, I planned my outfits months

ahead. No wonder she always looked such a mess.

We chatted a while longer and then I went off to the hair-dresser.

Alexandra arrived at our house fresh from Switzerland at seven. She dislikes me and I can't stand her, but of course Benjamin fails to see this. She looked as dull and plain as ever. It always amazes me how in this day and age a girl can look so utterly dowdy. Her hair scraped back, no make-up, uninteresting little wool dress. She's seventeen and yet manages to look years older.

Benjamin greeted her warmly. She's polite to him, but I'm sure she hates him for deserting 'Mummy'. He has a huge trust fund for her when she's twenty-one. She sipped an orange juice, and soon the others arrived—thank God!

I wore my new full-length white mink, and Vanessa loved it. I have no doubt she will shortly appear in a bad copy, she copies everything I have, but invariably it just doesn't suit her to wear my style, we are completely different types.

Dinner at 'Annabels' was fun. Lots of friends there. It was a terrible bore having Alexandra along, she was always looking at me with a sort of disdainful half smile. I wish she would stick with Mummy in the country instead of bothering us. Now she's talking of sharing a flat in London with a girl-friend, and Benjamin is insisting she come and live with us. How dare he! Thank God she's declining the invitation. Stupid child is starting a job as a secretary. What's the point with all her money?

Dinner lingered on. I danced with the old French goat who held me too tight and breathed garlic in my face. Delightful! I danced with Leonard, he's not bad although Vanessa's description of his activities in bed are very dull indeed. He probably saves it all up for his little popsie on the side. It's quite amazing how the most unimaginative of husbands can turn into a real Casanova in someone else's bed.

We finally set off for 'Hobo' I simply love it there. Such a marvellous mixture of people, always something going on. And Tony, well, Tony at work is a real sight. Absolutely everyone's best friend!

I must admit, it's when I like him best. He's king of the whole place, everyone wants him at their table, all the women want him.

He has a very sexy animal walk, almost as though he has a hidden erection. I wish he had as much confidence in bed, after all I've taught him his tastes are still a little on the suburban side, he can't seem to project any originality. To be a good lover you need a constant source of inspiration.

Of course his friends are unbelievable. They gather at his table like a clutch of male rejects. What a motley group!

The records are fabulous, so loud you can't even hear yourself think. I love dancing. The whole room is staring at my coat—one little dance in it won't be too hot. Let them all get a good look before I slip out of it.

Alexandra sits like a ton of bricks. I really can't stand her. Benjamin is so proud, he thinks she's so lovely. And as for the little bore he has fixed her up with, why his father's got more life in him than he has! Actually, he's just right for Alexandra, two dreary non-personalities together!

Oh no, he's not going to ask me to dance. Yes he is. Oh, how awful. Rich men's sons are all the same. Real smug little bores. This one's probably about the same age as Tony—only he's got about as much sex appeal as a flea. It's no use rubbing yourself up against me, sweetheart, you just haven't got what it takes.

'Let's sit down, Peter dear, it's so hot.'

He looked disappointed. I'd be disappointed if I had to go back and sit with Alexandra. Why, she wouldn't even dance with him. I must say, I love to dance. So lovely and uninhibited, Tony can't wait to dance with me and show me off to the whole room.

There was some sort of commotion going on over at the dance floor.

'It's some black girl completely nude!' Vanessa said excitedly. We both jumped up and rushed over. Mustn't miss a good show.

After, Vanessa and I went back to our table. 'You didn't say goodbye to Alexandra,' Benjamin said crossly.

'I didn't even know she was going,' I replied, delighted she had left.

'She had a headache,' then relenting he added, 'Perhaps you'll phone her tomorrow.' He squeezed my leg under the table. His hands were sweaty. He had grey hair, bald in patches, like a moth-eaten fur.

Tony was coming back in the room and I called him over. He looked very sexy tonight, God, those trousers he was wearing didn't leave much to the imagination!

He asked me to dance. Slow music was playing and he held me very tight.

'Aren't you being a little obvious?' I said indicating Benjamin, but he just held me tighter and I felt him and I wished we could do it there and then in front of everyone. Oh what bliss! But tonight was impossible. Benjamin was in town and *he* would probably want to do it. What an utter bore! Sex with Benjamin was so utterly dreary. I like young strong bodies, not old tired ones. He huffed and he puffed like he would never quite finish the show. Dear Benjamin was so monotonously the same in bed, he was unlovely and uninteresting. Fortunately he was quick.

We left 'Hobo' soon after and once in the privacy of our bedroom I flopped on the bed exhausted. What a day! Benjamin announced he had to leave for Paris the next afternoon. Did I want to come? Well, I wanted to come, but not to Paris. I decided I might pop over to New York to our flat for a few days, I adored the shops over there and I supposed I should visit Ray. He is an adorable looking hairdresser whom Benjamin has set up in his own salon there. I haven't spent time with Ray for ages. A few days with him might be fun.

Benjamin was pulling at my dress. He knew I hated that, I got up quickly and he backed away. Oh, poor old Benjamin, I'd frightened him. He was always frightened I'd say no—but of course I never did. I peeled off the dress and hung it up carefully, then I lay flat on the bed, the way he liked me to and waited for him. I closed my eyes and thought about Tony and Ray and Paul and it wasn't too bad. In fact, if he wasn't so goddamned fast it might not be bad at all. He washed himself after, a habit that drives me to distraction. I took off my make-up and put on my sleep mask. He was reading now. Oh, for separate bedrooms. What a joy!

FIVE

TONY

Sammy said, 'Watcha dancing with that old bag for?'

Sammy Schmuck! What did he know about class.

'I mean I know she owns the place but...'

'I think she's fantastic,' Janine interrupted, 'really fantastic, did you see that coat she had on?'

'What's a coat if there's nothing but skin and bone underneath?' Sammy chuckled at his own joke. 'Now that Italian number's not bad, nice pair of boobies.'

I should remark that Sammy has no conversation except about women. We have all heard clinical descriptions of every bird he's ever laid.

'Come on, darling, I'll do you a favour,' Sammy dragged Janine off to the packed dance floor.

Franklin looked miserable. 'Listen, long face,' I said, 'that's not for you, let Sammy have her, she's a pig.'

Massey said, 'I've got a beautiful little bird for you. Suki's sister—wouldn't she be great for Franklin?'

Suki nodded wide clown-like eyes. 'She's only fifteen but lovely.'

I had heard it all before. Everyone was always fixing Franklin up, but nothing ever worked out. He was too shy to make it with a bird. To get Franklin laid was one of our group projects. He would sit and listen to all our chat about women and agree with us when we told him he should blow his cherry, but nothing ever happened.

The evening was at its peak.

The place was so jammed that some tables' occupants had to take it in shifts to dance because there wasn't room for them all to sit down at the same time. It was always dodgy dancing at this time anyway. For one thing the tiny dance floor was so jam-packed you couldn't move, and for another you took a risk of losing your seat altogether.

I looked around with satisfaction. It was one of the more star-packed nights. There was a good sprinkling of top talent from most professions.

'The Must', current top rock group were all present. Long hair, tighter than tight clothes. They were nice boys, stoned out of their heads, but harmless, with their flaxen-haired girl-friends who all looked the same. It's a funny thing how in the rock world it's important to all to be on the same wavelength—you know—the long hair bit. They all look like out of the same mould. They try to look different from everyone else and bingo—there you go—all the same.

More people were crowding in, I got up and did the greeting bit. I wandered round a few tables having a scotch here and a scotch there. The world was starting to buzz. I could fancy something cuddly. Fontaine had left me with a sour taste in my mouth. As a matter of fact, I could fancy Vanessa, but that was impossible, there she was with hubby. I must remember to give her a ring, sneak in while nanny and the kidlets were out!

I kept on thinking of Miss Rich Bitch—she was so sort of different from other birds, she had this kind of aura of cool. I wondered if I'd see her again. Probably not, she looked like she hated it here.

Flowers grabbed hold of me—'Got to see you, man,' his eyes were distorted and nervous. He was flying on pot, probably needed more bread, that was always his problem. He was living with Tina, our Swedish receptionist. What a couple they made—he, dark and wild, she, white and quiet. There was a song there somewhere!

I lent him five pounds, listened to his bullshit about how grateful he was, and made a mental note to get it back from his next week's salary—otherwise I'd never see it again.

Miss Italian Movie Star and party were leaving—'Bye, Bye, Tonee,' she purred slowly through pearly white teeth, 'not long before we shall meet again huh?'

I loved her voice, it was a real turn on. 'Yeah,' I gave her the sincere stare. All the Italian waiters were going mad, hovering around to get a closer look. 'S'long, Tony, old boy,' the fag actor said. 'Bye, Tone,' the stunt-man said. They all wanted to know me, be my friend. The Italian producer muttered some Italian, gave me a dirty look, gripped Carla by the arm and they were gone. Good, I quickly had Franco put a visiting senator and party at their table.

So the evening reached its peak, and slowly around two-thirty it started to thin out, and by three-thirty only super swingers and odd-balls were left. Franklin said he was going and Janine said she wanted to stay, and they argued quietly and then he left. I caught him at the door. 'Listen, kid, we'll get you a date with Suki's sister. O.K.?' He shrugged. A waiter came at him with his check and I grabbed it. 'The cokes are on me tonight,' I said.

'Thanks, Tony.'

Back at the table Janine seemed to fancy me, and in spite of Sammy's frantic efforts she didn't want to know. She asked me to dance, and tossed the sad starlet's mane of red hair, and wriggled the sad starlet's curvy body, and the accent twanged disco-ordinately.

We ended up in my flat. I just don't dig going home alone. I was loaded and she didn't stop talking. I heard all about the movie she was doing, some bit part in a B film no doubt, and how Franklin was very sweet but such a baby, and how she loved London, and 'Hobo' was such a wild place, and just as I got it in, she said, 'Can I have a free membership?' So I gave it to her.

That's life.

SIX

ALEXANDRA

It's simply terrific to be home.

Madelaine and I flew back together. Her father and brother met us at the airport. Michael, her brother, is super. Of course I've known him for ages, we were all children together, but lately he really has become *so* attractive.

I daren't tell Maddy what I think of him because I suppose she wouldn't understand. I mean him being her brother and everything she most likely sees him in a different light. We always discuss boys together, not that there was too much chance in Switzerland, our school was run like a convent. However, Maddy had this huge crush on the school gardener. I used to unlock the hall window at night and she used to sneak out to meet him. We'd probably have both been expelled if we'd been found out. Anyway, she had a lovely time, he was quite old—about thirty, and they used to neck and once Maddy let him take her sweater off *and* her bra. But she said he went a bit berserk after that and used to try all sorts of things, so she didn't meet him any more. It was just as well because I didn't think he was much at all. Rather dour really.

On our last vacation we went with Maddy's parents to Monte Carlo and I met a gorgeous boy who sort of looked after our beach. He was so brown. He took Maddy and me dancing one night and kissed me goodnight. It was awful, he stuck his tongue in my mouth!

Anyway, here we are out of school at last! It's like a wonderful dream. No more school! Madelaine and I have a plan. She's going to work on her parents and I'm going to work on my mother and we're going to share a flat. In London!! In Chelsea!! We decided Chelsea was the best place, sort of swinging and everything. We'll both get jobs and have a terrific time.

After all, I've been seventeen two whole months now, I'm practically old! And nothing exciting has ever happened to me—nothing!

We went back to Maddy's house, it's in Virginia Water, and she's always lived there, with both parents. My parents are divorced. My father went off with an awful woman who lured him away from Mummy. I think it was really selfish of him. We were all so happy before, and my mother is great fun. Very sensible. I wish she wasn't so sensible, then perhaps she would have held on to him. I must admit that Daddy's new wife is quite glamorous. She hates me, I can just tell. Not that I care because I can't *stand* her, and fortunately I don't have to see them very much, only on occasions like tonight when I'm on my way home from school.

Maddy's father's going to drive me into town tonight for an evening out with Daddy and Fontaine, and then tomorrow morning I'm getting the train down to Mummy's. We live in a house near Newmarket, Mummy, my brother Max and me. We moved after the divorce because although Daddy would have let us stay in our old house it was too big, and anyway I don't think Mummy was very happy there any more.

Our new house is splendid, and has stables, I have my own horse. We have a swimming pool, although of course it's never warm enough to swim in. But somehow it's not the same. Anyway, the last year I've been in Switzerland and before that boarding school, so I really haven't spent that much time there. I'm sure Mummy will let me come to London, she's so understanding, and I'll be with Maddy so I don't see how she can object.

'What are you wearing tonight?' Maddy came into her room wrapped in a bath-towel. She always took ages in the bath. I had been waiting to get in the bathroom for half-an-hour.

'I'm not going to dress up,' I replied. Actually I didn't have anything to dress up in if I'd wanted to, 'cos we mostly lived in sweaters and skirts in Switzerland. Both Madelaine and I had to get ourselves kitted out, our clothes were awful and old-fashioned.

'I don't blame you,' Maddy said, 'I certainly wouldn't get dressed up for *her* either.'

We both shared a mutual loathing for Fontaine, although of course Maddy had never met her, but knew all about her from me.

I bathed, brushed my hair, and put on the cleanest dress I could find.

Maddy supplied some make-up. I didn't put on much, because quite frankly, I wasn't very good at it. I needed practice.

'Have a glorious time,' Maddy said when I was ready, 'see you later.' I was coming back to stay the night.

I went downstairs to find Mr Newcombe. He was going to a business dinner in London. He really is a nice father, I liked him awfully, and I wished *my* father was like him.

Oh good! Michael's coming too. He's very good-looking, tall, with lovely longish hair. He lives in London. I'm sure when Maddy and I get our flat in town we'll see lots and lots of him. Anyway, I hope so.

He sat in the front of the car with his father, and I was in the back, so there wasn't much chance for talking on the drive.

My father lives in a big house in Belgravia. Mummy says it's in very bad taste. It has a lot of white statues balanced about outside, and inside it's huge and not at all comfortable. There is even an awful indoor swimming pool which is in a sort of glass room, all dark and depressing, with hundreds of vines and plants growing around it. It's creepy. I loathe it.

I said goodbye to Mr Newcombe. Michael smiled at me.

I said, 'See you soon.'

Maybe he liked me too. Maddy was always talking about how he had heaps of girl-friends, maybe I could be one of them, or *the* one.

I mused on this as the butler let me in, and took my coat.

Fontaine came bearing down on me, 'Alexandra darling, how wonderful to see you.' She kissed me on the cheek. I knew she was only doing it for Daddy's sake. He hugged me. He seems to have grown shorter and older.

Suddenly I felt a warmth towards him and I hugged him back. Oh, if only he'd stayed with Mummy! Everyone knew Fontaine just loved him for his money.

'We're going to have a lovely evening,' my father said, 'how was school? Tell me all about it.'

We sat together on the sofa, and I wanted to cry because he did look so old and tired. I had seen him four months before and he had looked fine, but now—oh my goodness, what had she done to him?

'Are you well, Daddy?'

'Of course I'm well. Working very hard but that's what I like. I was never one for sitting about.'

He glanced over at Fontaine, but she was taking no notice of us. She was sipping champagne, and reading a fashion magazine.

'How's your mother?'

'Oh, I haven't been home yet, but I spoke to her tonight and

41

she sounded fine. She said she just got a letter from Ben and he's having a marvellous time.'

My brother Ben was at a University in America.

'Wonderful woman your mother, very strong...' He tailed off and I could still remember the day Mummy told us he was leaving. She hadn't cried or anything like that, but I knew he was breaking her heart. My mother is a pretty woman, about fifty. When she was young she had been gorgeous. In their wedding photos she was petite, with golden curling hair and a dimpled face. I knew that she had married my father long before he was so rich.

'I'll give Mummy your love,' I said, and wondered if that was the right thing to say. But it was all right because he just smiled, and patted me on the knee.

'I'm going to come and live in London,' I blurted out, 'I'm going to share a flat with Madelaine and get a job.'

'When did you decide all this?'

'Maddy and I have been thinking about it for ages. Actually it's not all set yet, but I've written off for three jobs and I've got interviews next week, and Maddy's got two flats to see. Don't you think it's a good idea?'

My father frowned. 'But if you want to come to London you can live here, you don't need to get a job. Fontaine and I would be more than delighted to have you here.'

'No, Daddy, you don't understand. I want to be independent and free. I'm eighteen now and I know at twenty-one I'll have heaps of money from my Trust. Well that's why I want to keep myself, sort of support myself for a few years. I don't just want to be a rich man's daughter. I want to think for myself and work for myself and then at twenty-one I'll be able to accept the responsibility of my money. I don't want to "come out" and be a deb. I want a few years as just an ordinary girl.'

There! I'd said it. The speech I'd prepared for my mother.

Father beamed, 'That's my girl,' he said, 'that's my little girl. But I could help you find a nice job, you could take your choice.'

'*No*, Daddy.'

Some more people arrived, and my father joined Fontaine in greeting them.

'Alexandra, I want you to meet Peter Lincoln Smith. He's kindly agreed to escort you this evening.'

My face burned. *Kindly* agreed to escort me! Oh, my father

was *so* embarrassing. I didn't want to be fixed up, it was so awful and old-fashioned, and my father hadn't even mentioned it to me.

Peter Lincoln Smith had a mean thin mouth and a limp handshake. I didn't like him, and I don't think he liked me.

There were two other couples, much older people. We had a long, dull dinner at 'Annabel's'. I wished I was with Michael, then it would have been wonderful.

Fontaine never stopped talking all night. I really don't know how my father can stand her, she's so loud.

Afterwards they all wanted to go to a discothèque and Peter and I had to go too. I don't think we had exchanged more than six words all evening.

I felt embarrassed trailing in behind Fontaine and everyone was staring. Oh, it was awful.

At one point the manager sat down and tried to be nice to me, for Daddy's sake I suppose. He asked me to dance and I said no. Honestly people are such phonies. Just because of my father they think they have to be nice to me. Well, they jolly well don't.

I felt very tired. It had been a long day and I had the ride back to Virginia Water. I asked Peter if he'd mind putting me in a taxi.

There was some commotion on the dance floor and Fontaine had rushed over to see what it was. So I said goodnight to Daddy and thankfully left.

Peter had a red M.G. which he had driven me to the club in.

'I'll run you down,' he said.

'Oh no, it's much too far and much too late.' I didn't want to face another hour of Peter's company.

'Nonsense,' he said, suddenly linking his arm in mine, 'no traffic at this time of night, won't take long.'

So I was stuck. I climbed in and we set off in silence.

Peter drove fast and I leaned back in the seat. I soon fell asleep. I must have slept for ages, because when I awoke we were parked in a country lane and Peter was kissing me.

I didn't know what to do, he had taken me by surprise and I didn't want to offend him. After all, he had driven me all this way. So I sat quietly while he kissed me, waiting for the right moment to push him away.

Oh no! Suddenly I felt his hand on my breast. Well, I

43

certainly wasn't going to just sit there now. I said, moving his hand away, 'Please stop that, Peter.'

But he didn't, and soon I found myself really struggling. His hands were everywhere. 'Don't fight me,' he said, as I managed to push his hands away again, 'just lie back and enjoy it.'

Oh, I hated him! He had one hand up my skirt now, and I swung my arm at his head with all the force I could muster.

He stopped at once, clutching his mouth where my blow had landed. 'You little bitch!' he exclaimed in surprise.

Well honestly! I couldn't wait to tell Madelaine. I jumped out of the car and ran off into the night. It was awfully dark, it wasn't a main road at all, and I had no idea where I was. Men are really disgusting, all they think about is one thing.

Suddenly I heard a car. It was Peter's, headlights full on, he was coming to find me.

I didn't know what to do. Maybe he wanted to rape and murder me! I mean things like that *do* happen, you read about it all the time. On second thoughts perhaps he was scared I would tell Daddy and wanted to take me home.

I didn't know what to do. Should I duck down and hide, and hope he wouldn't see me. Or should I climb in his car and demand he take me home.

It was cold and spitting with rain. I was completely lost. I stood quietly by the side of the road, with dignity I hoped. The car stopped beside me and Peter leaned over from the driving seat and flung open the door.

'It's all right, I'm not going to rape you,' he said as though reading my thoughts. 'Get in.'

I climbed back into the car. The least he could do was apologise. What a beast!

As it happened we were only about five minutes from Maddy's house and we both maintained a stony silence on the short drive. I climbed out as soon as he stopped the car. 'Goodnight,' I said coldly.

'Goodbye cock-teaser!' he yelled, and the car drove away.

Oh! Oh! I was *so* furious.

SEVEN

TONY

A week has passed. I saw four movies, had dinner at Trader Vic's, lost twenty-five pounds at roulette—bought three new shirts and got laid every night.

Fontaine has gone, taken off on one of her trips. She never tells me she's going, just buzzes off. I suppose she thinks it's good to keep me in suspense.

Janine has sort of moved herself in and I can't seem to get rid of her. 'The Twang' as I call her, seems to think she's here to stay. She comes to the club every night and sits with the gang and then she comes home with me and rushes off to the studio a few hours later, then she's back at seven—just about when I'm getting up. She's not a bad bird after all, very accommodating. But she'll have to go. I haven't even had a chance to call Sadie this week.

It's Saturday, big bright Saturday, busiest night of the week. It's eight p.m. and I'm seriously thinking of getting up. 'The Twang' is still asleep. Well, I mean she's knocking herself out, poor little bird. Not so little, she's built like a brick shithouse.

I would like a new flat. This pad I have now is very small. When Fontaine gets back we're going to have a serious talk about money. I need more, I deserve more. Every night except Sunday from ten p.m. till four a.m. is no joke.

I think I shall wear the black silk turtle neck and new black slacks tonight. That's where all my bread goes—on gear. Well, I like to look smart, keep up an image. It's important in my business, no use looking like one of those long hairs—dirty and all that. I reckon I've got a good look and I'm going to stick with it.

I mean I don't have short hair—not by any means. It sort of curls around the back of my collar—just right.

If I'm lucky, I can get out of here before 'The Twang' wakes up.

I wasn't lucky. She caught me at the door. 'Babee,' she squealed, 'wait for me, where are we going?'

Oh shit! that meant she expected me to buy her dinner.

I waited while she wriggled her starlet's body into a too-tight white dress and back-combed her hair and put on her eye-

45

lashes. She was definitely becoming a drag.

I called Sammy, he had a date, so we joined up with him at a little Italian bistro and dined royally on spaghetti and meatballs.

Sammy's date was fifteen if she was a day. He had picked her up at a bus stop. One of Sammy's habits was to cruise the streets in his secondhand E-type looking for likely birds. He never copped out, always came up with something. I guess they liked secondhand E-types. One of his favourite stories was of how he followed a bus from Baker Street to the Elephant and Castle because he fancied some little darling on it, and according to him he made it at the end of the ride!

One of these days he was going to get himself into a lot of trouble. Some tough father was going to ram a fist down his stupid throat. Anyway, until that day came, he was happy.

After dinner we went to the club. I liked to get there early on a Saturday. It was too soon for anyone to be in, Flowers was playing a few of the far out sounds which he dug, Franco was screaming in Italian at his waiters, Tina was polishing her nails.

'The Twang' and the fifteen-year-old went off to the ladies' room where they stayed at least half-an-hour.

'What do birds do to their faces that takes so long?' Sammy said. ' 'Ere, what's with you and this American bit, going a bit strong, isn't it?'

'Sammy, Sammy, you know me better than that, as a matter of fact I wondered if you wouldn't mind stepping in.'

Sammy shook his head sadly. 'She had her chance, anyway she's a bit old for me.'

Janine was all of twenty-five.

To tell the truth, I felt rather bad about Franklin, I knew he was choked about her latching on to me. I wish I could talk her into showing him the ropes—in other words, get him in the sack with her. He was a great-looking kid, some lucky girl was in for a thrill. I mean he'd been saving it up for a long time.

They started to come in. As usual, the ones who weren't too sure of a good table first. It always reminded me of a show. The audience files quietly in, sits down and waits, then here come the performers. Yelling greetings, kissing everyone, wearing maxis, minis, caftans, flowers, bells, you name it, they wear it. The beautiful people. An assorted group of high frequency talent, and every one of them my friend.

46

On Saturday you get the 'one night out a week' group too. Dressed to kill, they make a lot of uncool noise and most of the regular clientele send them up. However, they have the money and run up the really big bills, so you have to put up with them.

Here comes a group of them now. Hymie Verne Blatt, dress manufacturer, and his heavily jewelled wife Ethel Verne Blatt, with Jack Davidsonly, coat manufacturer, and even more heavily jewelled wife Bessie Davidsonly. What a group! Every time the wives went away, which was often, Hymie and Jack would appear with au pair ding-a-lings—proud as punch.

Meanwhile, from what I heard, Ethel and Bessie were making it with a couple of Spanish beach boys in Majorca!

However, tonight they were all a happy family. Neither couple had ever been known to appear anywhere alone, there were always the four of them, or the two guys or the two wives. Did they fuck together? We all wondered.

What a greeting I got when I went over to their table! You would think I was their closest dearest friend. These were the same four people who wouldn't look at me sideways when I was a waiter, many's the time I've seasoned their salad.

'Who's coming in tonight, Tony doll?' Ethel asked anxiously, she was the blonde one, Bessie was dark, they obviously thought they were a hot team together, appealing to all types.

I gave her a kiss on the cheek, standard procedure, 'You'll see, you'll see.' I had four types of greeting routines. Big stars I didn't know, firm handshake, sexy look. Big stars I did know, kiss kiss. Ding-a-lings and swingers (female or male) hug and a kiss, everyone else a kiss on the cheek.

The evening was starting to swing. It was going to be a good one. On a Saturday night we could do with a hundred more tables and fill them all. Who would have thought that people would fight and struggle to get into a hot smoky crowded atmosphere with deafening music, but they did and loved it.

Franklin arrived girl-less and sad-faced. He sat and stared at 'The Twang'.

Hal arrived with an American widow to whom he was showing the sights of London. What an operator! Always dressed to kill in the best Savile Row had to offer, hand-made shoes, Turnbull and Asser shirts, and a lot of gold from his fillings to his cufflinks.

Meanwhile he was flat on the heels of his ass, busted out, broke. His last fifty pounds had gone to the kid brother in New

Jersey.

He lived in the best hotels, promoting here, promoting there, and there was always some rich old bag to bail him out. This one tonight was a real horror. From the blue-rinsed hair to the sagging body. Oh boy, Hal certainly had to work somewhere along the line, and I didn't envy him.

Franco was patting me on the shoulder, we were reaching jamming up point and there were only a few emergency tables left. Someone at reception was asking for me. Shit! He knew I never went out front on a Saturday night. Too embarrassing turning people away. He muttered something about friends of Benjamin Khaled's. Well, they could go screw. No room, not on a Saturday baby. On second thoughts, maybe I should give them the bad news myself—people never said they were friends of Benjamin's, it was always—'Fontaine insisted we come by' —and then they would be shocked when they got a bill.

I went out front, there were two young guys, a sandy-haired girl, and another one talking to Tina.

'I'm awfully sorry,' I said, 'but we just don't have a table— you know it's ...'

The bird talking to Tina turned round.

My stomach did a somersault. It was Alexandra. She gazed at me with those wide brown eyes and tentatively smiled.

She had a gorgeous smile.

'Hello, do you remember me?'

Did I remember her—ha!

'Of course I do.' What should I call her? Alexandra? Miss Khaled? What?

She said, 'Couldn't you just squeeze us in somewhere? Daddy said it would be all right.'

As if I would turn her away, even without the threat of 'Daddy'. She looked different, prettier. Her auburn hair was loose, kept off her face with a green head band, and she wore a matching green sweater and tweedy slacks. Nothing flashy but she looked great.

'I'm sure we'll find room for you. How many? Four?'

She nodded, well pleased, and attached herself to the arm of one of the fellows. I hated him.

It was then I had a sudden flash of inspiration and decided to jam them all on to my table. What a great idea!

I led them in and told Sammy, etc., to move over. They all looked choked. The table was crowded as it was. But I managed to get the four of them seated. Then I offered them a

48

drink and was shocked when Alexandra agreed to drink wine with the other three. I had sort of imagined that she didn't drink. They chatted amongst themselves and I hovered by the table and Sammy pantomimed a face at me as much as to say—what the hell is this? I really don't know why I had flipped for this girl, but I had, and this time I wasn't going to let her get away.

I studied the schmuck she was with. Casually dressed, slightly long hair, much too good-looking in a slightly boyish way. He had an arm around her and was tapping her shoulder in time to the music. This was certainly no creepy little Peter Lincoln Smith. This was probably the boy-friend. Well, we would soon find out.

'The Twang' suddenly yelled at me across the table, 'Can we dance, sweetie?'

I froze her with a grim look. Stupid loud-mouthed cow! Got to get rid of her. 'Franklin, dance with Janine,' I said pleasantly. Silently I said—For Christ's sake give her a grope and get her interested in you.

They went off to dance. That was a start. I sat down. I stuck out my hand to Alexandra's boy-friend, forcing him to take his arm from around her. 'Tony Blake, glad to see you.'

Alexandra said, 'Oh, I'm sorry—this is Michael Newcombe' —then she indicated the other two, 'Michael's sister Madelaine, and Jonathan Roberts.'

We all shook hands.

'Super of you to squeeze us in,' Madelaine said, 'we didn't believe Alex when she said she could get us in. Michael's been trying to come here for ages!'

That made Michael out to be a right idiot.

'I hope you like it,' I said. 'Saturday night's a real killer.'

Sammy leaned over, his cockney accent cutting the air, 'Ere—take a look at that.'

We all turned to see Massey and Suki come in, she was wearing the shortest dress ever, split under the arms to below the waist at the side. It was a good job she was flat-chested. Even then, it was some dress.

Actually, with her huge made-up clown eyes, her mannish haircut and white face, she looked like she was in fancy dress.

Massey was cool as ever. 'Hey, man.'

They squashed down at the table and I could see Michael giving Suki a stare. Good. I performed introductions and soon everyone was talking away.

Alexandra had one of those classless beautifully spoken voices. She really was a knockout, and she was nice. She wasn't a stupid little rich bitch as I had thought. Her friends of course were a bit on the square side, hadn't been around much I reckoned.

From the conversation I gathered that Madelaine and Alexandra had been at this sort of finishing school in Switzerland together. Michael hadn't taken his eyes off Suki and I could see Alexandra getting a bit edgy. What an idiot he was to stare at a freak like Suki with a girl like Alexandra by his side. Still it was just as well, what did he know, he was your typical well-educated student type. I willed him to ask sweet little Suki to dance. Sweet little Suki indeed. She was your typical bony angular model girl, all legs and no tits. Massey and she had been going together for a few months on and off, and though they both appeared regularly with other dates, they had a nice scene going. Bingo. Michael, the jerk, was asking her to dance. I thought for a second the dumb face was going to refuse, but no, she couldn't resist the opportunity of wriggling her backside. She got up. Michael got up. Alexandra frowned.

Madelaine looked embarrassed and started to chatter loudly. I grabbed my opportunity like a sinking diver, 'Come and see round the club,' I said directly to Alexandra.

'Super,' Madelaine replied.

Alexandra shook her head, 'I think I'll stay here.'

I glared at Madelaine who had got up, and then to cap it all Jonathan asked Alexandra to dance and off they went.

Have you ever been choked?!

I caught Franco's eye. I said to Madelaine. 'We'll have to take a rain-check, I'm wanted out front.'

Tina was patiently turning people away. She smiled at me, she looked tired and pale. I guess it was no joke living with Flowers, he probably never quietened down. 'How's it going?' I gave her a pat.

'Fine, Mr Blake.' She brushed a lock of blonde hair off her forehead.

I felt sorry for her. 'Go home early tonight, you look tired— I'll get Franco to bring one of the boys out front.'

'Oh, thank you, Mr Blake, I don't feel too good . . .'

I went back inside and hovered by the dance floor. Alexandra was making an attempt to move. She wasn't very good at it. I studied her body partly visible through the folds of clothes. A nice full bosom, slim waist, small hips and long legs.

Was she or wasn't she? Did she or didn't she? I had a hard on to find out.

Madelaine was dancing with Sammy, and his teen-age wonder was nowhere to be seen. Probably back in the ladies' room.

Franklin and 'The Twang' were sitting down.

'Hi, Tony,' a girl I knew on her way back from dancing. She was very pretty. She squeezed my arm, 'When am I going to see you?'

I honestly couldn't remember if we'd made it or not. Some nights I was so loaded I wouldn't have known who it was wriggling about underneath me.

She was with a well-known singer, Steve Scott. One of the new breed, trying to project the sexy Englishman image and not doing a bad job. She was a dancer, a swinger, I did remember her. Her name was Carolyn something or other. I went over and sat with them and bought them a drink.

'Want to come to a party tomorrow?' Steve asked. 'My place, all you need is a bottle and a bird.'

'Yeah,' I was half catching glimpses of Alexandra dancing through the throng.

'You must come, it will be great,' Carolyn said. She jotted down Steve's address which I absentmindedly stuck in my pocket. Who needed parties on a Sunday anyway?

Flowers was launching into some slow soul sounds and when I glimpsed Alexandra again, she was clutched in the schmuck she was dancing with's arms. Well, Flowers could forget that. I rushed over to him and made him change mid record to something fast. Automatically Alexandra and partner jerked apart. I noticed happily that Suki and Michael didn't. Massey noticed too: 'Think I've lost her,' he joked when I sat down. 'Always knew she'd go off with the first white cat that came on strong.'

Now—how about Massey and 'The Twang'? No—she didn't like spades unless they were stars, and he didn't like busty chicks. Oh well . . .

Alexandra was coming back to the table. She looked flushed. 'It looks like we've been deserted, Jonathan,' she said with a wry grin to schmucko. I took her arm which she politely but immediately pulled away.

Oh God, her skin felt like velvet.

'Listen, I want to make you (should I add the rest of the sentence) a member. Let's go to the office.'

'Now?' she looked surprised. 'Besides, it's very nice of you but I don't think . . .'

I didn't let her finish, 'You've got to be a member, it will only take a minute and then you can come here anytime without having to go through the whole bit.'

'O.K.,' she got up. 'Come on, Jonathan.'

He got up and fast thinking I said, 'You stay here, otherwise the table will jam up and there will be nowhere for you to sit when we get back.'

He sat down. I had her.

This time I took a firm grip on her arm and propelled her through the crush. She was looking over to the dance floor to see Michael and Suki. I got her out to reception and then down one flight of stairs to the office. It was quite dark and only the faintest sounds of music reached us. I unlocked the door and switched on the light. It was a bare room with filing cabinets, a desk and a couple of chairs, very unromantic.

Alexandra stretched and yawned, her breasts leaned tautly against the sweater. I had a mad urge to grab her, strip her clothes off and make violent love to her. This little bird had really got under my skin. But it would never do to rush things. To get her out of my system I had to have her, and to have her I had to play it cool.

I lit a nervous cigarette and she sat down, tapped impatient buff nails on the desk and said, 'Who's that awful girl Michael's dancing with?'

I sang a few off key lines of an old song 'Jealousy', and she glared at me.

'I'm not jealous I can assure you,' she stuck her chin out, a gesture I immediately loved. 'But she's just ghastly. Who is she?'

'Some dopy little model girl. Is Michael your boy-friend?'

'Oh no,' she flushed. 'Actually, we've known each other ages, him being Madelaine's brother and everything, but this is the first time we've been out together.'

The scene became clear, schoolgirl crush, fancied him since she was a little girl bit. Well, we would soon get rid of him.

I found a membership form and doodled on it with a chewed pencil that was on the desk. She looked at me expectantly, wide brown eyes, beautiful eyes.

'What's your address?' I asked. You know this bird made me nervous.

'I wonder if I should give you Mummy's address,' she

52

mused aloud, 'I shall probably be there every weekend and it is my proper address.'

I didn't want Mummy's address. I wanted her improper address. She licked her lips, they were very full and shiny with some kind of lip gloss, very sexy.

'No, perhaps I should give you my address here although I don't know how permanent it will be.'

Was she a virgin? No, impossible. There are no virgins left over the age of fourteen in London, even Sammy hasn't come across one yet.

'Madelaine and I are sharing a flat,' she said, rather proudly, 'can Madelaine be a member too? The address is 14 Dundee Court, Chelsea.'

Chelsea yet! What did she want to go and set herself up amongst all that mob for? Oh well, at least she was in London and not living either with Mummy or Daddy. 'Phone number?' I asked, silently rehearsing what I would say the first time I phoned.

She gave me the number and I said, 'That's great, we'll send you the card this week and then I expect to see lots of you.'

She blushed. There are actually girls that still know how to blush. 'I doubt it,' she said standing up. 'I start my job on Monday, and I have to be there by nine every day.'

'Nine in the morning?' My voice was incredulous. Nine in the morning was ridiculous.

She smiled, 'That's right, I'm a secretary.'

Was I going mad, or was there a definite note of pride in her voice?

A secretary indeed! Could this possibly be Benjamin Khaled's daughter? I was choked, but so what, I still fancied her even if she didn't have any money. The old bastard, fancy not giving his own daughter any money and making her go out to work. Fontaine was clad from head to toe in mink, and this poor little bird had to go out to work. What a game.

Still it was just as well, if she'd had money everyone would have thought I was after that.

She was at the door, anxious to get back to see what Michael was up to, no doubt. I stayed sitting at the desk like an idiot.

'Shall we go back?' she enquired politely.

Didn't she realise I fancied her? Couldn't she tell? She treated me like I was nobody special. I mean, I don't want to sound big-headed but I do run the gaff and everybody digs a chat up by me. And I do have a good look, and she should

53

bloody well pay me *some* attention. Running after some little long-haired student, the girl was mad.

We went upstairs and Tina gave me a knowing smile.

At the table Sammy said loud-voiced as ever, ' 'Ere, where you bin?' and then 'The Twang' had the nerve to say, 'Tony babee, you're neglecting me, let's have a dance.'

That was the end of her. She had gone far enough. She could pack her false eyelashes and hank of hair and go.

Alexandra said a trifle irritably, 'Is Michael still dancing?'

Madelaine nodded and looked embarrassed. I seized the opportunity and grabbing Alexandra before she could sit down said, 'If you can't beat 'em, join 'em,' and I whipped her off to the dance floor.

I vaguely heard 'The Twang' shrieking in astonishment, 'Sonofabitch!'

Alexandra let me hold her at a discreet arm's length to the beat of 'Jimmy Mack'. I signalled Flowers to put on some slow sounds, and she said, 'Your girl-friend's furious.'

'My girl-friend.' I looked amazed. 'I've never seen her before tonight.'

She smiled, that insane innocent smile, and I pulled her a little closer as Flowers switched to 'Groovin' and she struggled a bit but I had her in a tight grip and I wasn't letting go. She smelt of clean hair and toothpaste, and I could feel her full breasts against me and her narrow waist was firm against my hands. She felt every bit as good as I'd expected her to.

'Isn't that Steve Scott?' she asked suddenly. He and Carolyn were wrapped casually around each other close by.

'Yeah—why? You like him?'

'Oh yes,' she was like a little schoolgirl, 'I always buy all his records, I think he's a terrific singer.'

Any second I expected her to produce an autograph book. She was a real sweet little innocent.

Suddenly I had a great idea, 'I'll tell you what I'll do for you since you're so nice.'

She looked at me with those big brown eyes.

'How would you like to go to a party at Steve Scott's house tomorrow?'

'Really? You mean I'd actually meet him?'

'Sure, I'll take you. How's that?'

She pondered a bit, 'Have you been invited?'

Oh, this girl was too much! I nodded seriously. 'Of course. We'll go, O.K.?'

'Can Madelaine come?'

Fuck bloody Madelaine, I was getting good and fed up with her, 'Well, that might be a bit tricky, but we'll go anyway.'

She made a snap decision, 'All right, but I can't stay out late.'

Had I made a wise move? Steve's parties were always a bit of an orgy. Well, that was O.K. We could always leave and go somewhere else—a nice romantic little restaurant, or my place, my sumptuous gaff off the Edgware Road. I kept on meaning to move, but who had the bread.

Flowers gave me a freaky look as we danced by, 'Man, who is the disc jockey tonight?' he muttered, rolling mad eyeballs. Sometimes he got very temperamental. He would go on kicks of playing far out sounds that nobody knew and then when he was told to play something a little more 'in' he would sulk for days. Then at times he was so stoned he didn't even know what he was playing. But when he was good, forget it. He could make the room move like nobody else. He was great.

Alexandra said, 'What shall I wear?'

All birds are for ever asking that question and you know they already have the whole outfit planned.

'Nothing dressy, whatever you fancy.'

Perhaps she would fancy something with a long back zip that I could get her out of in next to no time.

I must say I had been neglecting the club since Alexandra had arrived, but it suddenly came to my notice that a great struggle was going on in the corner, and all I could see was the backs of about three waiters and a worried-looking Franco. Alexandra felt so good I didn't want to let her go, but there was always tomorrow. Business was business. I gave her a gentle push in the direction of our table, 'Be a good girl and go sit down. I sense a little trouble.' Stewart Wade, bum drunken actor, was sitting on the floor screaming every four-letter word at the waiters while they answered angrily back in Italian. They were trying to pick him up and he was landing a drunken punch anywhere he could.

'What's the trouble?' I asked Franco.

He waved a lot of arms around, Italians when they get excited always seem to produce lots of arms. 'The punk, 'ee no wanna pay 'ees bill, 'ee broke one of my boys' noses, 'ee say 'ee never pay bill anywhere.'

I pushed through the waiters.

'Come on, baby,' I said, 'let's not cause a scene. On your feet.'

'Ah, Tony,' he had one of those booming Shakespearean voices. 'Tell these frigging morons to leave me alone.'

'Come on, sweetheart, let's go and talk about it outside.'

'I want to stay here.' He sat there, all two hundred pounds of him with a childish drunken smile. 'Fuck the lot of you,' he shouted gleefully. 'I'm Stewart Wade, *the* Stewart Wade, I never pay, so fuck you.'

The waiters were muttering angrily amongst themselves.

'Pick him up and throw him out,' I said. I'd had enough. Customers like him we didn't need.

Happy in their work, the four waiters grabbed him by the legs and arms and proceeded to carry him out bodily while he bellowed—'I'll get the frigging police,' and then he passed out cold. A large scrubber in a micro-mini with legs like a football player scurried out after him.

Franco and I looked at each other and shrugged. You get used to anything in our business.

Back at our table Michael and Suki had finally returned. Alexandra was saying she wanted to go, and so were Madelaine and Jonathan, but Michael was saying nothing, just looking a bit glassy-eyed in Suki's direction as she studied her face in a Mary Quant make-up box.

'I say, could we get the bill?' Jonathan asked.

'That's all right,' I looked at Alexandra who was looking at Michael, 'it's on me.'

'Oh, that's awfully nice of you,' Madelaine said. She wasn't bad in a debby sort of way. A suitable room-mate for Alexandra, not flighty, a bit plain and plump.

They all got up and exchanged goodbyes around the table. I walked them out front. I managed to pull Alexandra to the side, 'I'll pick you up around eight p.m.'

'Oh fine.' She looked like she had forgotten all about it.

They piled into the lift and left. The last glimpse I got of her she was staring accusingly at Michael. She opened her mouth to say something, but the lift doors closed.

I stretched in anticipation of the following night. I would soon have her forgetting all about Michael.

It was two a.m., peak time. Flowers came strolling out, the group had just gone. 'Just going round the corner, man,' he said. Off to get high, at least he had enough sense not to smoke in the club.

Hal appeared with his blue-rinsed bag. I had to admire him, he certainly had a lot of style. 'We're going to play a little chemmy,' he announced giving me the wink. That meant *he* was going to play a little chemmy with *her* money. He was a mad gambler and sometimes won a bundle which he would immediately blow on new gear.

She smiled at me, rows of nicotine-stained teeth, 'I just love your little old club, honey.'

Hal said, 'Mamie's got a girl-friend coming in next week if you want to make up a foursome.'

A girl-friend yet! She was about sixty! I shook my head seriously, 'I'm engaged.'

'Oh, what a shame, honey, she would have loved you.'

He was a bum. He knew I didn't go for the rich old widow scene, yet he never gave up, he was always trying to recruit me.

'You and I as a team, Tony, we'd destroy them,' he would say.

Fontaine was enough for me, thank you. I could just about make it with her, although it was becoming more and more difficult.

Fontaine—I had forgotten about her with her being away and all. But I glumly supposed she would be back soon. How would she feel about me and Alexandra? I pondered on this fact and decided she wouldn't like it. She wouldn't like it at all. It was a tricky situation. If I had any sense I wouldn't go near Miss Alexandra Al Khaled with a barge-pole. But I had flipped for her, she had really knocked me out. So let's face it, I wasn't playing it too smart, but so what, Fontaine would never find out, and Alexandra and I could have a fast affaire, then bye-bye. 'Schmuck,' a little voice kept saying in my ear, but I ignored it.

'Well, baby, I guess you and I can call it quits,' a furious voice said. It was 'The Twang', all quivering, sexy five foot five of her.

I wanted to say, 'Yes, you're right,' but Alexandra had put me in the mood, and 'The Twang' was there and ready, and there didn't seem to be much else available stock around. One more night with her wouldn't be too much of a hardship. I patted her sexy bum, 'Customers, my lovely, I've got to be nice to the paying people.' She pouted, and I put my arm around her, 'Let's dance.'

EIGHT

ALEXANDRA

What a week! It has simply rushed by, and *so* much has happened. Maddy and I are actually sitting here in our *own* flat, in *Chelsea*! And on Monday I start a *job*! And tonight I've got a date with Michael! ! It's all too super, and I just feel *so* lucky. Mummy was first class about the whole thing. She said, 'Just be sure to live a good life, and come home every weekend so I can be certain you get some proper food.' She gave me fifty pounds to put away, and she also came to town and looked at the flat with Maddy and me before we took it. We had lunch at Fortnum & Mason, and Mummy bought us a tea-set and some cutlery. Our flat is furnished, but Mummy said we shouldn't eat with old knives and forks. She should have seen what we ate with at boarding school.

Maddy and I have thoroughly discussed the Peter Lincoln Smith incident and came to the conclusion that he behaved like an utter pig! Maddy said I should tell Daddy. But I'm not a telltale, anyway I'd be too embarrassed and it would be childish.

We have both made up our minds that with the right boy it would be all right. Actually we have both decided that we *should* sort of—well you know—*sleep* with the right male. I mean sex is supposed to be so wonderful. Being a virgin is definitely out of date.

I have secretly decided that Michael and I should have an affair. Maddy and I discussed birth control for hours. Maddy says we should find a nice old doctor to prescribe us the pill. It certainly sounds a lot nicer than all the other undignified methods. I mean they all seem so *complicated*.

Between us our sexual experience is very limited. I have been kissed by about three boys, including Peter, and Maddy about the same, although, of course, she has been sort of semi-stripped when the school gardener got her bra and sweater off. We talked about that a lot. Maddy said she felt all sort of weak-kneed and super and he had kissed her there and sucked on her nipples like a baby. But then he had been so angry when she wouldn't let him go any further.

Maddy has small breasts. Mine are bigger. I feel all embarrassed when I think of Michael looking at them.

'I wonder what this Jonathan Roberts is like,' Madelaine suddenly said. 'Isn't it funny that Michael wants to be your date. Maybe I'll have you as a sister-in-law!' She giggled.

I blushed. 'Don't be so silly. He's just being nice to us I expect because we don't know anyone in London.'

'Huh! Michael's never been nice to me before. In fact, he's very selfish. *I* think he's after your body, your pure white virgin skin.'

Honestly, Madelaine could be so infuriating at times.

Michael had telephoned the day before and said that he and a friend of his were going to take us out. Maddy had answered the phone and I was trying to listen. 'Do you want to go?' she had whispered to me.

'Yes,' I whispered back. 'Of course I do.'

So it was settled, much to my delight, and they were picking us up at eight.

Michael had instructed his sister that we were to wear something casual. I had rushed down the Kings Road and found a Jaeger shop where I got some green tweed slacks and a matching sweater. There were lots of other shops with incredible clothes in the windows, but Mummy had always said, 'Buy quality' and I knew Jaeger was quality.

Michael and his friend Jonathan were half-an-hour late. I felt terrible waiting and thought they had forgotten all about us.

Jonathan seemed quite nice, and Madelaine looked pleased. Michael said, 'Well, girls, we're going to show you the town.' He looked terrific in a yellow roll-neck sweater and black trousers. Honestly, he is *so* good-looking!

We all piled into Jonathan's Mini, Maddy and me in the back. They took us to a very small cellar restaurant, absolutely jammed with people, and we sat at a corner table, scrubbed pine with a black candle in a glass holder. *Very* romantic, but rather noisy.

I was sitting opposite Michael and he leaned across and said, 'You don't look too bad tonight, London suits you.'

Oh, what a wonderful evening!

We drank red wine and ate chicken casserole. Madelaine got on awfully well with Jonathan, and Michael was really nice to me. In fact, the best thing was when he said to me at the end of the meal, 'You know I always thought you were a bit stupid, but for a girl you're quite intelligent.'

59

It was past twelve when we left, and Michael held my hand. I felt marvellous.

'What shall we do now?' Jonathan questioned Michael, 'Want to pop into "Judie's" and have a bit of a dance?'

'Oh God, I can't stand that place, it's always filled with such a grim crew.'

'How about "Hobo"?' I ventured. It hadn't been much fun for me before, but with Michael it would be different.

'I'm not a member,' he said, 'and they're very sticky about that.'

'That's all right,' I said, 'my father sort of has money in it, I'm sure we'll get in.'

'Not on a Saturday night, sweetie,' Jonathan said, 'that's the hottest place in town.'

'Oh, I'm *sure* it will be all right.' I felt rather proud of the fact that they all seemed to think the place was so exclusive. I tried to remember the name of the manager. Tony something —Beard, Bird—I wasn't quite sure.

'Look, if Alex says it's O.K., let's go,' Madelaine said.

'Well, it will be a wasted trip,' Jonathan said, 'that place is impossible. You've got to be Marlon Brando at least.'

'Come on, Marlon,' Michael said with a grin, squeezing my hand. 'Show us the impossible!'

By this time I was a bit nervous. What if I couldn't get us in? I wished I hadn't said anything.

Outside the club cars were double parked all down the street. Jonathan dropped us and we waited outside while he went off to park.

A beautiful girl arrived in a black sports car. She left it smack in the middle of the road and strode into the club. Michael turned to stare at her. I felt a horrible pang of jealousy.

Soon Jonathan got back and we all marched in, me in the front.

'Yes?' a blonde girl behind a desk questioned me.

'Er, we're friends of 'er—Benjamin Khaleds. He said it would be all right.'

'Did you book?' she enquired.

'Well no, but . . .'

'I'm sorry,' she shrugged, 'if you didn't book I can't help you.'

'I told you,' Jonathan jeered. 'Come on, let's go.'

'Just a minute,' I said, determined not to be embarrassed. 'Is

Mr Bird here?'

'Mr Who?' the girl behind the desk said.

'Mr Tony Beard.'

'Oh, you mean Mr Blake.' She pressed a buzzer on the desk and a waiter appeared. 'Luigi, tell Mr Blake—*if he's here*—that there's some people who say they're friends of Mr Khaleds.'

The girl smiled at me sympathetically. 'Saturday night you *must* book,' she said, 'and also a member has to sign you in. If I were you I'd talk to Mr Khaled, I ...'

I heard a voice behind me say, 'I'm awfully sorry but we just don't have a table.'

I turned quickly. It was the Manager. I smiled, 'Hello, do you remember me?'

Oh thank goodness, he's smiling back. 'Of course I do.'

'Couldn't you just squeeze us in somewhere? Daddy said it would be all right.'

I waited with a tense smile. Oh, how awful if he turned us away! But it was all right. He said he would find room for us somewhere and took hold of Michael's arm. I grinned triumphantly. We followed him in.

What a terrific place it is, with the loud music and frantic dancers. Oh, how super it is to be here with Michael.

We were crowded on to an already full table and I was absolutely jammed next to Michael. He took my hand and said slowly, 'Very, very good.'

It was all absolutely great until some awful funny girl appeared and started ogling Michael, and then he danced with her practically all night.

Oh, it was just too bad. The only good thing that happened was that I saw Steve Scott—in the flesh!! And Tony Blake invited me to a party at Steve Scott's house!

I was very quiet on the drive back to our flat, and then Jonathan parked the car and he and Maddy started talking in low voices. I was trapped in the back seat with Michael.

He said, 'Well, little Alex, we'll have to do this again.'

Little Alex! I was furious!

'I say, Maddy,' I said in a loud voice, 'we've been invited to a party at Steve Scott's tomorrow night. Tony Blake's going to take us.'

Maddy squealed. 'Oh, marvie! How did you manage that?'

Michael said, 'You can't go out with Tony Blake.'

'Why not?' I asked, my heart fluttering.

'You just can't,' Michael said. 'Two silly little kids like you, he'll eat you for dinner!'

Honestly! 'Come on, Mads, let's go in.' How dare he call us silly little kids.

'Thank you for dinner,' I added, and then rushed into our entrance, not even waiting for Maddy.

Tears were stinging my eyes.

I think I am in love!

NINE

FONTAINE

New York is cold. The people in the streets and shops are boring. They all seem to discover you're English and to them this means instant friendship, they think they can chat to you for hours about their dreary grandma in Scunthorpe. Today a perfect stranger came up to me in 'Bendels', and demanded in a deep Southern drawl where had I got my dinky chinchilla. Why she practically ripped it off my back with her eyes. However, they are chic, the very rich women.

Ray has become the darling of the society set. They all pop into him for their sets and comb-outs. Actually, he's become a bit effeminate, I'm shocked! He who was always so virile. Maybe it's my imagination, but I'm not usually wrong about these things. He hasn't even approached me about going to bed together. Success had definitely gone to his head. I shall have to talk to Benjamin about him, take the salon away or something like that.

After a week here I find myself thinking about Tony. A week of nothing sexually, only a short two-hour affaire with the husband of a friend of mine. Nothing special, rather boring actually.

It would be rather amusing to have Tony come over for a few days. Show the sexy animal off. I could tell Benjamin I wanted Tony to see New York, to find out what he thinks about opening 'Hobo' here. Tony would love it. I could buy him some clothes, show him the city.

Yes, I shall call Benjamin tonight and have him arrange the whole thing. Tony could be here by Monday and we can fly back the following weekend together.

I dressed carefully. Lunch with Sarah at the '21', wife of the man I'd had the two-hour affaire with. I knew she wanted to tell me about her latest lover. The gossip around town said he was a Chinese waiter. Well Sarah has always been kinky, so I wasn't surprised. Sarah would adore Tony. She's a very well educated society matron in her thirties, thin and beautiful, we used to model together. She married a Texan oil millionaire, then a Californian property millionaire, and now Allen, attractive unsuccessful writer. She has loads of money and Allen spends it well. They both have affaires and neither seems to mind. Actually she would be rather pleased if I told her about Allen and me. He wasn't very good though, a disappointment.

Sarah looked divine. If ever I decided to turn lesbian she would be my choice. Thin slavic face, jet black hair dramatically plastered down with a centre parting. She wore yellow, this year's Dior, I was a little more avant garde in Yves Saint Laurent.

We started with champagne cocktails and ordered melon and steak. Life is a permanent diet.

'Tell me all,' I demanded.

She smiled dreamily, 'Fontaine, my darling, if you haven't tried the mysteries of the East you haven't lived.'

I smiled back, 'I like my men a little—shall we say taller?'

She giggled, 'It's the quality not the quantity.'

'Give me quantity, to hell with quality!'

It was a pleasant lunch, I always enjoyed being with Sarah. We are alike in many ways.

Later I called Benjamin, 'Darling, I've got a marvellous idea. What about a "Hobo" here? Yes, here in New York. Can you arrange to have Tony Blake sent over for a few days? Now, immediately, tomorrow if possible. You're wonderful, of course I miss you. Yes, darling, have your secretary call me back with the details. Yes, of course I'll be home soon. I love you too, 'bye.' Poor old Benjamin. He really believed I loved him. I mean how could he? Didn't he ever look at himself?

Oh well, a party at the Sidwells tonight. Better dazzle them with the new Courrèges. Soon I would be dazzling them all with Tony. Quelle fun!

TEN

TONY

It's four o'clock in the afternoon and there's no getting rid of
'The Twang'. It's her day of rest and she's making the most of
it. Fast asleep like a lump of clay, unmade-up face hidden
beneath a tangle of hair. In the daylight it's orange and quite
revolting, she says it photographs fantastically. She's very
ambitious. I'm also ambitious, ambitious to get her out of my
bed and on her way.

I gave her a gentle tap on the shoulder, she snuggled down
in the bed and snored softly. Oh man, the only thing that was
going to wake her was something I didn't feel like giving her
this morning.

I went in the bathroom and had a wash. She slept on. I made
coffee and turned the telly up loud. She didn't stir. I gave her a
shove. She sighed and stretched out tarantula arms. I ignored
them. She opened sleep-filled eyes and said, 'C'mon back to
bed, baby.'

Really, she and Sammy would have been great together.

'Get up, Janine,' I said, 'my mother's coming to visit.'

'Your mother,' her eyes snapped wide open and she sat up
revealing full orange-tipped boobs fresh out of the centre spread
in *Playboy*.

'Yeah, my mother, she takes it into her head once a year to
come—today's the day.'

'Oh shit,' Janine twanged and got up.

She was built. Although without her make-up her face was
puffy and washed out. It's amazing what make-up can do for
a girl. She stomped into the bathroom and closed the door. I
congratulated myself on the mother bit, and tidied up. I could
go out, get something to eat and then get ready to pick up
Alexandra. I wanted the pad to be in good shape in case she
wanted to view it.

Janine emerged an hour later face in place, figure in sweater,
and too short skirt. Her kind of figure didn't go with mini-
mini's. She was playing it cool, trying to look like she didn't
care too much. I had gathered her things together in case she
hadn't twigged.

She smiled at me coolly, 'Bye, sweetheart,' she said, 'see you around.' And exit 'The Twang'.

I phoned Sammy.

'What a night,' he moaned, 'the little raver wouldn't leave me alone.'

'You want to grab something to eat?' I asked him.

'Yeah, pick me up.'

I pulled on old gear, and drove over to his place five minutes away. I was driving some decrepit old mini that a girl-friend had left with me to look after while she did a dancing tour of the Far East. I wondered if Sammy could be conned into lending me his E-type for tonight. Very sexy the E-type, a low slung roaring phallic symbol.

Sammy looked terrible, still in his dressing-gown, unshaven and seedy eyed. 'I'm giving up the young ones,' he announced, 'too much bloody energy.'

We went to a little salt beef hangout nearby and I listened to the tale of Miss fifteen-year-old's sexy acrobatics.

'And to top it all,' Sammy concluded, 'she pinched a fiver from beside the bed when she left. Liberty!' By this time it was half past six and I wanted to get home and changed for Alexandra.

'What are you doing tonight, Samuel?'

'Going to bed, I'm knocked out.'

'Can I borrow your car?'

'What for? You've got the mini.'

'Oh, come on, Sammy, I've got an important date, I couldn't possibly take her in that.'

'Who is it?' Sammy was like a nosey old woman.

I kept my voice casual, 'You know, the little bird from last night, Alexandra.'

'She's not your style,' Sammy said in surprise. 'You like flashier models than that.'

'I like her,' I said shortly. 'Can I borrow it?'

'Sure, only I've got to 'ave it by eight tomorrow morning.'

He tossed me the keys and I gave him the keys of the mini. He was all right Sammy was.

At home the phone was ringing and under my door was a telegram. I picked up the receiver and flipped open the buff coloured envelope.

'Mr Blake?' a crisp efficient bird's voice, 'this is Alice, Benjamin Khaled's secretary, I've been trying to get you all day but your line's been out of order.'

I always take the phone off the hook when I'm asleep.

'Yeah,' I said. Maybe Fontaine had had an accident.

'Mr Khaled requires that you fly to New York to investigate the suitability of opening a "Hobo" there.'

'Oh!' I was stunned.

'Mrs Khaled suggests you come immediately, I actually had you booked on the eight p.m. flight, but I shouldn't think you'll make that now. Of course if you rushed ...'

I interrupted, 'I can't go tonight, death in the family you know,' I always have been an exaggerated liar.

'Oh,' the crisp voice paused, 'Well, how about seven-forty-five tomorrow morning?'

What the hell was this? What was all the urgency? Of course I would love to see New York, but what was the panic? I scanned the wire quickly.

Need you here. Benjamin will explain. Make it fast. Fontaine.

'How long am I supposed to go for?' I asked Alice.

'A few days I believe, is the seven-forty-five all right?'

'Yes, that's O.K.'

'Fine, a car will pick you up at six a.m., everything will be taken care of this end, a car will meet you on arrival. Bon voyage!' Alice's crisp voice hung up. I sat back a bit stunned. New York. I'd always wanted to go there. What about visas and everything? I thought it took months. What should I take? 'Hobo' in New York. What a scene that would be!

There was no time to waste, I didn't want to be late for Alexandra. I'm off to New York in the morning—sounded good.

I sorted out some things to take, counted my money, only twenty quid, well I supposed Fontaine would take care of that. Then I dressed. Best casual clobber. Groomed the barnet. I was ready.

Alexandra and Madelaine lived in a big grim block of flats. I rang the bell of No. 14 and waited. I was shocked when Madelaine's brother Michael answered. He was unconcerned at seeing me, and invited me into an old-fashioned large living-room. Madelaine bounced in next, dressed in a flouncy blue dress, she said, 'Is it going to be all right for me to come too?'

I looked sad. 'Sorry, darling, absolutely not. I warned Alex.'

'Oh,' Madelaine's bounce sagged a bit, but she lit a cigarette and choked. Then she brightened, 'Well, Alex can tell me all about it anyway.' She wasn't a bad little bird, certainly understanding.

Michael offered me a drink. He acted like he lived there. Then, enter Alexandra. She looked lovely in one of those Victorian-type dresses with all frills everywhere, her hair was tied back and she really looked so young and pretty. I was knocked out.

Michael said, 'You've got everything but the kitchen stove on.'

She glared at him and replied, 'Better than wearing the minimum.'

Rather clever I thought. I said, 'I think you look great,' and she smiled triumphantly at Michael.

I was getting a bit fed up with the whole thing between her and the idiot, so I quickly downed the weak scotch he had given me and said, 'Come on, we can't be late.'

Then followed a whole explanation about why Madelaine couldn't come too. I was in trouble if Steve Scott blew his big mouth off about open house. Finally we got out of there and she admired Sammy's E-type, I forgot to mention it wasn't mine, I mean why confuse things? And then we were off.

It suddenly struck me we were much too early to go to the party. I mean nine-thirty would be earliest we could possibly appear, and then we'd probably be the first anyway.

A nice cosy drink somewhere was the thing. I decided the rooftop bar at the Hilton was suitably romantic. London shimmering and shining below us was a good scene. Or maybe I should destroy her with one of those wild drinks at Trader Vic's.

She was sitting demurely, the ribbon tying back her hair gave her a real little girl look. To tell the truth, I was a bit worried about taking her to Steve's. His parties got very wild, plenty of booze and birds and everyone turning on. I don't go for the pot scene myself—cannot see what all the fuss is about—it doesn't do anything for me. Just give me a few scotches and I'm all right. Of course, in my business, to certain people, I have to pretend I turn on—otherwise they would think I wasn't cool, and you've got to keep a hip image going. Fontaine and friends smoke occasionally. It's like a gang of children having naughty fun. They think they are so decadent. I have found that the really cool pot smokers just get on with it and don't make a whole group scene. Hal was always high, but he never discussed it.

'It's a shame Madelaine couldn't come,' Alexandra said.

'Yeah, sorry about that. Listen, I thought we'd grab a fast drink, we're early for the party.'

'Oh, what time does it start?' She fiddled with a few of her Victorian frills.

'About nine. Is the Hilton O.K. for you?'

She nodded. 'I've never been there.'

I was amazed, I'd never met anyone who hadn't been in the Hilton.

I took her to the rooftop bar. If she'd never been there this was something she had to see. The view was a knockout.

I could see she couldn't decide what to drink so I ordered her a champagne cocktail and I had a double scotch and coke. We attacked the nuts and she giggled a bit and said, 'What a super place!'

'Have you really never been here?' I was still surprised.

'No,' she shook her head. 'Actually I haven't spent very much time in London at all, Mummy hates it, so we never came. But now I've finished school I wanted to come so much and Mummy simply had to agree to let me share a flat with Madelaine—you see Madelaine's mother and mine are best friends.'

'What about your father?' I asked.

'Oh, Daddy,' she shrugged. 'Well, since he married that awful woman we haven't really spent much time with him,' she stopped, then rushed on, 'I suppose I shouldn't call her an awful woman, but she is.'

If she had stuck her tongue out and added—so there—I wouldn't have been surprised.

I wondered what Alexandra would have said if she'd known about the affaire Fontaine and I were having.

She sipped her champagne cocktail and I gulped my scotch. Her dress didn't reveal any flesh at all, even her arms were covered and the skirt wasn't particularly short. As if she sensed me thinking this she said, 'Now that I'm in London I must shorten my skirts, I feel like an old frump. In Switzerland we had to wear a regulation skirt length and that was that.'

'You don't need your skirt any shorter,' I said quickly. Quite frankly, I was fed up to the teeth with all the birds around practically exposing their knicks. On a clear night in the club you could see for ever. I didn't want Alexandra joining the ranks of the ass flashers. Really a very short skirt only looks good on a seventeen-year-old flat-chested girl with great legs (thin) and how many of those are there around? Not many I can tell you.

Alexandra finished her drink, 'What time can we go to the party?' she asked brightly.

I glanced at my watch—one of Fontaine's very few presents —Roman numerals, black croc strap—it was nearly nine, so I figured it would be all right.

Just as I asked for the cheque, a loud voice yelled, 'Tony, honey pie,' and arms were thrown around me. It was Molly Mandy. Just what I needed. She was wearing a multi-coloured jersey dress cut out everywhere, and as I tried to disentangle myself from her I noticed Alexandra's look of—well—amazement I guess. Molly finished her greeting, flashed very white teeth in a friendly smile at Alexandra, winked, said, 'Have a ball,' laughed, and swung off back to her escort, a soberly dressed old man, her speciality. God knows where she found them and God knows why they wanted to be seen out with her.

'Who's that?' Alexandra asked a bit breathlessly.

'Just a girl that comes into the club, a dress designer. Come on.'

I took hold of her hand, it went a bit stiff, but she didn't pull it away. We set off for the elevator. Oh, if Fontaine could see me now. I thought I had better cover my tracks.

'Listen, you know your father might not approve of my taking you out. I work for him in a roundabout way and he just might not like it, so I think it's best not to mention it. Right?'

'All right,' she replied, a bit surprised.

'I'd like to see you a lot more,' I added quickly. 'What do you think?'

I was making a right berk of myself. Never acted so stupid with a girl. The right way to go about it with someone you like is at the end of the evening to mumble casually, 'I'll call you' and then don't call for two weeks. That always gets them going. But I thought this girl was wonderful and sweet and warm and I wanted her to know how I felt. We were outside. 'Party time,' I said, and helped her into the car.

I was right, we were too early. Steve lounged to the door in his underpants and a sweater.

'Come on in,' he said, 'just finished boffing, where's your bottle?'

I'd forgotten he'd said to bring a bottle. Carolyn appeared wrapping a pink dressing-gown around her. She had nothing underneath and I noticed the firmness of her small breasts and I remembered the night we'd had together. She was a right raver.

'Tony, you're so bloody cheap,' she said, 'no bottle indeed, I suppose you forgot.' She smiled at Alexandra. 'Hi, I'm Carolyn.'

Alexandra smiled back and I noticed her eyes wandering to Steve's nether regions, in fact he was nearly hanging out. I started a slow burn.

'Make yourselves at home,' Steve said, 'we're going to dress. Answer the door if it rings.'

'He's terrific,' Alexandra whispered when he'd gone.

'Yes, I could see you liked him,' I replied drily, but it was lost on her.

I fixed her a vodka, all I could find. She made a face, but sipped it all the same. I couldn't see any food. Steve was the one that was cheap.

Soon the mob started to arrive. All the familiar faces. What a small town London really is. I spread the word I was off to New York to open a joint. Everyone was suitably impressed. Steve's parties were O.K. when they started, it was only after a couple of hours that they went to rack and ruin.

Alexandra seemed quite happy sitting with her vodka (third one, I aimed to get her smashed).

Steve said to me, 'Who's the sweet little pussy cat?'

Dirty bastard—I hadn't thought she would be his type. He was chatting her a bit and I was choked. I didn't leave her side, and then who should walk in but 'The Twang'.

'Ooh, Tony, is that your mother?' she asked in her loud nasal voice. I could have killed her. 'You're a lousy sonofabitch,' she said in a lower voice, 'I could take my choice, you know—I don't need you.'

Well, why didn't she leave me alone then? I figured it was time to go. I didn't want Alexandra involved in the pot scene that was starting.

'Come on,' I said, 'the time has come to find food.'

'I feel awful,' Alexandra said, 'sort of buzzy.'

I got her up and she leaned on me, and I realised she was loaded, my fault.

Janine said, 'Bye-bye, lover boy.' She really had a big mouth.

71

Outside the cold air hit Alexandra like a ton of bricks and she clung to my jacket and said, 'I feel sick.' Then she was sick, narrowly missing my jacket by inches, then she started to cry and I felt like the world's worst shit.

'Please take me home,' she moaned.

So much for an evening of fun. I got her in the car and she huddled miserably on her seat, 'I'm so embarrassed,' she said weakly, 'it's so awful. I've never done anything like that before.'

'Don't worry about it,' I said, 'it happens to everybody you just had a little bit over the odds, you'll soon feel better.'

'I'm so sorry.' She really was in a state.

'I'll tell you what, we'll go back to my place and I'll fix you some eggs and you can rest up a bit.'

She made a face, 'I couldn't eat, ugh! I just want to crawl into bed and hide.'

Didn't she realise that's what I had in mind? 'Well, how about some coffee then, nice strong black coffee?'

She nodded and I headed the phallic E-type in the direction of my pad. I switched the car radio on, a touch of Aretha Franklin at her most soulful—very nice. Things were looking up.

We arrived and Alexandra said, 'Where are we?'

'My place, going to make you some nice hot coffee.'

'Oh, Tony, I'm being such a bother. I can make some coffee, you don't have to go to all this trouble. Just drop me home, and I'll be off your hands.' Was she very smart or genuinely an innocent?

I got out of the car and helped her out. 'It's no bother.'

She looked a bit pale, but being sick had obviously done her good. We stood by the car, 'I'd rather go home,' she said, 'I'd feel much happier.'

'Don't be silly,' I was determined to get her to my flat, 'you'll feel better after some coffee.'

'No, really, Tony, I simply must go home.' She started to climb back into the car. Well, I couldn't stand there arguing all night. Mummy had probably warned her about going to big bad men's apartments, and Mummy was dead right. I got into the car too.

She smiled at me, 'You're being very kind.'

How could I resist those liquid brown eyes. I took her home, saw her to the front door. Shook her hand (her idea, not mine), kissed her on the cheek (my idea), said goodbye and promised to phone her as soon as I got back from New York.

'Super,' she said, and was inside her flat with the door closed in my face quick as a flash. Charming!

But she was a lovely little bird, and I could wait.

ELEVEN

ALEXANDRA

Madelaine and I discussed it. I was forced to tell her how I felt about Michael, because I had to tell someone, and since she was his sister and my best friend perhaps she could help.

She roared with laughter when she heard. 'Michael. Soppy old Michael! You're joking, I hope.' But then she could see that I wasn't joking and she got very serious and said, 'Alex, he's terrible with girls. He just wants them for one thing and then drops them.'

I didn't see how Maddy could know that. After all, she had been away at school with me for most of the year. Anyway if he wanted one thing he could have it.

We sat up late on Saturday night talking and Maddy came to the conclusion that the best thing to do was make him jealous. 'I think he quite likes you,' she said, 'only I don't think he looks on you as a potential girl-friend. After all, you've known each other since we were all kids together.'

'He still thinks I am a kid,' I said miserably, 'he said so.'

'We've just got to make him realise how gorgeous and desirable you are.' Maddy's eyes were gleaming, she loved organising things. 'Tomorrow night, when Tony comes to fetch us—we'll get Michael to be here, and you'll sweep past him looking absolutely fantastic and sort of act very cold and off-hand with him.'

'How do I look absolutely fantastic? I haven't got anything to wear.'

We went through my wardrobe and the only thing remotely glamorous I possessed was a frilly terylene dressing-gown.

'You can wear that!' Maddy exclaimed. 'Put a belt around it and no one will know.'

I tried it on, and with shoes and a belt it really did look quite good. So I decided I would wear that and we finally got to bed at three a.m. I was exhausted.

Maddy phoned Michael the next morning. Actually it was about twelve o'clock as we both overslept.

'We're in frightful trouble,' she wailed, 'we've blown a fuse and I can't work the television, and the stopper's jammed in the bath.'

'Oh hell,' Michael said. I was listening on the extension 'all right, I'll come over when I get up.'

'We've got to pop out now. Do you think you could make it about seven?'

'Seven. Where the bloody hell are you going?'

'Oh, we have to go and see Alex's father. Is seven O.K., then?'

'Yes, I suppose so, but I can't take you for dinner if that's what you're getting at. I've got a date.'

'That's O.K.,' Maddy said sweetly, and she hung up giggling. 'All fixed,' she declared. 'Now you've got to really devastate him.'

We spent the afternoon in preparation. I washed my hair and Maddy set it. I washed the dressing-gown and Maddy ironed it. It was fun having a flat of our own. We had bacon sandwiches for lunch, and pears and cream for tea washed down with heaps of Coca-Cola. What a thrill to be able to do what you like!

When Michael arrived I was shut in the bedroom with my hair in rollers trying to do a proper make-up. My hand shook and I smudged the eyeliner, so I had to take it all off and start again.

Maddy was all ready, and she had promised to keep Michael busy until Tony arrived. I wasn't supposed to come out of the bedroom until Tony got there, then I was supposed to just glide out and practically ignore Michael.

I do hope Maddy knows what she's doing. Maybe Michael will think I'm the most awful snob or something like that.

I was only just ready by eight, and then I heard the doorbell and I counted a slow sixty as arranged (it felt like six thousand and sixty!) I then walked casually (my heart was beating so loud I was surprised no one mentioned it!) into the living-room.

Michael was sprawled in a chair.

'I can't come,' Madelaine wailed, 'Tony said he tried to get me invited too, but it's just not possible.'

'Oh no! What a shame.' I didn't really want to go without Madelaine, especially now.

'Sorry, girls,' Tony said, 'just one of those things. Come on, we can't be late.'

I looked at Michael. Was he just going to let me walk out of here with a comparative stranger to a wild pop star's party and not say anything? Apparently he was.

75

'Goodbye,' I said.

Madelaine smiled half-heartedly, and Michael said, 'Don't forget to get his autograph!'

Tony had a very nice car. Actually he was really being awfully sweet to me. I wonder why he's bothering. Because of Daddy, I suppose. Lots of people are nice to me because of Daddy, him being so rich and everything.

Mummy always says, 'Having money doesn't make you any better than the next person.'

Tony said, 'We'll go to the Hilton for a drink first.'

It was rather fun and I drank champagne.

Tony seemed awfully popular. He joked with the barman and kept on saying hello to people. He made me feel very comfortable and he was funny. I wished Michael could be as nice as him.

I suppose a lot of girls would consider him very good-looking. He had lovely black curly hair, but he's really not my type, and goodnes, I'm sure I'm not his!

'What time can we go to the party?' I asked.

The champagne had made me feel good and I was determined to forget about Michael and have a nice time.

When we left, Tony held my hand. We went to the lift, then Tony said the most surprising thing, he said that Daddy might not approve of his taking me out and would I please not tell him. Well, that confused me. I mean I had thought that was the reason for his taking me out—to sort of get in Daddy's good books.

'All right,' I said, wondering why on earth he *was* taking me out.

Steve Scott's party was wonderful. We were the first ones there and he answered the front door practically naked. Then he and his girl-friend went off to dress and Tony gave me a drink, I don't know what it was but it tasted vile. I swallowed it down, anyway.

Tony was sweet, he stayed by my side most of the evening and I felt so sort of light-headed and witty. I felt I could talk to anyone, I even knew exactly what I would say to Michael if he was there.

Steve Scott was terrific. Once, when Tony was fetching me another drink, he sat on the arm of my chair and said, 'I bet you've never had it.'

'Had what?' I replied, smiling excitedly.

'Oh baby,' he laughed, 'I could show you a thing or two.

76

You and I could really fly.'

Then Tony came back, and Steve said, 'Who's the sweet little pussy cat?'

Tony said, 'Hands off, lover boy.'

Then Tony's girl-friend appeared and started yelling at him, and I drank some more of my drink, it was about my fifth, and Steve said, 'What's your phone number, sweetheart. Little girls like you are far too rare.'

So I gave him my phone number, and Tony came back and said we should go. Just when the party was getting to be fun. I couldn't wait to tell Madelaine that Steve Scott had asked for my phone number!!

As soon as I stood up I felt definitely and horribly sick.

Tony put his arm around me and helped me outside, and then—talk about being embarrassed—I *was* sick and could have died! Why didn't the pavement just open up and swallow me!

'Please take me home,' I begged Tony, hardly daring to look at him. I must say he really was very nice about it, kept on talking about going for coffee and food. Ugh! I couldn't face food. Really I couldn't face anything, I just wanted to get home and into bed.

He drove somewhere and stopped the car.

'Where are we?' I asked.

'My place, I'm going to make you some nice hot coffee.'

He got me out of the car and I got back in and insisted it was too much trouble and I *had* to go home.

He was very nice about it. I don't expect he really wanted to be bothered making me coffee anyway. After all, he was off on a trip to America the next day and I expect he had to get up early.

Oh, the relief of saying goodnight to Tony, dashing into our flat, and throwing up again.

He was probably glad to be rid of me, anyway.

TWELVE

FONTAINE

The thought of struggling along some crowded freeway with a talkative chauffeur is an utter bore.

I did want to see Tony, and although I hadn't planned to go to the airport, I suddenly decided it might be fun. So I cancelled lunch with friends, managed to sit through the boring drive to Kennedy International, and here comes Tony now. I can see him through the glass standing in line for Customs. He has a cheap suitcase—nothing worse, a give-away immediately. I must take him into Gucci.

He does look attractive, rather white in the daylight, he has an eerie night-club pallor which makes an exciting contrast to his jet black hair. What a shame he's not a bit more intelligent, though if he was he wouldn't be wasting his life away in a discothèque.

Poor Tony. Poor stud. What will happen to him when his hard body and curly hair are gone? Who will want him then?

At last he's through Customs and hurrying towards me smiling. He's not subtle, I can see he's going to kiss me, so I fend him off with a handshake—stupid boy, there are always photographers lurking.

'How was your trip?'

'Great,' he yawned, exhibiting his tonsils to America, 'saw a movie, boozed a bit, what's this all about anyway?'

I shrugged, 'Just an idea of mine.' It was best not to tell him I wanted to see him, it would go to his head and he would become impossible.

'Have you got a location or what?'

'Oh no, we're not that advanced, I thought I would hear your opinions and see what you think. We can visit all the competition and you can decide if it would be a good idea.'

He laughed, he had good strong white teeth, 'You mean all the panic was just for me to look around?'

'Yes, actually it was, I thought you would be thrilled to see New York.'

'Yeah—but did I have to leave like a shot out of a gun?'

'Really Tony, I'm surprised at you, you wanted to come while I was still here, didn't you?'

We were in the car by this time and I told the chauffeur to go to my apartment. Alice had arranged a room for Tony at a hotel, but he could damn well accommodate me before going there. I laid my hand lightly over his, 'How's "Hobo"? Have any of my friends been in?'

Tony shook his head. He didn't look as delighted with this trip as I had thought he would be. He was probably tired from the journey.

'What about Vanessa and Leonard?'

'Haven't seen them.'

'Not even her?'

He looked at me, guilty as hell, probably been screwing the life out of her.

Oh well, *I* had him now.

I certainly wasn't going to force the conversation, let him be uncommunicative and sulky. I leaned back in the car and closed my eyes.

Tony Blake should be kissing my feet. I had found him. If it wasn't for me he'd still be a waiter, bowing and scraping all over the place, full of phoney smiles and running for a tip. The trouble with people is that they never appreciate what you do for them.

Tony probably thought he would still have been successful without me. I mean, really, 'Hobo' was all my idea. I could have taken any one of hundreds of good-looking studs, installed them there and each one of them would have been as popular as Tony.

'This is wild!' Oh goody, the great oaf was finally talking. We were entering the city and Tony was window gazing at the tall buildings, rushing people and general din. Big dirty New York, the city of fairy tales and garbage cans, society balls and riots. You could get anything or do anything here, as long as you had the money of course.

'I thought I'd take you to my apartment first, and then the chauffeur will take you to your hotel. I've got all sorts of exciting things planned for tonight.'

'Great,' his voice lacked enthusiasm. Tony was definitely not himself.

Benjamin had done rather well for me in the Big City. I suppose you could say I have one of the best apartments here. Of course Tony's eyes fell out as soon as he saw it. It's one of my favourite homes, small—only three bedrooms—but with this marvellous four-sided terrace which goes all around, alive with rose bushes, winter flowers, and an adorable lemon tree, very pretty. Adamo—our Vietnamese man, takes care of it. He bowed us in and produced martinis.

'Lunch is laid out in the blue room, Madam,' he spoke like an English butler, perfect. All my friends were trying to steal him, but he liked working for Benjamin and me, after all we are hardly ever here.

'Fine Adams, you may go, I'll buzz if I need you.'

'Very good, Madam.'

He lived in the basement of the building, very convenient, easy to summon and easy to get rid of.

Tony was prowling around. 'This is fabulous,' he said, 'I've never seen anything like it, this view is the end.'

'How about this view?' I unbuttoned my dress.

One thing I'll say for Tony—he knows his part—and tired or not, he'll play.

We embraced very slowly and then he pushed me to the floor and took off the rest of my clothes.

'Welcome to New York,' I whispered.

He *was* a stud.

THIRTEEN

TONY

I don't think I've ever met a girl like Alexandra before. She's so sort of innocent and girlish and pretty and soft. She looks great. Clean and tidy and young, I really like her, I really do. Even the thought of New York doesn't turn me on too much and Fontaine doesn't turn me on at all any more. In view of the close relationship involved I'd be much better off to avoid Fontaine completely. (Impossible) My only chance is to get away from 'Hobo' and open up on my own. But there's that old problem—money.

I fancy the hostess wriggling up and down the aisle in that tight skirt. I bet she's got something waiting for *her* in New York. Sammy says he's made it on a plane, on a night trip to the South of France. According to him, he had it off with the hostess in the loo—bit crowded I bet.

'Can I get you anything?' She smiled at me, ignoring the old lady in the seat beside me.

'Yeah—but I don't think it's on the menu.'

She giggled, getting the message immediately. These airhostesses weren't slow.

'Do you wish to see the movie?' She smoothed down her tight skirt.

'Any other suggestions?'

Another giggle. 'Well, some of the passengers come and sit at the back if they have already seen the film.'

There's no doubt about it, I'm irresistible to women! 'I'll come and sit at the back then.'

'Good.' Another smile, and then wiping it off, she leaned across to the old lady and said briskly, 'If you care to see the film there will be a slight charge!' I got a whiff of perfume— cheap but clean.

We had only been in the air an hour, but I reckoned I was going to be all right.

After a decent interval of three minutes I followed Miss Tight Skirt to the back of the plane. She was busy with another girl getting tin foil trays of cold roast beef, congealed potato salad and hard-boiled eggs that had seen better days.

'Need any help?' I asked, trying to squeeze into the tiny

kitchen.

'Sorry, you're not allowed in here,' but she smiled to take away the sting. 'You can sit in any of the back row seats if you like, I'll be free when the movie starts.'

The other girl grinned at me too, she had a suntan and freckles. It looks like being a jolly afternoon.

I sat down near the window, viewed the grey expanse of sky and sea, and fell asleep.

I was woken up by Miss Tight Skirt sitting beside me. I kept on thinking of Sammy's experience. 'Ever done any night flight to Nice?' I asked casually.

'Why yes, as a matter of fact I used to be on that run.'

Oh no, it couldn't be true!

The movie was on and the plane was pretty dark. We were sitting on the inside two seats of a three-seater, and there was no one across the aisle.

'What's happening?' I asked.

'Anything you like,' she replied.

I mean, it had to be the same girl.

I thought of Alexandra so sweet and innocent. I guess I wouldn't be being unfaithful, because nothing had happened with her—yet. I put a hand on the hostess's knee.

'Oh come on,' she said, 'you can do better than that.' She pulled a big regulation rug across us. 'Shirley will warn us if anyone comes back to go to the loo.'

What a scene! Under the rug I fought my hand up the tight skirt. She wriggled down in the seat helping me. She had nothing on underneath, making things very easy she was! I unhooked her bra under her prim blouse, her breasts were small but nice, I wished I could see them but there we were all huddled up under the rug.

She unzipped my trousers and with a deft movement twisted herself towards me, and then I was up up and away!

'What about the pilot and stewards?' I asked. She was wriggling and squirming at a good pace.

'It's all right, they're all boozing up front,' she gasped.

Charming, the pilots were boozing up front, and the hostess was screwing at the back. I wouldn't travel on this airline again! Next time it would be British or American for me—less exhausting!

'Quick, someone's coming,' a whispered voice said. It was Shirley, and how right she was!

Oh boy—fun at twenty-six thousand feet, I was hardly

finished when Tight Skirt pulled out and all in one movement was standing, smoothing her skirt down, and smiling at the passenger who was on his way to the loo.

'Everything all right, sir?'

He nodded. 'Er, I'd like a whisky and soda, is that possible?'

She winked at me, destroyed under the blanket. 'Everything's possible on this airline, sir.'

She deftly hooked her bra as he carried on to the john. 'I don't know your name,' she said to me, 'but I hope you'll fly with us again.'

I went back to my seat, there seemed no point in hanging around. The old lady smiled and nodded to me. 'Lovely trip,' she said.

'It certainly was!'

'I beg your pardon?'

'Nothing.' I slouched down in my seat and watched the end of a silent Doris Day movie. A silent Doris Day is better than a talkative one. Man, I was tired, I fell off to sleep until Tight Skirt appeared pushing my shoulder and saying, 'Fasten your safety belt, please, we're coming in to land.'

She had freshened up and added a jacket and matching cap. Very smart and efficient.

I yawned and inspected the view. New York was spread out beneath me. What a sight! I wondered what Alexandra was doing now. Poor little chick getting sick like that. I scribbled her a fast postcard conveniently supplied along with a paper bag to throw up in.

'Dear A. Dull flight. Had any good vodka lately? See you soon—Tony.'

On the way out I handed it to Tight Skirt to post.

'What are you doing tonight?' I asked, more for conversation than anything else.

She gave me a wide grin, 'Going on the town with my fiancé, he's the pilot you know.'

Charming!

I went through Immigration and Customs. An emergency visa had been waiting for me at London airport, along with a vaccination. Money can buy anything.

Fontaine was there to meet me, wrapped in mink, shod in crocodile. I was surprised, I didn't think airports were her scene. I forced a smile and set off in her direction. Everyone was taking a second look, she was that kind of woman. She wanted me to kiss her, she offered that elegant chiselled face,

83

but I wasn't going to fall for that with everybody looking our way. Benjamin could be having her followed or anything and I wasn't going to be a patsy. We shook hands and chatted about the journey. I was dying to find out what this trip was all about, but she was giving nothing away.

We rode in silent luxury to her apartment. She kept on questioning me about who had been in, but that was all.

What a great apartment! Huge and very modern on the top floor of the tallest building I've ever seen, surrounded by a wild garden with a not-to-be believed oriental butler dressed in flowing robes with an English accent. Too much!

It was the usual scene with her, servant bowing and scraping, serving drinks and then vanishing. This one backed out of the apartment with such an inane grin on his face that I thought he would trip over his robe.

It was the same old Fontaine. He had hardly closed the front door when she was stripping off her clothes and making a grab for me.

'On the floor,' she whispered.

Oh no, after last night, and the trip, and her relationship to Alexandra, I didn't know if I could make it. But strength will tell, and I managed to do my best. I felt like a heel but what could I do? Alexandra wouldn't forgive me for this, but what *could* I do? My mind was going in sixteen different directions, all the opposite way from the lady under me. That awful woman as Alex described her. And she *was* an awful woman. She had dazzled me at first with all her glamour and fame, but now I saw right through her. A social nymphomaniac, that's what she was.

'You're out of practice, Tony,' her voice was cold and edgy. I finished before she was ready, and she was choked. Little did she know she was lucky to get anything at all, what with the scene on the plane and everything.

'Yeah, well what do you expect with you away and everything.'

'Oh, please, Tony, let's not play the innocent virgin with each other.'

She shifted about on the floor, 'Finish the job for God's sake.'

I obliged.

This really is a wild city. Great hotel, fantastic T.V. in the room with lots of channels. Since the chauffeur brought me here two hours ago I've changed stations ten times. Take your choice—quiz show, old English movie, cowboys and Indians. It's all too much! And about room service, great! Club sandwiches I've only dreamed about, I've ordered three times already.

This is the life. I lay on a king-sized bed after a shower watching a blonde chick in a plastic raincoat announce the weather on T.V. Fontaine was picking me up at seven, I had an hour yet.

I wanted to phone A. But Benjamin would be paying the bill and I didn't want him checking through and finding phone calls to his daughter.

I tell you married women disgust me, they're all out for a piece of action away from their husbands. There's hardly one married woman I know that I couldn't truthfully say I could have if I wanted. It makes a man think twice about getting married.

What was I thinking about marriage for anyway? It's not for me, not after all the things I've seen. If I ever did get married it would be to a sweet innocent little girl like Alexandra. My lovely lovely Alexandra. And she had no money anyway, so where would that be going? Not that I minded about her having no money—I mean I did think it was a bit strong on Benjamin's part—but I had no money either, so I couldn't even think about getting married. Alexandra Blake. Hmm—not too lyrical but nice, very nice. I imagined Sadie and Sam's faces if I married a girl that wasn't—'a nice Jewish girl'. They would go mad, but so what, I was a big boy now.

The time had come to get dressed. Fontaine had plans for the evening's entertainment—she had reeled off a list of things we were going to do that made me dizzy. We were to start off with a cocktail party, and then go to some friends of her's apartment, and then to dinner, and then a round of discothèques, and then there were a couple of other parties we might attend.

I chose my suit carefully, this would be the first time I had been out with Fontaine socially. I guess under normal circumstances I would be flattered, but things were different now, it all seemed a bit of a drag. It had been quite a day.

I decided on a pale lilac shirt from Turnbull and Asser, handmade, of course. Actually it had been made for Hal, but he didn't like the colour on himself so I bought it from him. We took the same size in shirts which was useful. He had some great gear which he got fed up with in a hurry—then I would buy it from him at half the original price. He made bread that way 'cos some old dear had probably bought it for him in the first place. Good old Hal. The last of the great promoters!

To go with the shirt I had a toning polka dot tie. The suit was black and it had a groovy waistcoat and then pearl cufflinks and tie clip, black socks and shoes. Even though I say it myself, I looked pretty damn good.

The desk rang to tell me a car was waiting. Great—New York City here I come!

FOURTEEN

FONTAINE

After Tony left and the chauffeur returned I went for my massage. Bliss. Hot sweaty hands pounding and pummelling my white skin. Then a delicious steam bath, followed by a soft massage with oil of pine, its odours sinking into my body.

Oh what luxury, almost as good as sex. Wrapped in pink towelling I had my hair washed, then lay on a floating pink couch while it was dried by concealed jets of air.

This is 'M'lady's Parlour', the very latest beauty house, and I must say, very impressive.

Sarah dragged me here immediately I arrived. 'It's so divine, darling, you'll come eighteen times.'

It's beauty is an aphrodisiac atmosphere. All the boys here are queens, it's like a harem with eunuchs preparing you for the night's fantasy.

Roger did my hair, small petite Roger with a mass of golden curls and pursed bitchy lips. 'Darling, do you believe what Clarissa wore to the premiere last night? She looked like a baby yellow elephant! Ridiculous! My friend says her dress was a Rudi Genreich, but I can't believe that Rudi would be that wicked.'

I smiled. The good thing about Roger was the fact that one could relax and listen to all the gossip. His bitcheries could go on for ever.

He continued, 'Saw a terrible late movie last night, I couldn't believe the clothes though, terribly now. You'd look divine in white satin with lots of fox fur. I think I'm going to do your hair very Grecian. Strand it with some pearls and things.'

I felt so good from the massage, my body tingled. Oh God, if all these little twits could see Tony they'd cream themselves!

He was getting a rather attractive quality of self-confidence. With me he had always been so fawning and adoring, now he seemed to treat me in a slightly cooler fashion. Although of course he was still a boy scout when it came to material things. Why the way his mouth had popped open when he saw my apartment! The stud prowling around and sniffing the luxury!

Of course I know eventually he will begin to flap his wings, but I'm sure this trip will cool him down a little and make him realise exactly who he's mixing with. After all there aren't many women like me around, and however many little affaires he has to indulge in, he'll soon find that out.

Roger could certainly do wonders with my hair, only two pieces and it really looks marvellous.

'Have a lovely time,' he said, stepping back and admiring his work.

I went home and phoned Sarah, we were all to dine together. I hadn't told her about Tony, I had just said a business associate of Benjamin's was joining us. I couldn't wait to see her face!

'What are you wearing?' she asked.

'I haven't decided yet,' I replied, although I was going to wear the black silk backless Cardin.

'Neither have I.' What a liar she was.

'We'll see you about eight, going to pop into the Carlton's party first.'

'What a bore. They're so show business, Allen can't stand them.'

Actually I knew that Sarah and Allen hadn't been invited, as Salamanda Smith, a Hollywood film star and Allen had been a very hot item indeed the previous summer, and Peter Carlton, whom she had since married, was terribly jealous. Oh, the intricacies of the social set!

'Are the Bells and Sidwells meeting at your place too?'

'Yes, everything's arranged,' Sarah lowered her voice, 'I had a wonderful afternoon. Have you ever tried yoga?'

I didn't want to get involved in one of Sarah's sexual discussions, they always began with a lowered voice.

'Yes, darling, often. See you later.' I hung up.

Tony looked refreshed. He also looked flashy and a bit cheap, but I was prepared to forgive him that. It was the terrible tie he had on that did it, change that and he wouldn't look too bad. I slid the glass down between me and the chauffeur and said, 'Stop at Saks.'

They were still open. I smiled at Tony and said, 'Let's pop in a minute, I want to get you a little something.'

Everyone stared at us. Well, Roger had gone a bit avant garde with my hair, divine for evening but not quite suitable for a flit through Saks. People who say that nobody stares at you in New York are mad. They stare more than anywhere else. Blue-haired mink-stoled ladies with beaded handbags and plastic rhinestone studded shoes are the first to say, 'Oh ma Gawd, lookit her!'

In the men's department I picked out six divine imported ties and made Tony put one on. He looked heaps better. 'We'll come here tomorrow and do some more shopping.' The salesman goggled at me and gave Tony the package.

'Didn't you like my tie?' He was surly.

'It was lovely, I just like this one better.' Oh God, don't tell me he was going to sulk. He should be delighted with six new fifteen-dollar ties.

The party was a shambles, so many people. Salamanda, floaty in pink chiffon. Tony was impressed. He still got awed by meeting film stars. She gushed over to us, 'Gee, so great of you to come, Mrs Khaled,' she held the smile for the hovering photographer.

What a dull pretty little face she had, not a bone worth anything in the whole structure.

Her puffy eyes surrounded in caked mascara were studying my diamonds.

'Tony Blake, our hostess, Mrs Peter Carlton,' I said.

He beamed, 'I loved your last film,' he said almost stuttering. 'How did you manage so long in the desert?'

Oh God, save me from the film fan!

She blinked, 'Gee, it was O.K. Petey came down on the weekends!'

'All that way?'

'We made it just outside of Vegas—hey,' she started to laugh, 'wacha think, we made it in the Sahara or somethin'? They wouldn't get lil ole me there, honey.'

I really think Tony is a cretinous bore. I can't imagine why I wanted him here. I left the two of them and looked around. The same old faces, oh God, sometimes *everything* is so boring.

FIFTEEN

TONY

Fontaine is the biggest put-down merchant of all time. Here I am, looking great, feeling great, ready to go, and she gives me one of those tight little smiles of hers and says, 'Tony, darling, we'll simply have to stop and get you a decent tie. You just can't go out like that.' I mean screw her, sitting there with her hair looking like a Carnival Queen. Who does she think she is? She doesn't own me, and pretty soon she's going to find that out. She dragged me into some store and lumbered me with six of the dreariest ties you could imagine. Imported yet, probably couldn't find a buyer for them in their own country. I put on the best of the bunch, to keep her happy, and silently fumed.

Fontaine was a cow. An old cow. I contemplated telling her to take a running jump, but I had no money to pay the hotel and I'm sure if I did that, no job to return to in good old Blighty. Fontaine Khaled had me by the short and curlies, and what was worse she bloody well knew it.

We arrived at the party, it was pretty jammed, but everyone turned to take a look at us. Fontaine hadn't bothered to tell me whose party it was, but I soon got the message when Salamanda Smith, *the* Salamanda Smith, came wafting over.

She was a gorgeous bird, curvy and blonde with a pair of bristols that fair knocked your eyes out. I'd just seen her in a wild desert movie, full of sex and sand type of thing. She was bowled over by Fontaine, but I could see she had an eye (baby blue) for me, and we got to chatting about her last movie.

She had to go to greet some more people and Fontaine had done a vanish, so there I was on my todd. I scouted around and got hold of a scotch from a white-coated guy who called me 'bud' and was really loaded.

Was he a waiter? The way he was acting I wasn't quite sure. But he picked up a tray, belched, and set off in the direction of some guests, so I guessed he was.

He weaved into a fake marble column, and it swayed, but stood its ground, then he staggered with his tray over to some people and hands stretched out like vultures relieving him of the glasses. He came rolling back in my direction—'S'elluva party,' he mumbled, 'lotsa cooze.'

Then he was off again towards Salamanda, and dropping his tray with a loud crash, he grabbed hold of her with one hand, and with the other unzipped his fly and said, 'Get a load of this, honey!'

There was a short silence while she struggled to free herself, and then three guys jumped on the waiter and he disappeared beneath a torrent of blows.

It was a funny scene really. Salamanda took a deep breath and smiled, and the waiter was dragged, blood dripping from his face, out of the room. Great! I counted ten knowing that Fontaine would appear at my side, anxious to hear all.

Fontaine—the last of the great gossips. She was there on the stroke of nine. 'What happened?' her silver-lidded eyes glistened anxiously.

'Just some drunk waiter, nothing exciting.'

'Oh,' she was disappointed, 'is that all?'

Salamanda was now retelling the story to a small group surrounding her, and Fontaine went over. I trailed behind. She was just saying, 'and there was his enormous *thing*! Just staring me in the face!'

Fontaine shot me a dirty look, I'd left out the best bits.

I wished I could phone Alexandra. I looked around for a phone, nobody would notice me making a quick call to London with this group. I strolled out of the door, looked about and found an empty bedroom with a shiny gold bedside model. I grabbed it quick. 'Overseas please—London England—a personal call to Miss Alexandra Khaled—8934434. No, I'll hang on.'

A beautiful girl came into the room, long straight black hair, long straight black body. She looked directly at me, 'You going to Marcellos after?'

'Who's Marcello?'

Her eyes were stony, unsmiling. 'You putting me on?'

'Nope,' I shook my head and winked. 'Who is he? I'm a stranger here.'

'Ah God almighty,' she smoothed down her long black hair. 'Marcellos is a restaurant, man, everyone seems to be going there, I'm looking for someone to take me. You interested?'

I was interested all right, but unavailable. 'I'm with someone. How about another night?'

Her eyes swept over me. 'Yeah, maybe.'

Just then the operator said, 'I'm putting you through now, your party's on the line.'

Then Alexandra's voice, clear and sweet, 'Hello?'

The girl was combing her hair at a mirror.

'Hello, baby, and how are you today?'

'Oh, Tony, how super of you to phone me all the way from America. I'm feeling much better, thank you. I feel such an idiot about last night.'

A warm glow came over me, 'Don't give it another thought. It was my fault for taking you to a lousy party like that. What are you doing?'

'I'm in bed actually.'

I imagined her with brushed shining hair and a fluffy pink nightdress. 'That's the best place to be.' I glanced over at the girl, she was hanging around. I covered the mouthpiece of the phone, 'Write down your number,' I hissed at her. I said back into the phone, 'I miss you.'

I did miss her. The girl wrote Norma and a number on some book matches and threw them at me, then she went out.

There was silence from Alexandra. 'I said I miss you.'

'I know,' her voice was a whisper.

'Well?'

'Well, what?'

'Well, do you miss me?'

'I don't know. I mean, you've only been gone a day, and after all we don't know each other very well.' She paused. 'Yes, I do miss you.'

My heart did a little skip, 'I'm going to be back soon, then we'll get to know each other really well. Be a good girl.'

'Yes,' she had such a lovely accent.

'See you soon.' I hung up. It was good to be alive. I peered at myself in the mirror. I looked good but wished I had a suntan. Maybe Fontaine would fancy a few days in Florida.

I went back into the party and found Fontaine, she was holding court, her clipped British tones ringing round the room. When she paused for air, she noticed me. 'Oh there you are, we've got to be going.' She wasn't as friendly towards me as she had been. You never knew with Fontaine, she blew hot and cold. Maybe she didn't like having me out with her, maybe she thought I wasn't good enough. All right for a fuck, but not for her friends. I scowled. She glared. We left.

In the car she said testily, 'You know, Tony, you shouldn't

92

act so star-struck I would have thought that by now you would have been used to meeting celebrities.'

Me—star-struck! I was choked! That was the *last* thing I was.

She tapped talon-like nails on her small gold (real, of course) handbag and added, 'You made a fool of yourself with Salamanda, you acted like a film fan. Don't you realise five years ago she was a stripper, and you—anyone—could have had her for ten dollars.'

I've learnt one lesson in life. Never argue with a woman when she's putting down another woman.

'Yeah, you're right,' I conceded. Well who needed an argument?

Fontaine softened up a bit. 'Just don't forget—you'll probably meet many big stars while you're here. Don't mention their work or anything about it, socially that's just not on.'

Silly cow! I yawned. 'I'd love to go to Florida.'

She ignored me.

We arrived at a big apartment house, and the doorman nearly broke his neck getting her ladyship out of the car.

'These are my dearest friends in New York,' Fontaine said, 'Sarah and Allen Grant, a wonderful couple. Don't embarrass me.'

I mean, what did she think I was going to do—pee on the carpet or something?

We went into a fantastic pad on the ground floor. Big, dark, crammed with antiques, stuffed animals and tall plants. Very groovy. What a scene you could have here!

This lady came to greet us, bony face, with pulled back black hair and whiter than white skin. She looked like she was suffering from a touch of malnutrition. She and Fontaine kissed, summing each other's oufits up with their eyes. Then Fontaine said, 'Sarah, I want you to meet Tony, Benjamin sent him over.'

Man, she made me sound like a package! Sarah looked me over. She had wild black eyes that burned right through you. Her lips were thin and painted dark red. I guessed she must be about forty. If you like skeleton thin older chicks she was a knockout. Personally I don't. Her glance jumped between me and Fontaine, and she smiled slightly. 'Well, what a surprise.'

Fontaine smiled too, 'Yes,' she said, and they linked arms and walked over to the bar, leaving me standing there like a right berk.

There were four or five other people sitting about, and a guy got up and came over to me. He had what women's magazines would call a craggy handsome face. He wore a shapeless grey suit, 'Allen Grant,' he said, shaking hands and giving me an amused squint.

'Tony Blake.'

'Come and have a drink.' He took me over to the bar and fixed me a very large scotch on the rocks. He fixed himself an even bigger one and disposed of it in three hefty gulps. Then he made himself another and said, 'Who are you?'

Charming! I mean I love questions like that from a complete stranger. What do you say? The Pope—Gunga Din— 'I'm over here for Ben Khaled, looking for—er—properties.'

'Oh. Are you having an affair with the lovely Mrs K. then?'

I mean was I supposed to hit him or what? Fortunately Fontaine came over. 'Allen, you naughty boy, what are you saying?'

Fontaine was flirting, a pose of hers that drove me mad.

He laughed. 'Nothing. How are you my sweet?'

'I'm fine.' Their eyes met in the sort of intimacy usually reserved for lovers. They probably were, that would just about be Fontaine's scene, knocking off her best friend's husband. I didn't care. My little Alexandra was tucked up at home in bed, and that's all I cared about.

Sarah suddenly took my arm, 'Come, Tony, come and meet the others.'

I racked my brain to find out where I'd seen her before. I pride myself on never forgetting a face, and I knew I'd seen this one somewhere. She hadn't been in the club, that I was sure of. She was certainly very striking, although as I said before, not my type at all. Her hand was brittle on my arm, skeleton fingers digging in. Suddenly it struck me where I knew her from. American Vogue three months ago, a big layout of her in Bermuda or somewhere modelling beach exotica. I told you I have a great memory. Sarah Grant—society bigwig—New York City.

'Fontaine never told me about you,' she said in a deep husky voice, 'you're divine.'

Instant lay, better watch out, didn't want to upset her ladyship.

I was then introduced to the others, your average rich

94

couples—neither of the women could hold a candle to Fontaine or Sarah, and the men were balding and moved in a cloud of cigar smoke.

After some boring small talk we left, a convoy of chauffeured cars.

First stop was dinner, an exclusive restaurant off Fifth Avenue, with hothouse plants growing wild, and gold-jacketed waiters.

I sat between Fontaine and Sarah, fighting a losing battle to taste my food against the fumes of their respective perfumes.

They both ignored me, making polite small talk around the rest of the table. I couldn't join in as I didn't know who or what they were talking about. I mean are you ready for 'Fleur met Itsy in St Moritz and they had a terrible fight and he ended up with Poopsie at Mooeys.'

Allen was the only one who spoke to me. I had a feeling he was as bored as I was.

So this was New York—social circuit number one. You can have it and stick it. I wished I was with Norma at 'Marcellos', wherever that might be.

Dinner dragged on and on and I was getting a bad case of yawning.

At last Fontaine said, 'I think we'd better get Tony to "Picketts" before he falls asleep on us.' She shot me a dark look to let me know she was furious about my yawning all night.

'Picketts' was the newest disco to open and make it big. I had heard all about it, but all the same it was a shock. The whole interior of the club was like a huge monster's open mouth. Fangs and cobwebs hung from everywhere, and in a transparent tooth hanging like a light fixture from the ceiling, a near-naked female freaked out to the blaring sounds of James Brown. There was an assortment of waitresses dressed in flimsy bits of cobwebs and lots of glimpses of a tit here, an ass there. Pretty wild, but not what I'd call a cool scene. I mean who needs gimmicks? The customers are supposed to make the fun.

Fontaine made her usual grand entrance, the guy running the joint nearly kissed her feet. He was small, dark and nervous looking. No competition there.

We were sat round a table shaped like a huge withered hand, and a little tenny bopper, happy in her cobweb gear, took our order. Champagne all round and a scotch for me, 'Why fight it,' Allen murmured, 'why not get used to her habits?'

'I only drink scotch,' I answered.

'Come on, Allen sweetie, let's show 'em.' Fontaine was getting all frisky as she dragged Allen off to dance.

'Shall we?' Sarah asked with arched eyebrows, already getting up without waiting for my reply.

I followed her on to the dance floor, and she was even more embarrassing stiff-assed than Fontaine.

What the hell was I doing here? Six months before I would have given anything to be involved in this scene with these people, in fact I wouldn't have believed it was possible. But now—well, who needed it? I had everything going for me in London, I didn't need this trailing behind Fontaine bag.

We stayed at 'Picketts' an hour, and then on to 'The Flower Mission', a wild mass of psychedelic symbols and freak-out light effects.

By this time the other two couples had dropped out and it was just Fontaine, Sarah, Allen and me against the world. We were all well smashed.

'Have you ever studied yoga?' Sarah asked me, black eyes piercing and probing.

'Er—no.'

'You should. You have a powerful body. I'm sure you would excel at it.'

'Tony,' Fontaine said excitedly, 'Allen's met a man here who can get us some cigarettes,' her voice lowered on the word cigarettes and I knew with a sinking feeling she meant pot. That's all I needed, one of her 'aren't we being wicked' pot-smoking scenes. I just didn't dig it, it didn't do a thing for me except make me go to sleep, and from the way Fontaine was carrying on, me going to sleep was not what she had in mind.

'We'll go to Sarah and Allen's, shall we?' she said it not so much as a question, more like a statement.

So we left and chauffeured all the way to the Grant pad.

Once there the two women disappeared and Allen made a beeline for the bar. He wasn't talking, just knocking back a large glass of brandy and looking hollow-eyed.

'What's the action?' I asked helping myself to a drink as he didn't seem to be offering.

'God knows,' he said, 'you're lucky, at least you're not married to yours.'

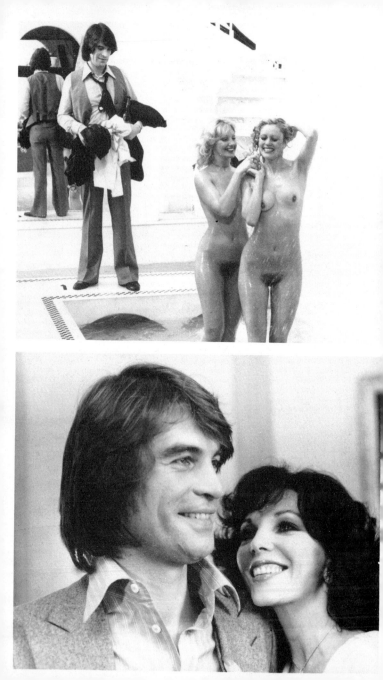

What did *that* mean?

I glanced at my watch, it was three a.m. I was bushed. I tried to calculate what time it was in London. Five hours difference but I couldn't remember which way.

Sarah came back in first. She had changed into a full-length brocade sort of caftan, and her jet-black hair was combed straight down. She looked vaguely Indian.

Fontaine followed, her hair was still piled high on her head, but she had changed into a long white floating thing, slightly transparent, and I could see the outline of her small naked breasts.

'Allen,' Sarah said, 'why don't you and Tony put on these?' She handed us each a black silk sort of short Japanese kimono.

'Come on,' Allen said resignedly.

I followed him into another room, and he stripped off his clothes and put on the black silk kimono.

He smiled grimly, 'I know why I'm doing this, how about you?'

I felt well choked about the whole thing, but what the hell, in a way it was rather exciting.

I put on the kimono, the silk felt great. I wished it wasn't so short, it just about covered my balls!

We went back inside. Fontaine and Sarah were smoking already, taking long thin-lipped drags. I went to sit beside Fontaine but she motioned me over to Sarah. Oh boy—if the regulars could see me now!

There was some weird Japanese music playing, and Sarah offered me her cigarette. I took a drag. We were sitting on a sofa, and opposite on another sofa were Fontaine and Allen.

I handed the cigarette back to Sarah. She puffed and leaned back blowing little smoke rings to the ceiling.

My turn, this wasn't too bad, I felt a certain numbness creep over me and the music sounded fantastic. I put the cigarette back in her mouth, and she leaned over and put her hands under the kimono. Her fingers felt like burning tongs as they fled around my flesh.

I glanced over at Fontaine. She was lying against the cushions and Allen was peeling the white thing off her. I watched fascinated as her body came into view and he started to kiss her. Her legs were spread and she moaned softly.

Meanwhile Sarah's hands manipulated me, and she took off my kimono, and man I felt great, and then I started to fly and

97

I was pounding into someone and when I looked it was Fontaine and then Sarah and then both of them were all over me. It was a kaleidoscope of faces and, man, for the first time I was really stoned.

SIXTEEN

ALEXANDRA

My first day at McLaughton & Co. was awful. To start off
with I was late, unforgivable on one's first day; secondly, I felt
dreadful, with what I supposed I could consider as my first
hangover; and thirdly, according to Madelaine all Michael had
said about me the previous evening was, 'What a ridiculous
dress'. I wasn't sure that I liked working too much either. It
was awfully dull just sitting at a pokey desk typing, perhaps I
should have let Daddy help me to get an interesting job.

I couldn't wait for five o'clock when I could rush home and
have a proper chat with Maddy. When were we going to see
Michael? Would Steve Scott phone? Of course Maddy had
flipped when I told her about him.

Fortunately five o'clock finally came and I was very ex-
travagant and took a taxi home. Maddy was lolling about reading magazines, the lucky thing didn't start her job until next
week.

'What was it like?' she asked excitedly. 'Have you got a
super boss who looks at your legs when you take dictation?'

'No, I've got a grumpy old man who doesn't even know
what legs are!'

We both laughed. 'What's for dinner?' We had planned to
take it in turns to organise meals, and today was Maddy's turn.
It was fun actually as we could try out all the recipes we had
learnt at school.

'Roast beef and Yorkshire pud, and to start puréed Avocado
pear, and to finish crème caramel, and we've overspent on our
budget and Michael and Jonathan are coming to dinner. I
thought you'd be pleased.'

'Oh great! How did you fix that?'

'Easy. I just asked them. My brother's not one to turn down
a free meal.'

I was delighted. 'What can I wear?' I wailed. Clothes in
London were a great problem. I *had* to go shopping.

'Oh, just pop on some slacks and a tight sweater. Let him
see your bosom, maybe that will attract him.'

I suppose my bosom *was* one of my best features. When I
was about twelve at school four of us went into the toilet and

99

compared bosoms. They had laughed at me then because mine were full and firm, but they had stayed that way, and Maddy said if any man saw them he would go mad.

I didn't have any tight sweaters, so I borrowed one of Maddy's. It *did* look good, but I felt slightly embarrassed.

'Wow!' Maddy said. 'Are you wearing a bra?'

'Of course.'

'Take it off. Men find it much more exciting if you're not.'

'I couldn't Maddy.'

'You want to get him in your evil clutches, don't you?'

I went back in the bedroom and took off my bra, and slipped the sweater back on. You could tell I wasn't wearing one, they bobbed a little when I walked.

I must say Maddy had prepared a really gorgeous dinner.

Michael and Jonathan came, watched a detective serial on television and devoured every mouthful of the food.

Michael, who had ignored me all evening, finally said, 'How was the party last night?'

'Oh, it was very nice, but I got s . . .'

Before I could finish Maddy blurted in with, 'She's got a date with Steve Scott, he's mad about her.'

'Oh, Maddy!' I blushed. How could she tell such awful lies.

'You really are seeing London,' Michael said grimly, 'moving with the crowd already. I bet your mother wouldn't be too pleased with the company you're keeping.'

Oh! He was insufferable! They watched a bit more television and then went.

I decided I hated him. Madelaine giggled as soon as they were gone. 'It's working,' she said, 'I think he's jealous.'

'He's not, he's *so* sarcastic to me.'

'No, that's good. At least he's *aware* of you now, you're not a little kid he's known for ages any more. And he couldn't take his eyes off your sweater. You see, he'll ask you out.'

'Yes, I bet.'

We cleared up the mess—one bad thing about not living at home, the washing up was ghastly! I was really exhausted. What with my hangover, and the first day at work, and the dinner. Oh well, at least Michael had looked at my sweater.

I had a bath, brushed my hair and collapsed into bed. I was soon asleep, and dreaming a really awful dream where I appeared at work stark naked and lots of fingers were typing on my body, then my breasts turned into typewriters, and Michael came and looked at me and turned his back in disgust, and a

100

bell started to jangle louder and louder, and I woke up. It was the telephone.

Maddy reached it before I did. 'It's for you,' she said sleepily, 'Tony Blake phoning you from New York. Do you know it's one-thirty. You certainly made a hit with him.'

I took the phone and Maddy leaned close so she could listen. Why on earth was Tony phoning me?

He was very friendly, wanting to know if I felt better and everything, then he said he missed me, and Maddy hissed, 'Say you miss him too.' So I did.

He said goodbye then, and I turned to Maddy exasperated, 'What did you want me to say that for?'

She smiled, 'Well, if he's spending all that money phoning you, you may as well be nice to him. I think he likes you, actually I think he's rather divine!'

'You can have him then,' I said crossly, 'I don't miss him, and I wish I hadn't said I did. Honestly sometimes I think you're mad.'

'You won't think I'm mad when I tell Michael about it, he'll be green if he thinks Tony Blake is after you *and* Steve Scott.'

'Maddy, let's go to sleep.'

'All right, but you'll see, you'll get your man in the end!'

SEVENTEEN

TONY

I opened my eyes and I was in my room at the hotel lying on top of the bed with all my gear on. How did I get back?

That bloody bitch Fontaine was a real balls breaker, and her skinny friend—Miss No Tits society bag. All right, so we'd had a big scene and there wasn't a gun at my head, but how could I have done it? What about Alexandra? What about Sadie and Sam my nice respectable parents? What if they ever knew, could see? I've always had this funny sort of thought that after you die you sit in a room and like watching a movie your whole life plays across the screen and all the people you know get to watch it. Charming! Last night's scene would make lovely viewing. Shit! Making it with Fontaine is one thing, but having a show with her so-called friends is another.

That faggot husband of Sarah's tried to sneak it in while the two women crawled all over me. But I caught him at that little game, thank you very much. I remember Fontaine saying, 'Let him do it, Tony, you'll love it.' Wow, she was *really* stoned. Bitch!

It was two o'clock and I was starving. I had a shower and ordered three eggs and a hamburger from room service. What was I supposed to do? Hang around until her ladyship decided to call me? I viewed television. Maybe I should call the club later. Maybe I should call Alexandra now. What the hell am I doing here anyway? It's a long way from the Elephant and Castle.

I guess I fell asleep again, 'cos when I woke up the T.V. screen was alive with sweaty teenagers and the phone was ringing.

'Yeah?'

'My, my. Aren't we American already!'

I glanced quickly at my watch, five-fifteen, and she was only just calling, 'What's happening?' I asked.

'Well, darling, all sorts of exciting things. Did you enjoy last night?'

'No.'

Her voice went very cold. 'Oh—why?'

'It's not my scene, Fontaine, I don't dig that one little bit.

You shouldn't put yourself in that position. It's, well, it's not right.'

Her laugh was amused, 'Oh, Tony, you're such a little suburbanite. It was fun. If you relaxed it could be a lot more fun.'

'I don't want to do it again, O.K.?'

Her voice was sarcastic. 'Yes sir, we will not indulge ourselves in any more naughty little orgies.'

There was silence. I knew she hated being criticised, but God almighty, somebody had to tell her. It was bad enough screwing around on her husband, but this beat the band.

'What's happening then?' I asked.

'I don't want to corrupt you, Tony dear, but I thought you might like to come over for an hour or so, then there's two parties and I thought perhaps dinner with Sarah and Allen.'

Oh Christ! I certainly didn't want to face Sarah and Allen again. What were we all supposed to do—discuss positions?

'Look, I don't want to see them. I'll come to the parties with you, then maybe I should just roam around on my own, get the feel of things.'

'Tony, really you can be such a bore! All right then, do that. Be here in half-an-hour.'

She slammed the phone down. How did I ever get myself into this?

It was too early to phone the club, but Alexandra should be home. Was it a clever move to risk a phone call? No.

I thought of her pretty little wide-eyed face and her soft auburn hair. She was the sort of girl who would still look good in ten or even twenty years.

When I got back to London I decided I would take her down to the Elephant and Castle and introduce her to Sadie and Sam. What a shock they'd get to see me with such a lovely girl. They thought I only ever went out with showgirls and 'tarty bits of fluff' as my Ma always said. How many times had they both said to me—find yourself a nice Jewish girl and settle down. So what difference Jewish smooish as long as she was nice. They would love pretty little Alex.

I got dressed. Polo-necked striped silk shirt, one of Hal's best buys, and my Dougie Hayward grey suit. I had to get some money from Fontaine. I was walking around with nothing. It was embarrassing, especially if I was going to take off on my own later.

On top of the T.V. with my comb and cigarettes were several

book matches I had picked up at various joints the previous evening. I liked things like that, lay them around the London pad and people knew you had travelled. Scribbled across the front of 'Lorenz—eat in style' was the name Norma and a number. Norma? I didn't know a Norma. Come to think of it I'd never been to a place called 'Lorenz' either. Norma, Norma, Norma. Ah yes, the tall lady with the long black hair at the party last night. Rather beautiful, a definite raver, very cool. I dialled the number and a guarded tired voice answered 'Yeah?'

'Is Norma there?'

'Wait a minute, I'll see. Who is it?'

'Tony Blake, but she doesn't know my name, we met at a party we ...'

'Hold it, baby, I don't want your life story. Hang on ...'

The guarded voice left me hanging on while I strained to hear the muffled conversation the other end. Then a voice identical to the first one got on and said, 'Yeah?'

'Norma?'

'Yeah?'

'We met at Salamanda Smith's party last night.' Nothing like dropping a name. 'I was on the phone in the bedroom remember?'

'Yeah.'

She was a wild conversationalist. 'Well, I thought I could see you later, like buy you a drink or something.'

'Sounds O.K., I'm having dinner with some guys, you can join us if you like.'

'Some guys' didn't sound too exciting. 'Look, if you're busy maybe some other night.'

'Suit yourself. We'll be at "Marcellos" if you change your mind.'

She hung up. Friendly girl, couldn't care less if I came or not.

I didn't even have the cab fare so I walked the few blocks to Fontaine's. She let me in herself, her hair hanging smoothly down her back, her face a mass of white cream but her eyes fully made up. She wore a thin silk dressing-gown.

'Come in the bedroom, I'm making up. Fix the champagne first, it's in the fridge.'

I went in the fully fitted oak panelled kitchen and opened several cupboards before locating the fridge, which was cleverly disguised as part of the wall. American kitchens are funny things, nobody seems to want to know what anything is.

I opened the champagne and took it in the bedroom. Fontaine was lying on the bed, the silk dressing-gown exposing her from the waist down so that the whole thing looked slightly obscene. She stretched her arms back behind her head.

'We won't need glasses,' she whispered, 'just bring the bottle, we'll drink it my way.'

I was excited in spite of myself. She repulsed me, but my body was responding to her.

I took off my suit and shirt, I certainly wasn't spoiling the outfit.

'Come on, Tony,' she said impatiently, 'I'm thirsty.'

When it was all over and the room stunk of champagne I lay on her bed watching her calmly get on with her make-up. I knew I couldn't make it any more. Oh, I could 'make it' in the physical sense, no problem there, but after—well, after I get this kind of unclean feeling, this sort of feeling of shame. With other women there's always some affection—something—even if it's just a casual lay. But Fontaine is cold as bloody ice, it's almost as if she's just using my body to suit herself. She's a bitch, and I've got to get away from her. Especially now with Alexandra in the picture.

'Can I shower?' I asked.

'Of course, you don't have to ask permission. Use the one in the guest-room.' She was painting her thin lips and didn't look up.

I showered the smell of the champagne off me and the smell of Fontaine, and then I just stood there turning the water on to icy cold. It felt good.

When I got back to London I was going to find someone to back me in a new club. It shouldn't be that difficult, I had a lot of connections, and me in a new club couldn't fail. I mean I'm not being conceited but 'Hobo' would never have made it without me. Maybe the new place could be called 'Tonys', or is that too obvious? I like it myself, sounds good. Find a location, find a backer, and kiss Fontaine Balls Breaker Khaled goodbye.

'Tony, are you ready?' Fontaine walked in wearing black satin and a lot of diamonds. She looked annoyed. 'What the hell are you doing in here?'

I got out of the shower quick, skin shrivelled by the cold.

'Come on, for God's sake. I hate hanging around waiting.' She swept out of the room.

I dressed quickly and found her gazing out on her terrace, smoking.

'Listen, since we'll be splitting up later I'd better have some money,' I said. 'I was rushed over here so quickly I couldn't arrange any.'

'I see.' She looked furious. I knew she hated parting with cash. 'Why on earth didn't you ask Benjamin's secretary?'

'I didn't meet her. The whole thing was arranged by phone.'

She opened her small evening bag and extracted three ten-dollar bills. 'That's all I have,' she said, 'I'll make some arrangements for you tomorrow.'

Charming! Thirty measly dollars to see New York on. That wasn't going to get me very far.

We went to the first party. Held in a restaurant the crush was terrible. I stood by the door watching Fontaine waft around. I drank three scotches. After half-an-hour she found me, gripped my arm and said, 'We've leaving. Do see if you can be a little more sociable at the next party. Klaus is coming with us.'

Klaus turned out to be a small faggot dressmaker, dressed to kill in frills, with rotting teeth and beady eyes. He sat between me and Fontaine in the car, pressing his thigh close to mine.

'Klaus has taken New York by storm with his thirties trouser-suits,' Fontaine remarked.

Well, good for little old beady-eyed Klaus. He may have taken New York by storm, but he was going to get a punch on the nose if he pressed his leg against mine any harder.

The second party was even worse. A faggot party. Droves of them. Scattered among them were the well-dressed ladies, and a few—very few—normal guys. At least they looked normal.

Klaus said, 'How divine. Everyone's here.'

Fontaine said, 'All the best designers in New York are gathered. You'd better stay close to me, Tony, I know how you feel about your precious ass!'

I hated her. So beautiful and elegant and bitchy.

I stayed there about ten minutes, but I was getting so many leers and coy glances I couldn't stand it any longer.

'I'm getting out of here,' I told Fontaine.

She brushed me aside with a cool, 'Bye-Bye,' and I wandered out into the New York night.

It was still early, before nine, and I tried to decide if it was too early to try 'Marcellos'. I was starving, with gnawing pains in my stomach. I walked into a hamburger joint and had three. That felt a lot better. What now? Seek out the wild Norma? There seemed to be nothing else to do. I hopped a cab and told him 'Marcellos', and he knew the place.

From the outside it looked all right. Small red and white awning, few steps down, pretty girl at reception desk. She smiled at me. 'You 'ave reservation, sir?' She was Italian. Should have known it when I saw those great big eyes.

'I thought I'd have a drink.'

'Certainly, sir—downstairs.' She smiled again. I smiled. If Norma didn't show I wondered what time this little darling finished.

Downstairs it was packed. The bar bordered the restaurant and every table was full.

I ordered a scotch and looked for Norma. She was easy to spot, her sleek black hair pulled back into a long plait and wearing huge horn-rimmed tinted glasses. She was at a table with three guys and I watched them a bit, before going over. She was a very striking girl, her features more Indian than Negro, her eyes, big, black and soulful.

'Hi there,' she said when I came over. She was authoritative, and got a waiter to bring another chair with a snap of her fingers. She nodded round the table: 'Mark—Terry—Davey— this is Tony.' Two of the guys were white, the other a very good-looking black guy with a beard.

'Hi man,' the bearded Davey greeted me.

The whole thing was a very warm scene. I could relax. Norma surveyed me coolly through her tinted lenses. 'Hey, what were you doin' at that *awful* party? What a giant sized drag!'

I nodded, 'Somebody took me.'

'Yeah, somebody took you all right,' she laughed. 'First time in my goddamn life I ever got stood up. Some prize jerk supposed to meet me there, and the sonofabitch never showed!'

'That will teach you to go with stars, girlie,' Davie said, grinning.

'You can bet your ass on that,' Norma agreed. 'Now to beat the band, the sonofabitch's secretary—secretary yet—hasn't even got the balls to call me himself—phones me today and says—quote—Mr Nicholas is *so* sorry he couldn't manage last night. Can I confirm your address as Mr Nicholas wishes to send you a colour television set. Man, I laughed and laughed.

Tell Mr Buck Nicholas to take his colour T.Vee and shove it right up his rude white ass, I said.' Everyone laughed. 'That guy is too much,' Norma continued. 'He can only make it with us black girls. He has some kind of hang up, cannot make it with a white lady. Then the poor bastard thinks he has to pay. I've got a little news for him—If I was planning on getting paid, a colour T.Vee wouldn't go anywhere near covering the cost! I should never have balled him, but he's so goddamned beautiful—umm—that body—wowee!!'

Buck Nicolas is a very famous movie actor, mostly appearing in tattered Tee shirts and tight Levi's to show off his equally famous body.

'You know we met before,' Norma said, lifting her glasses, balancing them in her hair and staring at me.

'We did?' I couldn't remember, and I had a good memory.

'Yeah, "Hobo", London. You used to run the joint, all the little girlies creaming themselves over you.'

I was sure I could never forget meeting a girl like Norma.

'Yeah, I still run "Hobo". When was it?'

'Coupla months back—you wouldn't remember me like I am now, I was wearing a blonde wig, you came over. I was with Steve Scott.'

Bingo! Could I ever forget her. What a night that had been, with every guy in the place fighting to meet her and Steve being very cool.

'Of course! You look completely different now.'

'Yeah—I only use the blonde wig when I want to really knock 'em in the aisles. I was only in London two days, crazy city, I'm going back soon. What are you doing here?'

'We might open up "Hobo". I'm sort of getting the feel of things.'

'Yeah? Great. Talk to Davey, he can *really* show you the town.'

She was right. After dinner (I just drank) Terry and Mark went off, and Norma, Davey and I saw New York. But I mean really saw it. We went all over in Davey's silver Porsche, uptown, downtown, Harlem, Chinatown. Norma was a wonderful girl. She talked in her laconic clipped style non-stop, and she danced like a mother, and she laughed a lot and drank a lot, and a six a.m. exhausted, drunk and happy we landed up at her apartment.

'Hey, you're O.K., she said laughing, undoing her plaited hair until it hung jet black and straight to her waist.

'You're pretty O.K. yourself,' I replied, putting my arms around her and pulling her close to me.

We were both a little loaded and both in the same happy mood. She was almost as tall as me, and I'm six one. She had on a clingy orange dress which I helped her out of.

Underneath there was a gorgeous brown skin and nothing else.

She laughed and moved out of my arms.

'Want a little drinkie?'

'Yeah, great.' I watched her move about the room pouring two scotches and clinking the ice in. She had a fantastic body, like a long supple panther.

I felt a little twinge of guilt about Alexandra, but this lady was so *beautiful*! A man can only take so much temptation. She came over to me and held the drink to my lips. I caught hold of one of her wild boobies. She took the drink away from me and put it carefully on a table.

'You want to swing, man—let's swing. I've got an insane bedroom. Only no hang-ups, huh?'

I covered her ass with my hands, 'No hang-ups.'

'O.K., let's go!'

She turned around and I followed her, my hands sticking to her backside, so high and round like a boy's.

Her bedroom was great. Leopardskin walls and a huge circular bed with a giant poster blow-up of Mick Jagger (Mick Jagger?!?) on the ceiling. She pressed a button and Ray Charles singing 'Eleanor Rigby' flooded the room.

I pushed her on to the bed and she stared up at me with amused black cat's eyes as I got undressed. I pinned her shoulders to the bed.

I started to kiss her, and we began to swing, and I could have bet Mick Jagger's eyes moved!

To me New York will always mean Norma. What a girl! I left her asleep at eleven the next morning and cabbed it back to my hotel. There was a message for me. 'Please be ready to leave on noon plane for London, Alice Clerk—secretary, for Benjamin Al Khaled. All tickets, etc., to be collected at Kennedy airport information desk.'

Charming! I was on the move again.

EIGHTEEN

FONTAINE

Reflecting on the whole thing it was a dreadful mistake. I should have left Tony where he was, he is nothing but an embarrassment here.

From the moment he arrived three days ago he has been gauche, naïve, star-struck, and a bore. Of course there was that one rather fun evening when we all got high, but he had the nerve to lecture me the next day about how I shouldn't involve myself in orgies, and that he certainly wasn't going to do it again. I mean, really, as far as I can remember he enjoyed it more than anyone!

Sarah thinks he's a bore. 'All cock and no brains,' she says. 'Really, Fontaine, find yourself an oriental.'

She is right. The stud is a dismal failure in New York. I have arranged for him to leave on the noon flight and this time I am *not* going to the airport.

Benjamin is flying in anyway. Dear rich, randy Benjamin.

There are a lot of things I need at 'Tiffany's'. Also I have seen a beautiful sable coat. And Saks have some divine Rudi Genreich originals.

Benjamin is arriving at the perfect time.

The phone rang and I waited for Adamo to announce who it was.

'Mr Blake, Madam.'

'Tony darling,' I may as well say goodbye with charm, the poor stud was probably shattered.

'Look, Fontaine, I just received a message that I'm supposed to be leaving.'

'Yes, darling. Well, Benjamin's coming into town, and I think you've seen enough to form some opinions. There's no point in you being away from "Hobo" too long.'

'Yeah, well I suppose you're right, But, Jesus Christ, I mean I'm shuttled around like luggage. Why didn't you mention it last night?'

'Oh, don't be boring, Tony. I didn't know last night. Anyway do give everyone my love, especially Vanessa. I'm sure you'll see Vanessa.' Oh God, he probably couldn't wait.

'Yeah. I'll see you in London then.'

110

'Ciaou, sweetie.'

That's got rid of him. Back to his little London dollies. He's so narrow-minded. After all I've taught him he still only knows one position! Stupid boy.

The phone again. 'Mr Grant, Madam.'

'Allen darling.'

'How about meeting today?'

'Where's Sarah?'

'Out. Well? Two o'clock the Plaza?'

'No, that's too late, Benjamin's coming in this afternoon. How about the St Regis at one?'

'Fine, I'll arrange it.'

'Allen.'

'Yes?'

'Bring your imagination.'

He laughed. Dear Allen wasn't so bad, not as equipped as Tony, but passable. After the little *ménage à quatre* of the other evening, I was really rather fond of him. It would be a pleasant way to pass the day until Benjamin arrived.

NINETEEN

ALEXANDRA

My second day at McLaughton & Co. was no better than the first. I can understand why girls become models and things, I mean just sitting here typing is worse than school. Mummy said I can take a Lucie Clayton course if I want to, and if I wasn't so determined to pay my own way, I would say yes. I don't suppose I would be a very good model anyway, I'm not thin enough, and my face is not unusual. But I don't think I can stick it at this job.

Maddy was all pleased with herself when I got home. She was a mass of Carmen rollers and face cream. 'I've got a date,' she announced, 'Jonathan phoned to thank me for dinner last night, and would I like to see a flick.'

'Great,' I said with as much enthusiasm as I could muster, 'what about Michael?'

Maddy immediately looked guilty. 'Oh sorry, Alex, Jonathan didn't mention him. But I promise I'll pump him tonight and find out all the gen. You know, what girls he sees and everything like that. It will be very useful to know all those things.'

'Yes, very.' I was acutely miserable.

Madelaine spent the next hour doing herself up and singing and generally being far too cheerful.

'Stay out of the way when Jonathan fetches me,' she said, 'I'll tell him you're at some party.'

'Thanks,' I said, shutting myself in the bedroom with a tin of cold baked beans.

I heard the doorbell and a mumble of voices and then the door slammed, and I was alone. I phoned Mummy. I wished I was at home.

'Why don't you bring some friends down with you this weekend?' Mummy asked. 'We could all go riding.'

'Perhaps I will. Can I let you know, please?'

I decided to invite Michael, whether Maddy thought it was a good idea or not. It was really ghastly being in the flat alone. I suppose this is the bad thing about living away from home. I even felt a bit nervous, sort of kept on hearing funny noises as it got later and darker.

I drew all the curtains, turned on the television and concentrated on a play. Then the phone rang.

'Is Alexandra Khaled there?' A husky mysterious voice.

'This is she.'

'Steve Scott. How are you?'

'Oh—I'm fine. How are you?' I felt myself blushing.

'All right. Sort of movin' along like a good boy. I thought you might want to come out.'

'Now?'

'I sort of thought tomorrow night, like dinner and that bit. You want to?'

'Yes, I'd like to.' Wait until Maddy heard about this!

'All right then, why don't you come round here about nine?'

'I'd love to.'

'See you then.'

'Oh, just a second,' I frantically searched for a pencil and some paper. 'Could you please tell me your address.'

He did so, adding, 'Don't dress up,' and was gone. How terrific! Although I would sooner it have been Michael, Steve Scott was a famous pop star, and very nice.

I couldn't wait to see Maddy's face, she would be green!

She was. Jonathan had plied her with too much wine after the film and she staggered in looking awful. She reminded me of how I had felt on Sunday night.

It was quite late, but I had stayed up reading purposely.

'Alex, I think I'm going to be sick!' she announced.

'For goodness sake, make sure it's in the bathroom.'

It was, and like me she felt a bit better afterwards. She lay on top of her bed groaning and I made some tea.

'I think I'm in love,' Maddy murmured between groans.

'What happened?'

'He tried to rape me in his mini. Of course he didn't, I pretended to faint and then he was *so* sweet, he even did my bra up and helped me to the door and kept on asking if I was all right.'

'How far did you go?' I asked anxiously.

'Far enough,' Maddy replied mysteriously, 'far enough.'

And with that she fell into a deep sleep, snoring loudly, with all her clothes on.

I managed to get her shoes and dress off but she was too heavy for me to get her properly undressed, so I pulled some covers over her and left her to her snores.

113

So much for my exciting news about Steve Scott. It would have to keep until morning. Funny old Maddy. I wondered how far she had gone. Whatever it was I had some catching up to do, and maybe tomorrow night would be my opportunity.

'Don't look so nervous, I'm not going to eat you.' Those were Steve Scott's opening words to me as I stood at his front door.

I must admit I was nervous. After all he *is* a star, and *so* dreamy looking. Not actually conventionally good-looking, but sort of exciting with his long wild hair, and very bright blue staring eyes.

'Come in then, don't stand there with your mouth hanging open.'

I shut my mouth quickly. I must say he is rather rude. Madelaine and I had discussed my date when she had blearily opened her eyes this morning. 'Whatever you do you must sleep with him,' she had announced dramatically, 'it's so dull being a virgin, and it would be marvellous for you to be able to say your first man was Steve Scott.'

'What's new, pussycat?' he asked.

'Er—nothing,' I replied. He had on a denim shirt and tight jeans.

'You're a funny little thing,' he said. 'How come you were with the big bad Tony, the other night?'

'He works for Daddy,' I stuttered, 'er—what I mean is my father sort of owns "Hobo".' I wished I hadn't said that, I sounded like some awful little rich girl.

'Who's Daddy, then?'

I didn't want to start boasting about Daddy. 'Nobody special, just a—er—er—businessman.'

'Oh,' said Steve, studying me with those bright eyes of his. 'What do you do, then? Model or actress?'

'Actually I'm neither, I'm a secretary.' That should stop any ideas he might have about me being rich. I hated people knowing I was rich, it embarrassed me.

'Great! Want to do some typing for me?'

'Yes—if you like.'

He laughed, 'I'm kidding. You know I think you're for real, a baby innocent.'

'I'm eighteen,' I lied.

'You're ancient,' he replied, still laughing. 'Where have you been?'

'I've been at school in Switzerland.'

He took my arm, 'You know for an eightteen-year-old bird you certainly manage to come across like fourteen.'

I was furious and pulled my arm away, but he gripped it again and said, 'Hey, I'm not knocking it, I like it. You don't know how unusual it is. Are you a virgin?'

I blushed.

'You are!' he said accusingly. 'I bet you are.'

How I wished I had never come. How could he ask me questions like that?

'Let's go and get some food,' he said, 'I want to hear all about Daddy and Switzerland and why you're still a virgin at your advanced age.'

He had a big old-fashioned Bentley, brightly polished. Everyone stared at us as we drove along.

Fortunately once we reached the restaurant he was descended on by various friends, and he didn't have a chance to question me during dinner.

He drank an awful lot, and the language at our table was incredible. Maddy wouldn't believe it, even the girls swore. I couldn't wait to get away. Perhaps I could just sneak off to the loo and not come back.

'Hey listen, everyone,' Steve suddenly said loudly, 'this girl's a virgin!' And he clapped his hand down on my shoulder and everyone stared at me.

Oh floor, please open up and swallow me!

'That's nice for you, Stevie,' one of the girl said, 'makes a change,' and she giggled.

I blushed beetroot. 'I think you're a pig!' I hissed at him. 'Please take me home.'

'It's nothing to be ashamed of,' Steve said surprised, 'you're probably the only bloody virgin of eighteen in England!'

I gulped my coffee down, and I was just deciding to get up and leave when who should walk in but Michael, my Michael —with that funny-looking girl he had danced with all night at 'Hobo'—Suki something or other.

She looked ridiculous in a silver tunic with silver knickers actually showing!

She came over to say hello to Steve. Michael walked behind her, saw me and looked amazed.

'Hello, Michael,' I waved gaily, I wished Steve would put his arm around me *now*.

'Hello, Alex,' Michael returned my greeting. I could see he was impressed I was with such an obviously 'in' group.

'See you later at "Hobo",' Suki said to Steve, and she and Michael went off to sit at a nearby table for two.

After a while, Steve said, 'So, what do you want to do? My pad? "Hobo"? or there's a poxy party going on somewhere?'

'I think I'd like to go to "Hobo",' I said, hoping that Michael would follow shortly.

'Let's go then.' He got up, and without even saying goodbye to anyone we left.

In his car he lit a cigarette and offered it to me.

'No, thank you, I don't smoke.'

'That's all right, take a drag, it will put you in good shape.'

I gingerly puffed on the cigarette. It had a funny taste and smelt vile.

'There you go, little girl, you're turning on nicely.'

'I really don't want any more,' I politely handed it back to him. I suppose it was one of those 'funny' cigarettes, I'm not exactly as dumb as he seems to think.

We sat in the car silently while he finished the cigarette.

I know I'm in love with Michael. Here I am sitting next to Steve Scott and *all* I can think of is Michael.

'All right, let's go,' Steve said, more to himself than to me, 'let us go out into the night and swing, little baby girl.'

I peeked quickly at my watch. It was nearly eleven-thirty. If this was going to be a late night how on earth was I going to get up for work tomorrow? I am one of those people that need masses of sleep.

'Hobo' wasn't very crowded. 'I like getting here early,' Steve said, 'you can feel it build that way.'

Soon we were joined by some of the people who had been with us at the restaurant, and others. I was determined not to get drunk so I was drinking Coca-Cola. I didn't really care how stupid Steve thought I was, I had decided that whatever Maddy said, I wasn't going to bed with him. He was much too personal and rude. I couldn't bear the thought of him seeing me without my clothes on. Honestly, the whole thing was going to be embarrassing enough without someone like him.

116

I watched the entrance, waiting for Michael, which of course was the only reason I was here.

'Come on, let's dance,' said Steve. 'You *can* dance, can't you?'

'Of course I can!'

On the dance floor after a few minutes he said, 'I thought you said you could dance.'

'I don't know why you wanted to take me out,' I said angrily, 'you've just been rude to me all night.'

'Oh come off it, little Miss Virgin, I'm only kidding you. Can't you take a joke?'

'I am *not* a virgin, and I *can't* take your sort of hurtful so-called jokes.'

With that I went and sat down, surprising, even myself.

Steve followed me laughing. 'Them there's fighting words little girl. Want another coke or shall we go back to my place and see who's right?'

'I would like another Coca-Cola please.'

At last Suki and Michael came in. She came straight over to Steve. 'Carolyn's downstairs,' she hissed.

'Oh shit!' he said quickly. 'She's supposed to be working tonight. Great!' He turned to me. 'See the trouble you're just about to get me in?'

'Why, what have I done?'

'Carolyn's my girl, she'll go mad if she sees me with another bird. Look, be a good girl and go over and sit with Suki. I'll see if I can get rid of her.'

'But ...'

'Go with Suki.'

Honestly!

Suki giggled. 'Carolyn would scratch your eyes out, come and sit with us.'

So to my complete embarrassment I had to go and sit with Michael and Suki.

Michael said, 'What's going on?' and Suki explained.

He wagged a finger at me, 'You're certainly getting around in your first week in London. How's the job going?'

'Fine.'

The three of us chatted a bit. Michael had his arm around Suki's waist and he kept on giving her little squeezes.

Oh, where was Steve? I didn't want to sit here playing gooseberry to the man I loved.

'Oh look!' Suki suddenly said. 'There's Jan and John, I must go and see them.' And she dashed off.

Michael said, 'Noisy here, isn't it?'

I nodded.

'Well, perhaps I'll take you to a nice quiet little place I know one night, that's if you can fit me into your busy schedule.'

'Oh yes,' I said, weakly. 'I could manage tomorrow.'

TWENTY

TONY

On the plane back to good old blighty I made several important decisions.

(1) Get out of 'Hobo' and into something else where I wasn't gripped tightly by the balls by a sex-mad nympho.

(2) Tell Alex how I feel about her (I do love her) and give up other girls.

(3) Save some money, if possible in case I should decide on marriage.

My mind was made up that a place called 'Tony's' would be fantastic. I had a lot of friends, and between them I could raise enough money—I didn't need one big backer. The new place would knock 'Hobo' right out. Make it very exclusive. I could picture it now.

First thing tomorrow I would be out searching for a suitable location. I think I can swing the whole thing for about ten thousand pounds. Now that shouldn't be hard to raise. If I can only get five people to come up with two thousand each. Sammy must have a couple of grand stashed away and Hal would be able to find it, and Franklin could talk to his old man. It was all going to work out great.

We landed about midnight and I decided to get a cab straight to the club. I only had one suitcase.

What a trip! I'd hardly even had time to take a pee before I was on the plane home again! Still it was good to be back. I would wait until the morning to phone Alexandra, she was probably deep in the land of nod. Poor little kid having to work at some lousy nine to five job. Maybe one of these days I'll marry her and then she can spend her time looking after me. Oh boy! Mustn't think about her like that. I can feel myself getting horny. I think the high altitude affects me, gives me a mad sexual urge.

Would it be wrong to bang one more lucky little bird tonight before giving it all up for Alexandra?

I took them all by surprise at the club. 'Flowers' was sitting chatting to his girl-friend at reception—sonofabitch. He jumped up like he had a candle under his ass when he saw me.

Franco was nowhere in sight. Inside a waiter was playing the records and I couldn't see another waiter in the room. I stormed into the kitchen where it was like an Italian wedding. Franco and the girl cashier were dancing—dancing yet! And the other waiters were slouched around watching. I couldn't leave the lousy place for a minute.

'Come on—come on, everyone,' I screamed, 'what's going on here.'

'Meester Blake!' Franco reeled like a startled rabbit. 'Meester Blake—we wasn't expecting you.'

'Yeah, I can see that. Get back into the room, you lazy slobs. Let's have a little action here, get some drinks moving.'

The waiters milled around in panic and confusion, and Franco suddenly started screaming at them in Italian. The cashier slunk back behind her desk.

Franco got rid of all the waiters and turned to me crestfallen, 'Meester Blake, I ...'

'Yeah, yeah, I know, Franco, you weren't expecting me.'

I went back inside. Flowers was at his stand, waiters were rushing around looking busy. We were back to normal.

I went over to the regulars' table. Sammy was there, arm around a horrific little black-eyed teeny bopper. 'Tony me boy, wacha doin' back? What happened? Good to see you.'

'Yeah,' I replied, 'have a drink, Sammy, I'm going to do the rounds, see you in a minute.'

I tell you 'Hobo' knocks spots off all those New York joints. It's got what I call classy flash—excitement—call it what you like, it's got it.

I bought a drink here, a drink there, shook a lot of hands, kissed a lot of faces, pinched a few bottoms. Then, wowee—pow! Alexandra sitting there as calm as you like. Pretty, she was very pretty, like a gorgeous cultured rose amongst a lot of dandelions. What the bloody hell is she doing here? I shook her hand, trying to keep cool. She smiled at me. She looked tired. She was with Ring-a-ding Suki and that schmucky student type. I sat down.

'Tell us all about New York,' Suki asked. Was she with the student or was Alex?

'How do you feel?' I asked my lovely Alex.

'Fine,' she said brightly. 'You certainly had a short trip.'

'Come on, darlin'—all fixed,' Steve Scott appeared. 'Hey, Tony, you back already?'

'Yeah, baby, I'm back.' We shook hands.

120

'Well, come on then,' he said to Suki, but Alex got up. I watched, shocked as he took her by the hand and pulled her off to another table. *My* Alex with that randy little singer—*my* Alex—*impossible*—there must be some mistake.

'What's she doing with him?' I asked the clown-faced Suki.

She shrugged, 'I don't know, I guess he's on another kick. You know, educated Miss Prim and Proper for a change.'

'You should be so bloody lucky as to be even a tenth as educated as she is,' I said burning. 'What is she—prim and proper because she doesn't screw on sight?'

'What's the matter, Tony, I only said . . .'

'I don't give a goddamn what you said, Suki, you're not fit to sit at the same table as her.' God, I was so angry. I got up and stormed over to Steve and his table of cronies.

'Tony, sit down, have a drink, tell us about the big bad New York scene.'

I could have smashed his stupid bloody face in.

'Alex, I want to talk to you,' I said trying to appear casual.

'Yes, Tony?' She questioned me with her wide brown eyes.

'Leave her alone,' Steve said loudly. 'She's mine tonight.'

'You're talking to a lady,' I said grimly, 'and if you don't mind I'd like to speak to her alone.'

Alex got up quickly. She was blushing. I took her out on the terrace and held her very gently by the shoulders.

'Look,' I said quietly, 'you can tell me to mind my own business, but a girl like you shouldn't be out with a shit bag like Steve Scott.'

She brushed her hair back with her hand, 'He is rather awful,' she admitted, much to my great relief.

'Tell him goodbye then, I'll take you home.'

'I couldn't do that. I mean he has given me dinner and everything, I couldn't just be rude.'

'Listen, sweetheart, that animal doesn't even know what being rude is.'

'It's nice of you to be so concerned, but honestly I can manage.'

I couldn't stop myself, I suddenly grabbed her tightly and kissed her. I pressed my mouth against her lips hard, her mouth was dry and refused to open, but I pushed my tongue between her teeth and forced her to let me in. I put my hands on her breasts and felt their warmth and roundness through her dress. She struggled and pushed me away. Her cheeks were

121

flushed.

'Honestly!' She exclaimed, 'I thought you were warning me about Steve.'

'Can I see you tomorrow?' Young schmuck asking for date.

'I'm sorry, Tony, I'm busy.' She smoothed down her dress and looked at me in a funny way, 'I'd better get back inside.'

'Yeah,' I was destroyed, 'I guess you'd better.'

I felt like I'd been kicked in the stomach. First of all I was hot as hell after kissing her and feeling her fantastic body. Secondly, I knew I wasn't about to let Steve frigging Scott take her home.

I followed her back inside. She sat down beside Steve and he whispered something to her. Bastard! I was going to fix him. I went over to Suki who was busy feeling up her student boyfriend under the table. God, Massey was well rid of this freak.

'Who did Alexandra come here with?' I asked.

She was mad at me. 'I don't know.'

I exerted a bit of the famous Blake charm. 'Come on, Suki sweetheart, don't be so touchy.'

'She came with Steve—and then Carolyn was downstairs looking for him—well, he must have got rid of her because that's when he came back and took Miss Goody Two Shoes off again. Why are you so interested anyway?'

I shrugged. 'She's only a kid, I'm just keeping an eye on her.'

'Oooh!' Suki the Freak shrieked with laughter, 'Sir Galahad Blake!'

Michael butted in then, 'I expect she can look after herself.'

I glared at him. Who asked for his ten cents worth?

Anyway I had a plan. I went downstairs to the office and dialled Steve's home. As I thought, Carolyn answered, she had been sent home to wait.

I disguised my voice (I could have been a wild actor) 'Your boy-friend's at "Hobo" making it with another girl.' Then I hung up, went upstairs and waited.

Fifteen minutes later Carolyn came storming in, her wild red hair flowing, her eyes mean and narrow. Steve didn't even see her coming. She gave him a whack across the face that made me wince.

'You lousy sonofabitch,' she screamed, 'what the *fuck* is going on here? Giving me some story about you had to show the head of Gloom Records around. Some fucking head.' She paused and glared at Alex who looked quite cool and collected. 'It might interest you to know,' she continued, 'that this is my fucking husband you're sitting next to. We got married last week and I wasn't supposed to tell anyone because it might upset his fucking fans. So fuck off.'

Steve practically slid under the table. What a scene! But Carolyn wasn't finished yet, 'I'm three months pregnant too—so stick that up your jumper—you little cow!'

Alexandra had gone visibly pale in the dim of the club. She stood up. 'I'm so sorry,' she said quietly, 'I didn't know,' and with that she made for the exit.

She certainly had class, lots and lots of class.

I caught up with her outside. She was crying. I wanted to wrap her up in my arms and carry her somewhere safe. Silently I handed her my handkerchief and she blew her nose.

I called a cab and we got in. I gave the driver my address. This time I wasn't letting her escape. She didn't say anything until the cab reached my place, and then we went through the same old discussion:

'Oh, Tony, it's simply much too late, I must get home.'

'Just one quick brandy, you need it.'

'I hate brandy.'

'Well, a coffee then.'

'It will keep me awake. I'm sorry to be such a nuisance, but please take me home.'

The cab driver sat there, his ugly hawk face listening to every word.

'Look, just five minutes, we'll have a quick coffee, a little chat, and then I promise I'll take you right home.'

She sighed. 'All right.'

I paid the cab and he winked and muttered, 'Enjoy the quick coffee, guy.' Lousy dirty old man.

My flat smelt horrible, all the windows had been closed, and something had gone off in the fridge. I let some air in and stuck the kettle on. It was a horrible little pad. I had to move.

Alexandra sat on the sofa and I put on an Astrud Gilberto album.

Now that I had her here I didn't know what to do with her.

'This is a nice flat,' she said in her best polite voice, 'have you lived here very long?'

'A few months, it's too small. I want to move, get somewhere nicer.'

'Oh.'

We lapsed into silence until the whistle of the kettle boiling. Coffee was a mistake, I should have given her a drink, got her more relaxed.

'How about an Irish coffee?' I asked.

'I've never had that.'

Not that I had any cream or brown sugar or any of that jazz, but I could put a slug of whisky in it, better than plain coffee. 'You'll love it.'

Astrud was singing. 'The Shadow of Your Smile'. If I had been with any other bird by this time we would have been stripped off and hard at it.

'Did you have a nice time in America?' she asked.

'Yeah—great.' I finished the coffees and handed one to her. It tasted good—personally I don't think you need all that sugar and cream shit.

'You know, Alex, I've got a lot of things to tell you.'

She sipped her coffee and stared at a picture of me taken the opening night of 'Hobo'.

'Do you want to go to bed with me, Tony?' she enquired politely, as if asking what time the next bus home was.

I was stunned. I practically spilt my coffee. 'What?' I stuttered like an idiot.

She was blushing now and biting her lower lip. 'Well, *do* you?'

This wasn't exactly the way I had the whole thing planned. I had figured on telling her how I felt, maybe kissing and cuddling her a while. 'Yes, of course I do,' I said lamely. She had really caught me off guard.

'All right then,' she said calmly. We sat and stared at each other for a bit, and I noticed her hand was shaking as she drank the coffee.

I went to her and took the cup out of her hand and kissed her. This time her lips parted and she gave a little sigh.

I ran my hands around her body, feeling her squirm a little under my touch. She was wearing a brown woollen dress, high-necked with small buttons down the back. I started to undo them.

'Can we go in the bedroom?' she asked. 'Perhaps I can go in first.'

'Yeah, O.K.' She had me so excited I didn't know where I was at.

'I'll call you when I'm ready.'

She trotted off and left me in a state of shock. Wowee—I

had thought she was a little baby innocent. I still loved her though, in spite of the fact that she had obviously—well—been around.

I wondered should I strip off? I wished there was time to take a bath. I felt hot and sweaty from the plane trip.

'I'm ready, Tony,' a little voice called, 'please don't turn the light on.'

She was in my bed, covers up to her chin.

I took my clothes off clumsily, throwing them on the floor. I kept my pants on and jumped into bed beside her.

She had velvet skin, I swear to God her skin was actual velvet. I could only see her faintly in the darkened room, she had drawn the curtains and wouldn't let me pull the covers off her. I felt her slowly, her breasts were very high and full, her waist narrow and her hips curved out, all covered with this wild velvet skin. She lay on her back, her body tense, her hands gripping the covers.

'Relax, baby!' I whispered, 'take it easy, enjoy it.'

Her body hair was sparse and silky like a fine down, she tightened her thighs when she felt my hand there.

I rolled on top of her and forced the covers out of her grip. She was shivering. I stood up over her and took my pants off. She shut her eyes and I came back on top of her and worked to get her legs apart.

'Tony, I'm a virgin,' she suddenly said after a short silent struggle during which I couldn't shift her legs open. I felt myself go down like a punctured balloon.

She opened her eyes quickly, 'You don't mind, do you?'

Mind? Mind! I was delighted. Only it put another aspect on everything. She was a virgin, and she wanted to go to bed with me, which could only mean that she must love me.

'You silly kid, of course I don't mind, I think that's wonderful, perfect.'

'Oh good,' I felt her relax. I rolled off her and gathered her in my arms and held her.

'You see I don't know what I have to do, I don't know how not to have a baby or anything. It's—it's the first time I've ever seen a naked man.'

Well, they say that if you wait long enough, everything comes your way. I felt like a giant! A king!

We lay there for a bit. I was perfectly content just holding her beautiful body. I shut my eyes. I was a bit knocked out by the plane trip and everything.

125

'Tony, is everything all right? You're not disappointed or anything?'

I opened my eyes quickly. Wow—I was so comfortable and happy that I must have dropped off to sleep for a second.

She had escaped from my arms, and was kneeling on the bed holding a sheet in front of her.

'Of *course* it is, baby. Come back here.'

'I just mean—well, if you are disappointed and you don't want to, well—I quite understand.'

'You're kidding!' I pulled the sheet away from her and she quickly lay down. I kissed her face and stroked her hair and felt her unbelievably perfect breasts. She started to make little soft noises, like a kitten.

I had this funny sort of choking feeling. Christ! I loved this girl *so* much. It wasn't even sex, I wasn't so sure that I wanted to make love to her.

She was so pure and innocent, and I wanted her to stay that way. But she wanted me, she wanted to belong to me. She smelt so sweet, like summer flowers.

I was on top of her and showing her what to do. And she was gasping and biting her lower lip and staring at me with those wide brown innocent eyes.

Oh God! I pulled out just in time. It was fantastic! Then she rolled away from me and lay on her stomach.

She was mine.

TWENTY-ONE

FONTAINE

It is such a relief to be rid of the stud. I have learnt a little lesson, never take people out of their natural surroundings. My God, look at the zoo, all those poor animals locked up in cages neurotic as hell. In London in charge of 'Hobo', Tony is a man. Here he is nothing.

I spent a very entertaining afternoon with Allen. He has a lot of possibilities, and he *did* bring his imagination! He told me some absolutely shocking stories about himself and Salamanda Smith. *Très risqué*! I shall look at the little vapid blonde movie queen with new eyes.

Benjamin has arrived and he is showering and cleaning his teeth and gargling. God knows what else. Benjamin is immaculate. He washes his short round body at least three times a day. Whenever we make love he showers first and after, an infuriating habit, although very hygienic. He changes his underwear and socks twice a day—sometimes three times. As a business man Benjamin is a genius. But as a husband he is an infuriating, irritating bore!

Unfortunately only the Body Beautiful can really interest me, that and money of course. Benjamin and I have very little to say to each other. Social gossip doesn't interest him, and financial and business talk drives me to distraction. His children bore me to tears, and he hates discussing my clothes. Actually we are very rarely alone together.

Once he asked me if I would have a child. I told him that at his age it was a ridiculous idea. I don't like children. I find them time-consuming, dirty and noisy. Apart from which, they destroy your figure. Look at Vanessa, big cow-like Vanessa.

Yes, I must say, I am quite happy with my life the way it is. I really have everything.

It's so exciting finding new studs and watching their progress. Tony is a prime example—from waiter to my lover to— well, what exactly is he? A host I suppose one could call him.

There comes a time in every relationship I undertake when a man's body is not enough. I think I have reached that time with Tony. I think he must go. I'll throw him to all the little dollies who may not want him when he's no longer at 'Hobo'.

I must remember to get Benjamin to arrange to have him fired when we get back.

Of course what I really need is a *rich* stud, with a title and all the things that Benjamin has. Then I could divorce Benjamin and *really* be happy. I don't think I've ever come across a rich stud, they just don't seem to exist. All the men with *real* money and position are old, fat, and desperately boring—like Benjamin. Poor old Benjamin.

'Did you have a nice shower, darling?'

'Yes, very nice. Is my secretary here yet?'

'I don't know, I'll buzz Adamo. I've arranged dinner with Sarah and Allen. He's Sarah's latest husband, a writer, I'm sure you'll like him.'

'You know I can't stand Sarah.'

'Darling,' I went to him and started to pull off his bath towel which was tied round his middle. He looked ridiculous with his white hairy legs peeping out.

He turned away, 'Not now, Fontaine. My secretary should be here.'

Well, well! Independent Benjamin. At this stage, after any separation there had been, he was usually rarin' to go.

Deliberately I stepped out of my negligee and stretched. 'I think I'll have a bath while you're with dear old Miss Clerk. Do you think I'm getting too fat?'

I knew there wasn't an ounce of fat on my entire body. I knew the sight of my body excited old Benjamin like hell.

'No, you're not getting fat.' His beady little eyes flicked over me, and then abruptly he turned away for a second time.

Was he getting senile at last?

I rang Adamo on the intercom.

'Is Mr Khaled's secretary here?'

'Yes, Madam.'

Benjamin was busy getting dressed. 'She's here. You will be finished by six, won't you? I promised the Sidwells we would drop by for a drink.'

He grunted. I stretched my naked body and blew him a kiss, and went off into my bathroom.

After all, if the poor old fellow couldn't get it up, well what could one do?

TWENTY-TWO

TONY

I can remember when I was a kid seeing all those wild Hollywood movies where there would be some kind of great love scene—and then the hero (usually Gene Kelly) would say goodnight to his girl and rush off into the street singing and dancing it up a storm.

Well that's exactly what I feel like doing now. Man, I feel like Gene Kelly ten times larger than life.

What if I burst into song and dance in the middle of the Kings Road? I'd probably get nicked for being drunk!

I took my little Alexandra home in a cab. She was very quiet after, very lovable, very shy. In fact, she didn't say a word. She dressed in the bathroom while I snatched a quick kip, then she shook me awake and said please could she go home.

I didn't know what to say to her, I was so sort of knocked out by it all.

So we both sat quietly in the cab, and then I dropped her off and let the cab go, and here I am in Chelsea. It's three a.m. and now I'm wide awake and starving hungry and feeling great.

I picked up another taxi and rode over to 'Hobo'. They never learn—this time there was nobody out front. I raged inside, grabbed a frightened Franco and said, 'Where the hell is Tina?'

'Meester Blake—we wasn't expecting you back.'

'Yeah, baby, you're not telling me anything new.'

'I think Tina no feel good, she go home early.'

'Great Franco—great. So if you let her go home why not put someone else out front?'

'Of course I deed, Meester Blake. Frederico is there.'

'Frederico ain't there.'

Franco looked shocked. 'I keel that Frederico, I told 'im 'undred times to stay out front.'

I felt too good to argue any more. I just had to be there, that was all. Franco was fine when I was around.

Flowers was playing Lou Rawls. The place had that nice relaxed atmosphere at the end of a good night. There were about thirty people left in the room.

Sammy was still sitting with his juvenile wonder. He grabbed me. 'Where you bin? You missed all the excitement. It's a good job I was 'ere, I straightened things out a bit.'

'What happened?'

'That Carolyn's a mad bird. She started picking everything up in sight and throwing it at Steve, and 'e's trying to 'ide under the table, and the f-ing and blinding that was going on is nobody's business! So anyway I grab a hold of 'er and then she starts to cry and 'e goes running out of the club and then what do you know—the bleedin' newspapers arrive—some joker must 'ave phoned 'em. What a barny!'

I shrugged. I wasn't sorry I'd missed anything, because if I had stayed I'd probably have smashed that half assed pop singer to pieces.

Sammy's bird sat gloomily in the corner chewing on her thumb. 'Can we go?' she whined.

'In a minute, don't be so anxious, I'm going to give it to you.' Sammy replied, winking at me and mouthing—'a raver'!

Sammy was still chasing scrubbers. Why didn't he look around for a nice decent girl?

'Hey, Sammy, while I was in New York I was thinking.'

'Ye gods—'e's thinking yet!'

'No, Sammy, seriously. I've got this great idea for opening up a new place.'

'A new place? Watcha want to do that for? What's wrong with 'ere?'

'Well, you know, Sammy, I'm the last one to ever see any bread out of this place, it's making a bomb and I see about tuppence.'

'Yeah? Well, you're a schmuck, aren't you? Watcha want to make yourself a lousy deal for?'

'Because I wasn't in a position to make any deal when this joint opened. Anyway—who knew it was going to take off like it did?'

'Yeah, well—why doncha get 'em to pay you some more? You work 'ard enough—*when* you're 'ere, that is.'

'Why let them put *more* money in their pockets? This place is *me*—without me they'd be finished in a couple of weeks.'

'Hold on, boy, you mean a lot to the place, but it still managed very nicely while you were in New York.'

'Aw, come on Sammy, let's go,' said the whiney-voiced scrubber, 'I'm fed up with sitting here all night.'

'Yeah, you go Sammy, I'll talk to you tomorrow.' I could see that I wasn't going to get too much out of him.

'Meester Blake,' Franco was at my elbow, 'there ees Meester Ian Thaine outside with a party of ten, they want to come in, but we cannot serve any drinks now and 'ee is screaming 'bout that.'

'O.K., Franco, I'll handle it.'

Ian Thaine was a pain in the neck. He had made a fortune in so-called 'swinging London' gear—clothes, souvenirs, old uniforms, posters. He had 'Thaine' shops everywhere, and he made Sammy look like one of the aristocracy. He was about my age, thin and weedy-looking, out to better himself socially but never making it. I knew he hated me, because he saw me chatting to all-comers—film stars, lords, politicians. It killed him. He wanted to be someone. In fact, the rumour had it that he hired a permanent press agent to try to get his name in the gossip columns alongside the élite. I suppose he was worth a couple of million at least. He was usually with a motley crowd.

Tonight it was a couple of last season's debs, three members of a scruffy rock group, a once glamorous sexy actress with her nineteen-year-old 'Manager', a bit part actor, and two wide-eyed teeny boppers obviously culled from the streets of Piccadilly.

'Ian, m'boy,' I gave him the brotherly firm sincere handshake.

'Tony,' he sneered at me, 'is that right we can't get a pissing drink?'

'Sorry, Ian, that's right, got to think of our licence.'

'Well, balls to your licence,' he said peevishly 'we want drinks.'

I smiled pleasantly, 'You'll just have to go somewhere else then.'

Ian bit on his thin lower lip, 'Oh, all right, we'll suffer on Coca-Cola then. I can see I'm going to have to open a place of my own in this town before I can get a drink.'

Bingo! Lights flash. Ian Thaine. Why hadn't I thought of him before?

'Come on, Ian,' I put my arm around his shoulder, 'I'll buy you all Coca-Colas myself.'

My mind was working quickly. Ian was perfect—but perfect for the set-up I had in mind. He would jerk off at the thought of owning a successful joint. All I needed was a little sweet talk. He had the money, plenty of it. We could go fifty-fifty. He to put up all the money, me to put up myself.

'Hey, Ian,' I said, 'I've been thinking . . .'

TWENTY-THREE

ALEXANDRA

Maddy was fast asleep. It seems whenever I need her she's huddled in an immovable ball beneath her covers. I gave her a push, but she groaned and vanished under her eiderdown. The most important night of my life, and she didn't even want to hear about it.

I felt strangely weak at the knees, but studying my face in the mirror I really didn't look any different. Perhaps a little more sophisticated?

What an evening! First the terrible time with Steve Scott, then his *wife* appearing. I could have died with embarrassment. And Michael being there witnessing the whole thing. I must have looked such a fool.

Anyway, at least Tony was very nice coming after me and everything. He was so sweet and kind that when we were in the taxi outside his flat I suddenly decided that if I was going to go to bed with someone, *he* would be the perfect person. After all he's the only one who seems to pay any attention to me.

I think he was a bit shocked when I asked him if he wanted to make love to me. Honestly, I felt like a scarlet lady! *Me* approaching *him*!

But after all I had decided that I was going to lose my virginity and I was determined.

Michael likes women of the world. Am I a woman of the world now? It wasn't much fun. I mean I just sort of lay there while he climbed on top of me. He was awfully heavy and it hurt a bit. I don't know what all the fuss is about if that's all you do. And it's so messy—ugh! I didn't enjoy it at all. I can't ever imagine Mummy and Daddy doing it. Did they? I suppose they must have before they separated. But Mummy doing that, why it's so undignified.

I shook Maddy again, but she simply refused to budge. I'd never get to sleep until I told *someone*.

Of course, the most exciting thing is the fact that I have a date with Michael! A date! Just the two of us. He must like me if he wants to take me to a quiet place for dinner.

I felt a bit weak. I don't know how I'm going to face going

to work tomorrow. I'm not sure if I'm cut out to be a secretary after all.

Oh, Michael, have I done the right thing? I only did it for you.

What if I get pregnant? Tony said he'd been careful but how do I know? What does he think of me? I don't know if I can ever face him again. Surely it was better in the old days when a man was supposed to want his wife to be a virgin. Now the whole thing has changed, and it's awful to be a virgin. I feel so confused.

'Maddy, wake up!'

TWENTY-FOUR

TONY

Ian Thaine was easy. I couldn't understand why I hadn't thought of him before. He was craving to be a big man, dying to be friends with everyone, and what better way than to own a club?

I chatted him and he responded like a baby. I'd hardly ever given him the time of day before, because he was an obnoxious sonofabitch, but talking to him I realised just how much he wanted to be liked.

After an exhausting hour of costs and profits and all that jazz we shook hands.

'It's a deal,' Ian said.

Beautiful! He would put up all the money. I would do everything else and get a salary plus forty-nine per cent. I struggled for fifty, but Ian wasn't budging on that.

'We'll call it "Ian's",' he said.

'Yeah,' I muttered. We could argue about that later.

It was all too good to be true. It was late and the waiters were looking mutinous. Ian and party were the only customers left. One of the debs came and plonked herself on Ian's knee. He slid his hand up her skirt. The aged actress was in a tight clinch with her young manager. Nobody looked like budging.

I stood up. 'I think it's bedtime.'

Ian stood up, the ex-deb sliding in a furious heap on the floor. 'Yes, let's go.' Ian was now my friend.

To the waiters' relief the whole party got itself together and we all left.

Downstairs the three rock singers piled into a Ford with the two teeny boppers and roared off. The actress, her manager and the bit part actor got into a taxi. The two ex-debs, Ian and I were left. He was driving a white Lincoln Continental with gold fixtures and maroon upholstery.

'Where's your car?' he asked me.

'Er—in the garage being fixed.'

'I'll drop you then.'

'No, that's O.K., Ian, I can take a cab.'

'I said I'll drop you.' He took me to one side, 'Besides I want you to take Diana with you. You'll like her.' He whispered a speciality that she was expert at.

'Look, Ian, I don't want...'

But he ignored me. I climbed in the back of the car with Diana. She was horsey-faced, tall and skinny. I couldn't have fancied her on the best of nights.

'Where to?' Ian asked.

I told him. How the hell was I going to get out of this? I mean he obviously thought he was doing me a big favour. The best thing to do was play it by ear.

He dropped me off and Diana clambered out with me.

'See you at my office at three then,' Ian said. 'Have a good time.'

Shit! He drove off and Diana and I stood there. 'Where do you live?' I asked her when the car was out of sight.

'With Ian,' she replied slightly surprised. 'Why?'

It looked like I was lumbered. Why was I such a berk? Why hadn't I just taken Ian to one side and explained. I suppose because I wanted a deal, and if accepting one of his tatty girls was going to please him, well, I guess I would just have to accept her.

'Come on,' I said wearily.

Please forgive me, my wonderful Alexandra, but I'm doing it for us.

TWENTY-FIVE

FONTAINE

Benjamin is not himself. Surly and bad-tempered and positively rude to Sarah and Allen. I am absolutely furious. Why, I've never seen him like this. Of course I know he's an absolute monster in business, but, with me he has always been placid and polite, and had never verbally attacked my friends, which he did quite viciously last night, calling poor Allen 'a lily livered, poor man's Tennessee Williams'. Well I mean really! I didn't know he'd even read anything of Allen's.

Sarah was livid. I have rarely seen her angry, but last night her eyes were flashing and the words practically spitting from between her lips.

Needless to say we all parted outside 'Le Club' simply dreadful friends. I haven't spoken to Benjamin since. How dare he think that he can insult me and my friends!

Allen says he knows all about us. What nonsense! How could he possibly know? I'm always very discreet.

On top of everything else we have the added thrill of beastly little Ben junior joining us tonight. Alexandra is bad enough, looking down her nose at me all night, but Ben junior is impossible. Mutual hate abounds.

God knows why Benjamin insists I have to see his children. They're *his*, not mine. I want no part of them.

What I would actually like to do is go back to London. I expect I am missed there.

I have decided to wait a few weeks before having Benjamin fire Tony. After all, he is different in London and I may as well make use of him until I find another London stud. I must say I feel quite nostalgic about Vanessa and 'Hobo' and all the little intrigues in London.

Oh God, I suppose I shall have to make peace with Benjamin. Why the hell *I* should make peace I don't know, but I *do* want to buy that sable coat today and it *is* twelve thousand dollars. I'll put on my white mink over nothing and go and wake him.

Benjamin, of course, was already up and out and at his office. It is noon and he always rises at seven.

Adamo remained impassive at the sight of me wandering

around in my coat. Dear Adamo, the perfect servant.

Benjamin wouldn't appreciate me turning up at his office in my mink and nothing else. Actually it was rather a fun thing I would like to do. The erotic secret of being naked underneath was very exciting. But of course Benjamin was much too staid for that.

I phoned Sarah. 'Darling, I'm sorry, I'm just too upset for words.'

Sarah's voice was acid. 'I'm sorry for you, sweetie, you're married to him.'

'That's all right, darling. He's abject with remorse today. I'm just off to get a new sable.'

'They're more chic in Paris this year.'

Sarah was a bitch, but I could out-bitch anyone. 'Why don't you buy Allen one?'

She laughed coldly. 'You're so amusing, Fontaine, maybe I shall.'

We said our goodbyes, and I phoned Benjamin at his office.

'Yes, what is it? I'm busy.'

Oh my god, he was impossible. It crossed my mind to forget the coat and let him beg my forgiveness. But a sable coat is worth a slight effort.

'You're not still angry?'

'What is it, Fontaine? I'm busy and can't discuss that now.'

'Well, darling, I need some money.'

'Talk to my secretary, she'll send over what you need.'

'I need about twenty thousand.'

There was a pause. 'Twenty thousand dollars?'

'Yes, darling, I've seen a gorgeous sable coat, and I have to get a few other bits and bobs.'

'But I just bought you the white mink.'

'I know, darling, but I *need* a new sable.'

'No, Fontaine, we'll talk about it later.'

'What do you mean, no Fontaine?' I was shaking with fury.

'Goodbye,' he hung up on me.

I phoned back at once. 'Mr Khaled is in conference, and can't be disturbed,' an embarrassed secretary said.

'But this is Mrs Khaled.'

'I'm sorry, he said I wasn't to interrupt him for anyone.'

I slammed the receiver down. How dare he! How dare he! He would pay a lot more than a sable coat for this.

TWENTY-SIX

TONY

I think I'm a right bastard. What I should have done was told Ian Thaine to take his messy little ex-deb home with him and screw the fact that it might louse up our deal. If our deal depended on me knocking off one of his birds, then to hell with it—who needed it?

I did. Who even knew if he was going to come up with the money anyway? So far it was all conversation.

I really felt bad. Diana had gone, I had to force her to go. She was a dog, a disgusting dog. And I was disgusting too, laying back and letting her slobber all over me. Well, at least I hadn't touched *her*.

I have definitely decided I'm going to marry little Alex. It's a big decision, I know, but I love her, I truly love her. I think I would kill any bastard that tried to touch her.

The whole situation is very dodgy. I've got to get away from Fontaine and 'Hobo'. Christ, if Alex ever found out about me and Fontaine it would be all over. She's a girl of principles, she's so sweet and kind, and that body! Wowee! I've never seen such a gorgeous body, so shy, and a virgin. I can hardly believe it, and she's mine, all mine.

I think what I'm going to do is get up and dress and maybe take little Alex for lunch. Of course, I don't have her office number. I should have asked her last night, but maybe her girlfriend is home.

I dialled their flat, but there was no reply. Shit! I couldn't even remember the name of the firm she worked for. It's twelve o'clock, that means I've got to wait until five-thirty or six before she gets home.

I had to meet with Ian Thaine at three, that would pass the afternoon. Maybe Sammy would fancy a bite of lunch.

I couldn't track Sammy down, but I found Hal and Franklin in our favourite coffee bar, a nice little place where you could sit all day and watch the American tourists go by.

Hal said, 'Listen, baby, I've got a beautiful deal going. You remember Mamie? Well, her old man invested in this film company in Rome before he died, and now the company's nearly going bust and she's putting up a lot more bread and

I'm taking over. We're leaving for Rome tomorrow. Beautiful huh? If you're a good boy I'll put you in a movie, you're pretty enough!'

Hal came up with a deal like this every so often, but something always ballsed it up, usually him.

'That's great, Hal, you're going to be a big man.'

'Baby, I'm always a big man.' His smokey eyes surveyed two American ladies struggling with their mink stoles. He was always on the look out.

'So what's new, Tony baby? How was my town?'

'Great, Hal, great, I had a ball.'

'Yeah, one of these days I'll go back. I'm waiting for my bookie to die! Got to be a success in that city baby, otherwise you're nowhere—but nothing.'

My favourite waitress came scurrying over. 'Morning Mr Blake. Same as usual?'

'Yes, pretty, make sure the eggs are nice and firm.'

She dimpled a smile at me. 'I see your club made headlines today.'

'What?'

Hal said, 'Yeah, baby, didn't you see it. A load of shit about Steve Scott.'

'Oh,' I patted my waitress on the bottom. It felt like she had nothing on under the flimsy blue skirt and white apron. 'Be a darling and grab me the papers.'

'I'll try, Mr Blake. We're awfully busy just now.'

She returned in two minutes flat with three morning papers. I scanned them quickly. Steve Scott was on the front page of all of them. The headlines screamed about his secret marriage. I read the first one.

'Steve Scott (23) disclosed at London discothèque "Hobo" last night his secret marriage to actress and dancer Carolyn England (23) some time last week. Steve Scott found fame two years ago when his record "Laurie Baby" shot to the top of the charts. Since then his records have stayed consistently in the Top Ten. He has just finished recording his own Weekly T.V. Show and is due to start work shortly on his first film "MUD". Miss England has appeared countless times on your T.V. screens and was last year voted "The girl with the longest legs on T.V." The news was broken when Miss England surprised her new husband at "Hobo", where he was enjoying a quiet evening of fun with Alexandra Khaled, eighteen-year-old daughter of billionaire Benjamin Al Khaled. The new Mrs

139

Scott also announced the fact that they are expecting an addition to the family. The Steve Scott fan club hung a black flag from its windows early this morning. Steve Scott has no comment on his surprise marriage.'

There was a big picture of Carolyn leering sexily in a black fishnet cat-suit, and a small picture of Steve having his shirt ripped off by a band of fans.

I was really choked. Where the hell had they got their information about Alexandra? Why should her name be brought up? Lousy newspapers. They all carried more or less the same story.

My poor Alex was probably upset if she had seen it. Well, it did teach her a lesson for going out with the randy little bastard in the first place.

I attacked my eggs.

'Hello, mind if I sit here?'

It was Suki, dressed for the day in a thigh-length Indian shift and fringed jacket.

Franklin said, 'Where's your sister? You promised to fix me up.'

'Oh yes, sorry, I've been a bit busy and forgot all about it. I'll talk to her.'

I just didn't understand Franklin. He was a good-looking boy who had every opportunity to chat up all the birds at the club, but he never made a move. Now he was hanging his hopes on Suki's sister.

'If you promised him, do it,' I said, 'get a hold of your sister for tonight.'

'She might be busy,' Suki replied producing her compact and studying her freaky face. 'Anyone seen Massey lately?'

Under all the piles of weird make-up she was probably quite pretty.

'What do you want to know about Massey for? You've got you little student now,' I said.

'I just wondered if anyone had seen Massey, that's all,' she replied defensively, 'I thought he might be here today.'

I finished my eggs and ordered some cheese-cake. Eating is one of my favourite pastimes, but I never get fat. I stay in great shape. Twenty-five push-ups a day. My stomach's hard as a rock.

Just then who should walk in but Massey. Cool as ever in a white suit and brown polo-neck sweater. He's a great-looking guy.

'Tony, man,' he clapped me on the shoulder, 'good to have you back. Hello, Suki—Franklin—Hal.' He sat down at our rapidly expanding table.

Suki snapped her compact shut and put it away. 'Mass, can I come back?' she asked.

'No,' he said quietly, 'no, baby, you stick with your little white boy.'

Her clown eyes filled with tears. 'Oh come on, Mass, let me come back.'

'I said no, Suki.' And he turned to talk to me about New York.

Suki sat there a few minutes, then with two black tears hovering in her eyes, got up and left.

I ate her open cheese sandwich, which she hadn't touched.

'She thinks she can just come walking back to me when she gets a little bored with her sweet little white boy,' Massey said grimly. 'Well, she can just sweat it out.'

I think Massey was actually jealous.

I hung around there until it was nearly time to meet with Ian Thaine, then I walked the short distance to his office.

He sat on a black leather throne in front of a huge antique desk in a red room hung with pictures of himself. His opening words were, 'I told you you'd get a good job done, didn't I? Those little convent-educated bints are the ones.' His face was thin and evil and his eyes long yellow slits.

'Yeah, well thanks, Ian.'

'Nothing—it's nothing.'

He then proceeded to give me a full sex summary of the three birds he had living with him, including Diana. Then he unlocked a desk drawer and produced a stack of polaroid pictures of them in various stages of undress. They became obscene. I felt sick to my stomach.

'I took them all,' Ian said proudly. 'Sometimes I have little parties, next time I'll see you're invited.'

Here was a man after Fontaine's heart! Was I climbing from the frying pan into the fire? What about getting down to business? I flicked quickly through the rest of the polaroids and said, 'Very nice, Ian. Now what about contracts and things?'

'Contracts?' he said. 'What's the matter, don't you trust me?'

'Of course I trust you, but if I'm going to start knocking myself out looking for locations, I want to be sure everything's cool—you know, have it all down in black and white. Of course as soon as we find somewhere I'll leave "Hobo."'

141

One thing I was sure of. I wasn't going to be Tony Schmuck again. If I had to get involved with this slimy bastard it was all going to be legal, so that when he wanted me to attend any of his parties I could safely say no, without getting chucked out. Fontaine unwittingly had taught me to be smart.

'All right,' Ian said, 'I'll have an agreement drawn up. Meanwhile start looking. What about Mrs Khaled?'

I looked at him in surprise. How did he know about me and Fontaine?

'What about her?' I said suspiciously.

'Well, I mean shall I mention her in the agreement?'

'What for?' Now I was really surprised.

'She's your—er—partner, isn't she? She'll be in it with us, won't she?'

'Oh,' I was speechless.

Ian carried on. 'I'd like to meet her. When can I meet her?'

This was charming. When had I ever mentioned Fontaine?

'She's in New York,' I said vaguely.

'Now there's a beautiful woman,' Ian said admiringly, locking his polaroids away.

I stood up. 'O.K., Ian, I'll wait to hear from you then.'

'Yes, I'll have my solicitor draw something up. Shouldn't take long.'

'Fine, I'll start looking.'

We shook hands. I didn't trust him, but as long as he thought Fontaine was involved he'd probably come up with an agreement and the money. I don't know why he should think Fontaine was my partner, but if it was going to keep him sweet, let him think it. Why disillusion the poor schmuck before the time came?

I couldn't wait for my little Alex to come home from her office. What a drag. I didn't even know where it was. At least another two hours before she would be home.

I wondered what she would want to do tonight. I wasn't going to take her on any wild outings, just a nice quiet dinner, somewhere small, and a talk, a serious talk about us. Then she was going home to bed early. My darling must get some sleep. I figured I would drop by a few estate agents to pass the rest of the afternoon. May as well start the ball rolling.

TWENTY-SEVEN

ALEXANDRA

I don't think I've ever been so embarrassed in my life! Mr McLaughton, himself, summoned me into his office and I was shaking. I had been half-an-hour late in the morning, and I supposed this was it.

He was a huge man with bushy eyebrows from under which peered watery red eyes. I don't know why *he* had to fire me, I'd never even seen him before.

'Sit down, Alexandra,' he boomed. 'You don't mind me calling you Alexandra, do you?' and he chuckled.

I sat nervously. Daddy was right. I should have taken a job with one of his friends.

'Well, well, well,' Mr McLaughton said, suddenly lapsing into a fit of coughing, 'so we have a celebrity in our midst.'

'A celebrity, sir?' I questioned dimly.

'You are Ben Khaled's daughter are you not?'

How on earth had they found out?

'Yes, sir.'

'Well, well, well. You should have told us. Why so secretive?'

I blushed, 'I don't know, sir.'

Honestly, what was I expected to do? Come marching in for the job announcing to all and sundry that my father was Benjamin Khaled.

'I think we can give you a better position than you have,' Mr McLaughton said, beaming. 'I think we can bring you into my office as a junior personal assistant, at an extra three pounds a week. Not that the money matters to you, I'm sure.'

I didn't want to be brought into his office as a junior personal assistant at an extra three pounds a week just because they knew who Daddy was.

'Thank you, sir,' I muttered. I'm weak. I hate to cause scenes. I would have to phone up or get Maddy to phone and say I couldn't work there any more.

'My two daughters are great fans of Steve Scott, you'll have to get them his autograph.'

I looked at him in astonishment, 'Steve Scott...' I stammered.

He picked up a newspaper on his desk and waved it at me, 'Pretty girl he married,' he said, 'is she a friend of yours too?'

I took the newspaper from him. I read it quickly. Oh golly! The whole thing became clear. That's how they knew about me. What would Mummy say if she saw this, and Daddy? He would be furious.

'I haven't seen this,' I mumbled.

'Don't forget about the autographs. You can take the rest of the week off if you like, start your new job on Monday heh? Perhaps I can meet your father one night, have a little chat about his talented daughter.' He chuckled again.

'Yes, sir. Thank you, sir.' I fled.

By three o'clock I was home. Madelaine was out. I phoned Mummy. Apparently she hadn't seen the newspapers because she didn't mention anything about the whole mess.

'You are bringing some friends this weekend, aren't you?' she asked.

I hadn't even asked Michael yet, I hoped he would come. 'Yes, Mummy, just one.'

'All right, jolly good, darling. See you tomorrow then.'

Madelaine came in shortly after, laden with packages. 'I've been shopping,' she announced, 'got myself some terrific gear. What on earth are you doing home?'

We talked while she unwrapped her parcels and tried everything on. Madelaine is a super girl, absolutely my best friend, but she's really not the type for all the things she had bought. Mini culottes looked just awful on her as she had a big bottom. In any case they were far too short. A see-through crochet dress was the worst thing, and a brown maxi dress the best. Anyway, I suppose she at least was going to look 'with it'.

'You must get one of these crochet dresses,' Mandy enthused, 'they're so terrif, and with your figure it will look fabulous! If you like you can borrow mine tonight.'

Actually it did look a lot better on me.

Maddy had discovered via Jonathan that Suki had been sleeping at their flat, and that even worse she had moved lots of her things in.

'Jonathan's absolutely livid!' Maddy said. 'It's only a tiny flat and her things are everywhere. He says Michael is dotty about her. Sorry, old thing, but I'm sure it won't last.'

'Why is he taking me out tonight?'

She shrugged. 'Search me. I say, when are you seeing Tony again?'

'I don't know, never I hope.'

'Oh, Alex, he's nice, awfully good-looking. He's your lover anyway, you'll have to see him.'

'Of course I won't.'

We had discussed my losing my virginity from seven a.m. when Maddy finally woke up, to eight-thirty, when I had dashed off to the office. Maddy had asked a thousand questions. Did it hurt? Did I love him? Was he enormous? Did I scream? I couldn't really remember any details. I suppose he did have a nice body. Of course I didn't love him, I loved Michael. Michael, Michael, that's all I could think of.

At six o'clock Tony phoned. 'Well, beautiful, how do you feel?'

'Fine, thank you.'

'What time shall I fetch you?'

'Fetch me?' I racked my brains to think if I had made any arrangement with him for tonight, and I was sure I hadn't.

'How about eight o'clock? We'll just have dinner and then I'll bring you straight home.'

'Look, Tony, I'm awfully sorry but I am already going out.'

There was a long pause and then he said, 'You're kidding?'

'No, I've had this arranged for ages.'

There was another long pause and then he said, 'Well, break it.'

'Break what?'

'Your date, idiot. I'll fetch you at eight.'

'Tony, I can't, it's ...'

His voice was suddenly very angry. 'Who are you seeing that's so bloody important?'

I cringed. I hated people to be angry with me. 'I'm sorry, Tony, it's—it's family, I just can't get out of it.'

'Oh, Alex, Alex. What are you doing to me?'

'I'm not doing anything to you.'

'Are you angry with me about last night, is that it?'

'Tony, honestly I'm not angry. I'd really love to see you but it's just not possible tonight.'

'All right, little girl. How about later?'

'I'm not sure, I don't know ...'

'Look, I'll phone you at eleven. If you're not tired I'll pop round for an hour before going to the club. How's that?'

'That's terrific.' I breathed a sigh of relief to get him off the

145

phone without a nasty scene.

I borrowed Maddy's crochet dress and Michael actually gave a whistle when he saw me.

'You *are* growing up,' he commented.

He took me to a little restaurant, very dark and cosy, then he lectured me solidly about how I was mixing with bad company, and if I didn't watch it I would get into trouble, and all these people I was always with smoked drugs and things. Well, I *knew* that.

'I feel responsible for you,' he said. 'You can't come straight out of school and turn into the town swinger.'

Honestly!

'What have your parents said about the papers today?'

'Nothing,' I muttered, I was sulky and disappointed. I thought he had wanted to have dinner with me, but he just wanted to tell me what a silly little girl I was.

'Anyway, what about you and that awful funny girl?' I finally said, unable to keep quiet any longer, 'What do your parents think of *you* living with her!'

'I'm not seventeen years old,' he said grimly. 'I'm only trying to help you, Alex, you're only a kid.'

I hated him!

I was home by ten-thirty, having bid a cold goodbye to Michael immediately we finished dinner.

Tony phoned promptly at eleven. I would show Michael. I invited Tony to spend the weekend in the country at Mummy's house. Michael had called Tony common and loud. Well, let's see what he thought about this! If this didn't make him jealous I didn't know what would.

TWENTY-EIGHT

TONY

You drift through life from day to day and everything's cool. Life is good, things swing along nicely, plenty of birds, friends, food, enough bread to gamble a little, eat out every night, hand Sadie a fiver occasionally. Beautiful!

Of course I always wanted to do a bit better, get my own joint. But I knew I didn't have to push, it would all happen. I could just relax and enjoy life. It was such a blast to have names I'd only ever read about treat me like their long lost brother, and fantastic birds available.

Then along comes Miss Alexandra Khaled, auburn shining hair, big brown eyes, knockout body, young, innocent, classy, sweet, shy, kind. And I fall—POW!! In love.

It means an immediate change in my life. I need plenty more bread, not for gambling, or eating out, or handing more to Sadie. But I need to make a home. I have to have something to offer her.

She looks at me with those big trusting eyes and I melt. I never in my life felt this way before. I feel I must look after her, protect her from the big ugly world, take care of her.

When she said she couldn't see me tonight I was destroyed. My whole day had hinged around seeing her in the evening. I was angry and jealous and sick to my stomach. But she explained so nicely, so sweetly.

Oh boy, I never thought I'd get caught like this. I've known a lot of women and I thought as far as they were concerned I had it licked. Screw 'em and leave 'em wanting more. Never failed. But now I was caught in that well-known trap.

When she said she couldn't see me, it was a physical feeling of pain. Of course, I had to marry her. This was it. Put her in a little flat, give her a few children. I wonder if she can cook?

I spent a miserable evening with Sammy and his whiney-voiced scrubber from the night before. We ate at a steak house and I'll swear she was giving him a quick one under the table. She sucked her thumb between mouthfuls of food, and wiped her nose with the back of her hand. Charming!

Eventually she went to the loo and Sammy said, 'What's the matter with you—what are you dragging for?'

I shrugged, 'Nothing, I'm fine, everything's cool.' I wasn't about to tell *him* what the matter was.

'What do you think of my bird? Still at school, isn't she a little darlin'?'

'You won't be happy until you get caught, schmuck. She's under age.'

'Who's going to catch me, then? She says 'er parents never ask any questions. She can come and go when she wants.'

'Sammy,' I shook my head sadly, 'what do you want it for?'

'You're kidding, aren't you?'

She came back. She looked all of fifteen in her wisp of a dress and long stockinged legs.

Eleven o'clock came along very slowly. I tried to stay cool and phoned Alex.

She was adorable. 'I'm in bed, Tony. I've been home ages.'

'Can't I come round and read you a bedtime story?'

Oh God, I was coming out with lines I didn't even believe.

'I'm just going to sleep, but I'll tell you what, would you like to come to the country for the weekend?'

'When?' I asked stupidly.

'I thought tomorrow afternoon, and we could come back Sunday evening.'

'Yeah, that would be great.'

Screw the club, it would have to manage without me over the weekend. A whole three days with my Alex. Great.

'Shall we take the train?' she enquired. 'Or do you want to drive? It's only an hour's journey.'

I didn't think Sammy would see fit to part with his E-type over the weekend so I said, 'We'll take the train.'

'There's a four o'clock from King's Cross we could get. Mummy will meet us the other end.'

I had forgotten about dear old Mummy. That sort of put a dampener on things. What if Mummy told Daddy and Daddy told Fontaine? Oh well, I'd soon be away from 'Hobo'.

'Yeah, that's perfect. I'll pick you up around three.'

'What happened to you?' Sammy asked. 'You look like you found gold.'

'Yeah,' I laughed, 'let's go to the club.'

It was going to be one of those nights, jamming up early, plenty of faces. Franco on his toes, Flowers playing Wilson Pickett.

Hal, Franklin and Massey in already. Massey with a zoftic blonde, Franklin alone as usual, and Hal stoned, celebrating his last night of freedom before Rome and Mamie.

I socialised a bit. It was too soon to put out the word I would be opening on my own, but it was as well to spread my charm heavy. I must remember to pinch the members' list and get it copied.

'The Twang' came in with a film group, pouty lips, mane of tangled orange hair, she had got over her temper with me. She gave me a hug and a kiss. Her tits were hanging out of a black velvet dress. She wasn't a bad kid, we had had quite a lot of fun. She was certainly well built.

'Guess what, Tonee baby?' she squeaked, 'I'm starring in "MUD" with Steve Scott. Isn't that to much?"

'Yeah, that's great.' I felt full of goodness towards the world.

'What did she have to say?' Franklin asked when I sat down.

'She says she's starring with Steve Scott in "MUD".'

'Huh!' exclaimed Franklin. 'Candy Cook is the lead, she's probably got some bit part.'

Franklin still hadn't recovered from his encounter with 'The Twang'.

'Franklin,' I said seriously, 'what are we going to do about you?'

'What do you mean?'

'I mean you getting laid, that's what I mean. What are you saving it up for? Wow—if I was your age with your connections I'd be having a ball.'

'I just haven't met the right girl.'

'Shit, man, by this time *any* girl would be the right girl. You can't jerk off all your life you know.'

Franklin lapsed into silence and I went and had a scotch with one of the 'Must' just back from a record-breaking concert in Paris.

There's something about a scotch and Coke I like. It's a good long drink with hidden punch. I must have had about six or seven when I went to take a piss and realised I was well and truly loaded. I usually just get a little buzz on when I'm working, but tonight—like POW! it had really hit me.

I was sweating hot, having been dancing with Molly Mandy, who's a wild dancer. She had wandered in on her own and sat herself at our table. I had this vague idea of fixing her up with

149

Franklin, but God almighty, she'd eat him alive! Maybe that's what the kid needed.

Out of the blue I found myself dancing with 'The Twang'. She wriggled her hips like I didn't believe.

'Ooh! Tonee, this is fun,' she said, 'you never used to dance with me when we were together.'

'Funky Street.' Flowers freaking out at his stand. 'The Twang' shaking her boobies at me. Man, I was gone. Flowers grinning broadly. 'Jumpin' Jack Flash.' Sweat pouring off me. Hal having a screaming match with Franco. Everyone laughing. Everyone having a ball. Sammy doing it with his schoolgirl. 'Tramp.' Why did Otis Redding have to get it in a lousy plane crash? Flowers in mourning for weeks, more so than for Martin Luther King. 'You're Lookin' Good.' 'The Twang' falling out of her dress, giggling, tossing orange hair around. Suddenly she changed into Molly Mandy and I said, 'Do me a favour and ball Franklin.'

The music was getting slow, slower. Who was I dancing with? Carla Cassini, beautiful Italian movie star. She smelt fantastic, but ruined the whole thing with hairy armpits. 'You ees beeg man, yes?' 'I Left My Heart in San Francisco.' Was that Massey with Suki? And the zoftic blonde dancing with Hal? Hal never danced but he was swinging tonight. Who wasn't!

'My producer—he 'ave to return Roma for one day only, so I come to see you tonight. Good idea, yes?' She was an armful of woman. What about Alex? Would one more time be wrong? 'Who Can I Turn To?' She moulded her body into mine, rubbing a leg between my thighs. Christ, she caught me in the balls and it hurt. 'We must be careful,' she muttered, 'I am followed—'ee always has me followed.' Can't take my eyes off you. She churned her body into mine, keeping perfect time to the music.

'I stay at 102 Marlofield Street, a leetle 'ouse. You come in one 'alf hour to the back window—I arrange everything.'

Shit, man! Franco and the Italian waiters were hovering at the edge of the dance floor trying to get a better look.

'I go now,' she said abruptly, and left me standing there.

It never rains but it pours. I sat down.

Molly Mandy was hard at work whispering in Franklin's ear. He looked a bit stunned. Man, the room was turning. 'The Twang' appeared sitting next to me. 'How about tonight for old time's sake?' She whispered in my ear, wriggling her

150

tongue about in there at the same time.

Molly Mandy gave me a wink across the table. Massey and Suki came and sat down. A short fat guy who I didn't know came over to 'The Twang' and clamped a chubby hand on her shoulder. He had a cigar clamped between his teeth. 'You gonna stay with this jerk all night?'

'Oh, Chucky, sorry, I'll be right back.'

'You'd better,' he said.

'Who's that?' I asked.

'That's Chuck Van Marless Junior,' she said, 'the producer, I'd better get back.'

'So who's keeping you?'

She gave me a sad look. 'You're such a bastard, Tonee.'

Her voice got on my nerves. She wriggled her way back to Chucky junior, and the group she was with.

I love Alexandra. What number Marlofield did Carla say? After all I wasn't married—yet.

Franklin and Molly Mandy suddenly got up. 'We're going,' she announced with a big smile, flashing her gold fillings. Franklin studied the ground in embarrassment. At last, at last!

'What about my sister?' Suki said when they had gone.

'Where is your frigging sister?' I asked.

'She's here—somewhere. She saw some friends when we came in, but she'll be here soon and she thinks Franklin is her date.'

'Listen, baby,' Massey said, 'I don't think she's too anxious, you've been here an hour already and where is she?'

Suki shrugged. 'Let's dance.'

They went off, happy to be together again.

I couldn't remember the goddamn number—a hundred and something, a hundred and two, that was it. I was going. After all a movie star is a movie star, and what Alex didn't know wasn't going to hurt her. It certainly didn't mean I didn't love her. Anyway it's a well-known fact that fellows need it more than birds. So where did Fontaine come in then?

I grabbed a taxi, and remembering Carla's warning, had him drop me off in the square, where I wandered around looking for a hundred and two. It was impossible work finding the numbers, and pissing with rain, but I went from house to house peering at doors with my trusty cigarette lighter. Oh God, what one wouldn't do for a star!

I found it. I hoped she had some scotch and Coke. I needed

it. I pushed my way past clumps of trees to the back and started trying the windows. I was soaking.

Suddenly a light shone in my eyes and a loud voice said, 'I'd stay just where you are if I were you.' And then a big nasty copper loomed into view. 'What do you think you're doing then?' he enquired politely. One thing about our policemen, they've got lovely manners.

So there I stood wet through and just approaching a hangover in West London Central Police Station. Charming! The bloody copper had never heard of Carla Cassini, and nor had the couple who lived in one hundred and two Marlofield Square. Too late I realised it should have been Marlofield Street, but the sweet arm of the law didn't want to know about going along there.

I imagined Carla waiting for me in a clinging black slip, the sort of thing she wore in most of her movies.

I was in a right mess now.

Oh God, what a scene! After long arguments they finally sent someone round to check my story at a hundred and two Marlofield Street, and Carla, the bitch, denied she'd ever even heard of me!! So then more arguments until I finally got them to phone 'Hobo' and then Franco and Sammy came rushing over and identified me. Franco confirmed that Miss Carla Cassini had been in the club that night, and had been dancing with me, so they finally believed me and let me go.

Shit, man! Sammy was laughing so much that tears were rolling down his cheeks.

'I can just picture the scene,' he said, 'you trying to get in a window with an 'ard on, and the copper pouncing down on you!'

Oh very funny. Very funny indeed.

Franco was trying to look grave and concerned, wedged in the back of Sammy's E-type, but I knew as soon as we got back to the club the story was going to be all over.

'Now, I don't want this spread around,' I said grimly.

'Meester Blake!' Franco exclaimed in horror, 'I cut off my right arm eef I say anything.'

Lying sonofabitch!

TWENTY-NINE

FONTAINE

I sat and planned my revenge. It was about time Benjamin was taught a lesson. God almighty, he was treating me like a wife!

I got dressed and went out and bought the sable coat anyhow. Benjamin's credit was good, and they knew who I was. 'Send the bill to my husband's office,' I said, 'he always likes me to pick my own Christmas presents.' That would teach dear old Benjamin to say no. Doesn't the old fool realise how lucky he is to have a wife like me? I am beautiful, elegant, chic, famous. What more could anyone want from a woman?

Tonight, when he expects me to entertain his beastly son I shall make mincemeat of them both.

Oh no, old Benjamin can't expect to treat *me* that way and get away with it. First of all I intend to return to London tomorrow, with or without Benjamin. I will show him who calls the tune in *our* marriage.

My God, if he thinks he can push me around the way he used to treat his dreary first wife, he can think again.

I put on a white lace Courrèges cat suit. Roger came by and fixed my hair in a devastating style, then Adamo made me a champagne cocktail, and I awaited my darling husband's return.

He puffed in promptly at six, followed closely by Ben junior, who peered at me through owl-like glasses. 'Hello, Benjamin, darling,' I purred coldly, ignoring the son, '*so* sweet of you to call me back.'

'Did you see young Ben?' Benjamin said pointedly.

'Yes, I saw young Ben,' I replied in a sing-song voice.

'Fontaine, pull yourself together. We'll talk about it later.'

'There's nothing to talk about. Oh, by the way, I bought the coat—it's in the bedroom, it's absolutely divine. Thank you, darling.'

Benjamin's face sagged, but he was loath to argue in front of his precious son.

He turned brightly to Ben junior. 'Well now, what restaurant would you like to go to?'

'Anywhere, sir,' Ben junior replied, studying the floor in embarrassment at being caught in the middle of an argument.

'What about you?' Benjamin turned to me, desperately trying to keep the proceedings bright.

'I don't think I'll come.' I savoured his look of annoyance, 'I have a headache.'

There was a short delicious silence, then Benjamin said, 'Make yourself comfortable, Ben, have a drink, look at the magazines. I think there's a new "Playboy".' He winked at his son as only a decrepit old man can. 'Fontaine, why don't you come in the bedroom and show me your coat while I shower?'

Oh, I see. He was going to forgive me for buying the coat if I came out to din-din like a good girl and was nice to dreary boring son.

I was right.

Benjamin: 'Fontaine, don't be a bitch!'

Me: 'A bitch?'

Benjamin: 'You know what I mean.'

Me: 'What?'

Benjamin: 'The boy is very sensitive, don't hurt him, make him at ease.'

Me: 'And how about *me*? I'm sensitive too, especially when some goddamn little secretary won't even put me through to you on the goddamn phone.'

Benjamin: 'You must understand ...'

Me: 'So must you. I don't expect to be treated like that.'

Benjamin: 'Well, you have the coat now, so at least you can be civil.'

Me: 'Yes—I have the coat *only* because I ignored you and got it anyway.'

Benjamin: 'Please, Fontaine, for the boy.'

Me: 'He's not a boy, Benjamin, don't baby him. He's probably bored stiff at having to have dinner with us anyway, and so am I—very bored by the whole thing.'

Benjamin: 'I'll see you get the rest of the money you wanted tomorrow morning.'

Me: 'Oh, all right then, but just remember to *never* treat me like that again.'

Benjamin pleadingly: 'All right, Fontaine, but please let us have a nice friendly amicable evening.'

I hate Benjamin. I hate a man you can tread all over.

His punishment wasn't over yet, he would see. As soon as he comes pawing me, expecting to go to bed with me, he will just have to wait. Just as he had to wait before we were married. Oh God, I had him mad for it then, and that's just the way it's going to be again. He'll have to beg for it. On his knees. Poor old bastard.

THIRTY

TONY

Charming! Hauled down to the police station like a common criminal! Sadie would have a thousand fits if she knew. All over some bird that, if you want the truth, I didn't even fancy! Well, not much anyway. I mean if she hadn't've been who she was I certainly wouldn't have gone creeping down to Marlofield Square—Street—or wherever it was. Really I don't fancy anyone except my darling little Alex.

It is two o'clock in the afternoon, and I'm shaved and dressed (very casual—white sweater, black slacks, suede jacket). I am wondering what kind of jazz to take with me. A suit in case my darling wants to go out? Pyjamas? I don't even have any, on account of the fact that I always kip in the raw—lets the skin breathe, y'know.

In the end I bundled a couple more sweaters and my shaving gear in a bag. After all, a weekend in the country was bound to be slopping about.

I didn't feel too fantastic. Slight touch of your actual hangover. But I looked good, with some overnight tan all over my face. I could have just got back from the South of France.

Alex was waiting for me. Very pretty in a green trouser suit, and her hair sort of tied on top of her head and tumbling around her lovely little face. She had a huge suitcase and, blushing, she said, 'I'm taking all my dirty washing home!'

Sweet!

'Do you want some coffee?' she asked.

'Well, I've got the cab waiting.'

'Oh, O.K. Maddy won't be a sec.'

Maddy?!? Don't tell me she was coming with us. What a lumber!

She was. Maddy in a mauve trouser suit, with a big fat bottom, a John Lennon cap and plain face.

I had been looking forward to a nice quiet chat with my Alex, but it was not to be. On the train Maddy kept up a non-stop stream of unintelligent conversation, all about clothes and some schmuck called Jonathan and wasn't Christmas going to be absolutely 'super'. I gathered from the conversation that

156

Alex was going to spend Christmas at Madelaine's home. Charming! I would have to talk her out of *that*.

'Mummy always goes to St Moritz for Christmas,' Alex remarked to me—*finally* including me in the conversation, 'it's so lovely there with the ski-ing and everything. This will be the first Christmas I haven't gone with her.'

'Golly, only another week and I haven't bought *one* present yet,' Madelaine exclaimed, 'what on earth do *you* want, Alex?'

Alex laughed. 'Nothing actually. Where are you spending Christmas, Tony?'

Where *was* I spending Christmas? The Elephant and Asshole I supposed. 'Er, I haven't decided yet.'

As a matter of fact Sadie and Sam don't keep Christmas—I mean, nothing special. Usually on Christmas Day I get up late and wander over to the Hilton with whatever bird I happen to be with, and eat up their special Christmas lunch. It's very nice. Then I usually wander home, get into kip and watch the telly.

I fell asleep to the sound of the girls' chatter. I would get Alex alone later, I could wait.

'Wake up, we're here!'

I staggered off the train behind the girls, carrying Alex's enormous suitcase, Madelaine's ton-weight overnight bag and my carryall.

Tony the porter. The girls raced off up the platform and I followed. Alex threw her arms around a fair-haired woman, standing beside a station wagon.

She smiled at me when I came lumbering up with all the gear.

Alex said, 'Mummy, I should like to introduce you to Tony Blake.'

'Mummy' gave me a friendly smile. I could see where Alex got her beautiful brown eyes from. Her mother was an attractive woman, a lot better than any of the old birds Hal ever appeared with.

'So glad to meet you, Mr Blake. You'll have to excuse my daughter leaving you to carry everything, she has absolutely no manners.'

We all laughed. I liked 'Mummy'.

We reached the house, and I was shown around a bit, then left alone in a mahogany lined guest-room with an adjoining marble bathroom. What a house! Stables, swimming pool—the lot. Servants darting around everywhere, three cars in the drive. I had imagined poor abandoned 'Mummy' living in a sweet little cottage with a daily help. Really, I was a bit choked. How could Alex have a billionaire father, and a mother that lived like this, and still work as a crummy secretary? I couldn't understand it. Were they all dead mean or what?

A butler came in with my bag. 'Shall I unpack for you, sir?' he enquired, looking disdainfully down his long thin nose.

Oh shit, man—if Sammy could see me now! Oh boy!

'No, that's all right,' I said airily, thinking of my two crumpled sweaters and a clean pair of pants with a hole in.

'Are you sure, sir?'

'Yeah, I'm sure,' I glared at him, hoping he would go away.

'Can I fetch you a drink, sir?'

Now that was more like it. 'Yes, I'll have a scotch and Coke, plenty of ice.

'Scotch *with* Coca-Cola, sir?'

'Yeah—*with* Coca-Cola.'

'Very good, sir.'

Skinny old bastard, didn't know what it was all about, stuck down in the country.

I opened my only piece of luggage and wished to hell I'd brought a suit.

Alex and Madelaine had deposited me in this room saying gaily, 'We're going to change for dinner—see you downstairs at seven.'

I had nothing to change into except another sweater, and I was saving that for tomorrow. I had an awful feeling that I'd brought the wrong gear. I hadn't even been alone with my baby Alex yet. Where the hell was her bedroom, anyway? I'd have to know that for later.

Long Thin Nose came back with a tiny slug of scotch in a glass, a full ice bucket and a bottle of Coke.

I downed the scotch in one fell swoop. Then I changed sweaters and went off in search of Alex.

It was a huge bloody house with massive oak doors everywhere—all closed. I went downstairs and in front of a roaring fire I found 'Mummy' in a blue chiffon cocktail gown, with a red faced giant of an old chap in a dinner jacket.

'Ah, Mr Blake,' 'Mummy' said. I wished she would cut out the Mr Blake jazz. 'I'd like to introduce you to Doctor Sutton.'

I shook hands. Well, at least they were going out somewhere, all dolled up like that.

'Mr Blake is a friend of Alexandra's from London.'

'Oh yes,' said Doctor Sutton, 'how do you do—yes, London, I shall be going there in three weeks time. Friend of Alexandra's, hump? Very nice. Charming girl, just like her mother, y'know—charming. Yes—very nice, very nice.'

'Would you care for a drink, Mr Blake?' asked 'Mummy'.

'Yeah—I mean yes, thank you, lovely, er I wish you'd call me Tony.'

'Certainly.' She smiled, she had a smile like Alex, only it was a little worn round the edges.

She summoned Long Thin Nose who smirked knowingly at me and said, 'Scotch *with* Coca-Cola, sir.'

'Yeah.'

'Now that's a funny drink.' Doctor Sutton wasn't one to miss out on a bit of conversation. 'Very funny, you drown the taste of the alcohol with the carbonated drink. You may just as well drink plain Coca-Cola.'

I wished the old goat would get going, and where was my Alex? As if on cue she came giggling in with Maddy. Both of them wearing quite dressy outfits. It suddenly dawned on me that maybe dressing for dinner meant dressing up for dinner.

Maddy confirmed my suspicions, 'Haven't you changed yet, Tony?' she asked, just as Old Long Nose was bringing me my drink.

'Hush, Madelaine,' 'Mummy' said, 'Mr Blake doesn't have to change.'

'Oh gosh, Tony,' Alex interrupted, 'I forgot to tell you we always dress for dinner. I thought you would know ...' she trailed off lamely. 'Oh golly, I'm so silly, please forgive me, why on earth should you?'

Yeah. Why on earth should I know? After all I'm only a lousy ex-waiter. I felt like a right berk.

'Don't worry about it, Mr Blake. You look quite respectable as you are,' said 'Mummy'.

So I stood there with egg on my face while they all inspected my black and white striped (at least it was Simpsons) sweater and tight black trousers.

Madelaine stifled a giggle. What she needed was a good stiff kick up her backside.

'Dinner is served, M'Lady.' Old Long Thin Nose was back. I

thought scenes like this only existed in the movies.

We all trooped into the dining-room, Alex holding my arm and whispering, 'Sorry!'

The dining-room table was loaded with enough silver to sink a ship. It's a good job I was once a waiter—otherwise I'd never have known which knives and forks and jazz to use.

Dinner was a gas, Doctor Sutton entertaining us with a story about a patient of his with a terminal disease; 'Mummy' telling us about how she was coming up to town for the January sales and what she was going to buy; and Alex and Madelaine occasionally giggling together.

I was well and truly fed up. After dinner, which dragged on, there was coffee in the study, then everyone started yawning and 'Mummy' said, 'we'd better all have an early night if we're to go riding in the morning.' I tried to catch Alex's eye, but she was in a huddle with her girl-friend as usual.

'You do ride, don't you, Mr Blake?' asked Mummy'. I'd kill her if she didn't stop calling me Mr Blake.

I felt like saying—'Yeach, baby, I ride, but not the way you have in mind!' Instead I said, 'No.'

'Oh what a pity, but you can have a nice lie-in and we shall be back by lunchtime.'

Oh very jolly.

Everyone said goodnight to everyone else and the girls and I started upstairs while Mummy saw the Doctor out.

'Where's your room?' I hissed at Alex.

'Oh!' she looked flustered. 'Maddy's in with me.'

Charming! 'Then you come to my room.'

'Tony I *can't*, not here.'

I took her sweet little hand and squeezed it, 'I just want to talk to you, only talk I promise.'

My body was talking already, I was as hard as a rock.

'All right, I'll try.'

I gave her a kiss on the cheek as Madelaine stood and stared.

'Make it soon.'

She nodded, 'If I can.' And then she was off with her girl-friend.

What a lousy situation. I mean what a drag this whole thing was. I was choked. I looked at my watch. It was only nine-thirty. I hadn't been to bed at nine-thirty since I was ten!

I went to my room. No television, no radio, no telephone. Someone had turned the bed down and unpacked my bag. Well what the hell—so what: I didn't care what some thin-nosed butler thought of me.

I lay on the bed and smoked a cigarette—then another one, then another.

This was ridiculous, nearly half an hour and no Alex.

I couldn't bear the thought that she wasn't going to come. My body was in a nervous sweat already. I would give her another five minutes—ten minutes—fifteen minutes. Goddamn it! Nearly an hour and where was she?

I went into the passage. No sign of life, just a dim light burning.

Like an idiot I had no idea where her room was. I peered through the keyhole of the door next to mine, the room was in darkness. Then the next keyhole—it was a john—then the next—a cupboard. I was making great progress.

The passage curved round a corner, and there was a door with light showing under it. I bent down to peer through the keyhole and jerked back with astonishment. Naughty old 'Mummy'. She was spread out on the bed, yards of blue chiffon round her waist, legs high in the air, and crouched above her was dear old Doctor Sutton. 'Mummy' was a right raver.

I couldn't help smiling. What a scene! Doctor Sutton still had most of his clothes on—couldn't be too comfortable! Well, well, well. I dragged myself away from the keyhole—I was a doer not a watcher.

Now I felt as horny as old Harry. Where was my little Alex baby?

I went down the other end of the passage and started the keyhole routine again. Her room was in the same position as her mother's, but *she* wasn't. She was lying asleep in a divan bed with a small table separating her from Madelaine, also asleep.

I looked at her for a while. I felt a thief. She was breathing softly with the covers pulled up to her neck and her hair spread out on the pillow. I had such a feeling of LOVE.

I kept a wary eye on Madelaine, who was giving out with a few snores, and I gently pulled the covers off Alex. She was wearing a white frilly nightgown and she sighed and turned on to her back. I was eating her up with my eyes. My body was choking to hold her.

I put my hand on to her breast, so soft and still. Her eyelids fluttered and I quickly took my hand away. She opened her eyes. 'Tony!'

'Sssh.' I didn't want the girl-friend awake. 'What happened to you?'

She looked a bit sheepish. 'I *meant* to come to talk to you but I must have fallen asleep.'

Very flattering—I mean she really must have the hots for me.

'Well, come on,' I whispered.

'But it's so late, and what about Maddy?' she protested. All the same she climbed out of bed and slipped on a pink quilted dressing-gown.

I took her hand. 'Maddy's fast asleep, and I'll have you back in bed in no time.' She didn't realise I meant my bed of course.

We crept off down the passage back to my room, and she curled up in a chair and stared at me with those big brown eyes.

I paced about a bit and turned all the lights off except for a bedside lamp.

'What do you want to talk about?' she asked sweetly.

I stood behind her chair and stroked her hair. If I didn't have her soon I was going to explode.

'I'm sorry about dinner,' she said, 'I should have warned you we always dress. Mummy's a stickler for doing things properly.'

Yeah, baby!

'Alex,' I said, my voice strangled. I started to undo the buttons of her dressing-gown. She pushed my hands away.

'It's a shame you can't ride,' she said in a high little voice.

Oh but I can—I can.

My hands reached her beautiful breasts and I squeezed her nipples. She wriggled around in the chair, trying to get away.

'Stay still—relax,' I said. I was shaking, I wanted her so badly. I was a fine one to tell *her* to relax.

'What about "Mummy"?' she asked desperately.

I ignored *that*, and managed to slip her nightie over her head. Her hands flew to cover herself and she started to shiver.

'Come on, let's get into bed.' Then I played the strong man and carried her over and plopped her on the middle of the bed. She still had on a pair of white panties and she lay quickly on her stomach, so all I could see was her velvet smooth back, rounded bottom through the panties, and long knockout legs.

I ripped my clothes off. If I wasn't quick I was going to blow the whole set-up. I lay on top of her. Oh Man, I could have made it all over those sexy legs! But I gathered a little control and pushed myself between the back of her thighs. She tried to push me off.

'Please, please, stop it, Tony, I don't want to—*please.*'

Birds were always saying no when they meant yes. Then she started to cry, loud sobs, and I suddenly felt like the world's worst heel. This wasn't some bird I was on the make for. This was the wonderful girl I wanted to marry. 'Hey,' I got off her and cuddled her softly. 'Quiet, darling, easy, if you don't want to, we won't—no problem.'

She stopped crying, 'I'm sorry, Tony.'

She got up and put her things on, then I took her to the door and kissed her. She smiled at me. She looked like a little girl. 'Goodnight, Tony. Thank you.' Then she was gone.

Man, this was love. If I could give up what I just gave up I really had it bad.

And now I was left with a problem, and not even a 'Playboy' magazine in sight!

THIRTY-ONE

ALEXANDRA

Maddy woke me in the morning by pummelling my back until I was forced to open my eyes. I yawned. 'What time is it?'

'It's seven, and where on earth were you last night? I got up to go to the loo and you were gone. Did the devastating Tony drag you off to his room? I tried to stay awake for you to come back but you were ages.'

'I wasn't.'

'Oh yes, you were. Did he ravish your innocent girlish body?'

'Maddy, shut up, you sound just like some ghastly magazine.'

'Did he screw you, then?'

'Maddy!'

I went off to the bathroom before she could bag it, and took a cold bath. Mummy says cold baths are better for you than hot ones.

I tried not to think about the previous evening with Tony.

Maddy was all huffy when I finished in the bathroom.

'You've become very secretive,' she remarked coldly.

We had a breakfast of scrambled eggs and bacon with Mummy, then we set off riding. It was glorious fun. I had my own horse, Pinto, and she was so pleased to see me.

I felt guilty about last night, guilty about upsetting Maddy, and guilty about everything in general.

We were riding through the woods and approaching a stream when suddenly Pinto reared up and I came tumbling off.

'Ouch!!'

Mummy and Maddy had already crossed the stream, but they stopped, and turned back.

I felt all right, nothing broken, but when I tried to stand my left leg gave way and I felt an awful pain.

'I think you've got a nasty sprain,' Mummy said.

'Oh, Alex, how ghastly!' Maddy lamented.

They piled me back on to Pinto who was now standing quietly, and back to the house we all went.

Mummy sent for Doctor Sutton, who came immediately. He

is such a sweet old man. He brought me into the world and has looked after me ever since.

It was a sprain, and a nasty one.

'Off your feet for five or six days at least,' Doctor Sutton pronounced.

'Poor Alex,' Maddy wailed.

Mummy was very businesslike. 'Can't be helped. I think there's a two o'clock train to town that Mr Blake had better take. What about you, Madelaine dear? Do you want to stay or leave then too?'

I groaned. I was beginning to feel a bit sick and awful. 'I think you had better go back, Maddy. I'm not going to be much fun.'

'If you're sure, Alex. I'll stay if you like.'

'No,' I shook my head. Doctor Sutton had given me some pain killer and sleeping pills and I was feeling very drowsy.

'Come along, Madelaine dear,' 'Mummy' said, 'she'll be much better if she has some sleep.'

They went out of the room and my leg throbbed and my head ached and my eyes were closing.

THIRTY-TWO

TONY

Too bloody much! Sitting on another train next to best friend dear old Madelaine, without so much as a last glimpse of my adorable, wonderful little Alex.

'Rotten luck, isn't it?' Madelaine questioned for the sixth time.

I think she gets some sort of perverted thrill seeing me so choked.

'Yeah,' I muttered, wishing she would shut up.

'What will you *do* tonight?'

'What I always do on a Saturday night, go to the club.'

'Oh, you're so lucky. I'm left absolutely in the lurch, my boyfriend's away and I hate staying in the flat alone.'

Tough!

We had five minutes of beautiful silence, then—

'I say, Tony, could I come to the club with you. I'd be ever so good, stay out of your way and everything.'

I frowned. Who needed her?

'Well no, Maddy, it would be a real drag for you, you'd get shoved around all over the joint, Saturday night's a madhouse.'

'*Please*, Tony, I don't mind. I'm sure Alex would want you to take me. In fact she did mention something about us sticking together.'

Sticking together? What was *that*?

Shit—why had my little darling gone and fallen off her goddamn horse?

'That's settled, then?'

Christ! Didn't she ever shut up? The poor guy that ever got lucky would probably have to gag her while he had it off.

'All right,' I said reluctantly. I didn't want her carrying tales to Alex about how I wouldn't take her to the club. She prattled on about God knows what, I was bored by her chubby legs in patterned stockings, and her 'plum in the left cheek' voice.

King's Cross at last!

'Can I share your taxi, Tony?'

Caught once more. She talked all the way to Chelsea and left me with—'Can you pick me up about eight o'clock?'

Oh no, definitely no.

'Sorry, Mads, I've got to pop over and visit my mum and dad. If you want to come to the club I'll be there from about twelve.'

That should fix her. Her face dropped.

'What a shame. I thought we could have a super dins first.'

'Sorry, darling, duty calls.'

'Oh, Alex will be disappointed when I tell her.'

Anyone would think it was Alex I was turning down!

'Well, you know how it is. Maybe I'll see you later.'

I hopped back in the cab and muttered at the driver to get moving.

'See you later then,' Madelaine shouted bravely.

She didn't intend to give up, but I doubted if she would come waltzing into the club alone at midnight.

I felt pretty blue. I'd been feeling like a king the night before on account of that whole scene with my darling, but now she was lying injured in bed and they hadn't even let me see her before I left. Dragtime. I had decided to talk to her about our plans, get everything settled over the rest of the weekend. I certainly wouldn't have minded staying at the house while she was in bed, but 'Mummy' had Madelaine and me out of there like a shot out of a gun.

My flat looked worse than ever. I could never expect Alex to move in here, even to start off with. Maybe if we got rid of Madelaine I could move in with Alex. That would be all right for a start—great idea.

I was thinking of perhaps Caxton Hall for the wedding, do it quickly before anyone could object. I'd have to talk to her about it as soon as I saw her again, and when would that be? With randy old Doctor Sutton in charge, who knew?

Anyway—come Monday morning I am going to be out and looking for a new club premises. As long as Alex is away I may as well get *something* settled.

THIRTY-THREE

FONTAINE

Benjamin and I flew back to London in silence.

Our whole relationship has been based on silence ever since that ghastly evening out with Ben Cretin junior.

When we were coming in to land, Benjamin suddenly gripped my arm and said, white-faced and shaking, 'I want a divorce, Fontaine.'

Well of course I was astounded! 'You want *what*?'

He cleared his throat and I studied the network of tiny aged lines all over his face.

'I want a divorce,' he repeated.

I gazed out of the window completely at a loss. The old fool asking *me* for a divorce! How ironic. How humiliating. How dare he!

I smiled coolly. 'Sorry, old boy, but I don't think I care for that idea.' Inwardly I was in a burning rage.

'You have no choice,' he said sourly, 'I've had you watched.' He produced a thick wad of papers from his briefcase. 'I know *all* about you and Allen Grant and Tony Blake. I even have photographs.'

He handed me a glossy ten by eight of me and Tony on the bed in the New York apartment.

Oh my God, I looked awful, and Tony so hairy, like a great ape—ugh!

'Where did you get this?' I asked pleasantly.

'Adamo.'

'Oh!' That little bastard! I couldn't think properly. I had to get a lawyer immediately.

'There will be two cars meeting us at the airport.' Benjamin said, 'I have a suite at Claridges, and you may stay at the house until it's sold.'

My head was spinning. What had I done to this old man that he could treat me like this?

'Of course I will make you a reasonable allowance, though I don't have to, and we'll call the sable coat a farewell gift.' He stored his evidence back in his briefcase, and the wheels of the plane touched gently down.

For some utterly stupid reason my eyes filled with tears and

I said, 'But I thought you loved me.'

He looked at me seriously, 'And I thought you loved me.' He unclicked his seat belt and stood up, 'Goodbye, Fontaine. Good luck.'

THIRTY-FOUR

TONY

I had a good kip. Didn't feel like seeing anybody, so went to a movie on my own and arrived down the club early. There was nobody in yet. I sat down and told Franco to have the chef fix me a steak and chips. Flowers wandered in and sat down beside me. He looked moody and miserable.

'How's it going?' I asked.

Flowers shrugged. 'Not good man, not good at all.' He has a terrible habit of chewing on his fingernails, which he was busy doing now.

'What's the problem then?' I knew it was bound to be a touch, but I wanted to keep him sweet as I had plans for him and Tina in the new joint.

'I need a fast fifty, need it for Tina, she's gone and got herself in trouble.'

Charming! A touch is a touch, but fifty?

He chewed on his fingernails some more and I did some quick thinking. Flowers made twenty a week, so if I gave him the fifty and took half of his salary, it would take me five weeks to get it back. On the other hand I did want them with me when I went, and what better way to guarantee that fact than by having him in my debt? Besides which, I liked Tina, she was a good, hard-working kid.

'O.K. I'll get it for you. Monday all right?'

'Yeah, man, that's cool.' Flowers beamed all over his face. 'You're great, Tony. I knew we could count on you.' He rushed off to tell Tina the good news.

I have a couple of hundred pounds roulette winnings stashed away under my mattress. I guess I will have to dip into that: my emergency tax free bread—the best kind. I have definitely decided to take Flowers, Tina and Franco with me. A good team. Of course I can do it without them, but having them along will help.

Fontaine will be definitely choked when I am gone, she will soon see I was worth a lot more than fifty lousy quid a week. I don't give 'Hobo' ten days without me. The plan was to set the new place up, have it all ready to go, and then bye bye, Mrs Khaled.

Where is Mrs K. anyway? Still in New York, I hope, enjoying her strange scenes.

The bread people started to arrive and were placed carefully out of the way. Flowers put on an early Antonio Carlos Jobim album. One of the 'Must' arrived alone and sat down with me. He was about the most intelligent of the group, but always high on acid. We discussed sounds and how the police were always raiding his joint, but he was too smart for them—he kept all his gear buried in the garden!

'Where's Lissy?' I asked. Lissy was his flaxen-haired sixteen-year-old-freaked-out wife.

'She's taking a health bath in Germany.'

'Oh.' I mean what else do you say to *that*?

Sammy bounced in alone. 'I've been workin' me bleedin' balls off!' He announced, 'I'll have a scotch and coke.'

I got up to greet some faces. A well known politician and his new wife. Who should they be with but mumsy old Vanessa and husband Leonard. She smiled nervously at me, huge tits escaping from purple tulle. Leonard shook my hand, good clean masculine stuff. I had a feeling he couldn't stand me. In this business you get a pretty reliable sixth sense about things like that.

Everybody started to arrive at once, and Franco got busy sorting them all out and getting them in the right pattern. There were certain places where certain people would sit, and certain places they would not. Franco knew exactly, and he was great at arranging them all.

I stayed near the entrance, greeting, kissing, cuddling, flattering. Vanessa came out to the Ladies room and whispered. 'Can I talk to you, Tony?'

'Yeah.' Why all the hush? We were well out of sight of hubby.

'Have you heard about Benjamin Khaled?'

'Heard what?'

'Well apparently, and I know this from a very good source, my hairdresser actually.'

'Get on with it.' I was impatient.

'You must promise not to breathe an itsy-bitsy word of this to Fontaine. Do you promise?'

'Yeah, I promise.' She was impossible.

'Actually he's been seeing another woman, and not just any other woman—Delores! My dear, Fontaine will be beside herself with utter rage when she hears. She would never dream

171

Benjamin could stray. Isn't it too, too frightful?'

Without tits, I would never have looked at Vanessa in the first place, now even with them I couldn't fancy her. Gossip gave me a pain. Who the hell cared? Good old Benjamin, getting one back on Fontaine was the best thing he could do. And with Delores yet! Sensational new model, on the cover of you name it she's on it. Yeah! Fontaine was going to be double choked!

I patted Vanessa on her sexy fat bottom and winked. 'Don't believe it.'

'But it's true! Honestly Tony. Delores goes to the same hairdresser as me and I heard that...'

'Still don't believe it.'

She pouted. 'Nanny takes the children out every day between three and five as before. Why don't you pop in to see me?'

I shrugged. That scene was definitely over. 'Yeah, maybe.'

She laughed nervously. 'Don't say maybe, say yes.'

I was saved by Sammy appearing. ''Ere, any loose stock around?'

Vanessa gave him a look of distaste and disappeared into the loo.

Sammy chuckled. 'You've always got a bird 'anging around you. What you got that I 'aven't?'

One of the good things about Sammy is that you never have to bother to answer him.

The evening roared on. I stayed sober, rejected a few girls and felt pretty pleased with myself. I wasn't going to be unfaithful to my darling Alex. I didn't want to be, and I wasn't going to. There's true love for you.

Just before one, Madelaine appeared. 'I've had a simply dreadful time getting in,' she complained. 'I came at twelve and that ghastly foreign girl said you weren't here yet, and she wouldn't even let me in to wait. Then I came back and she *still* said you weren't here, so I waited 'til she wasn't looking and just came right on in. Really, I do think you should fire her.'

She looked lumpy in some sort of crochet dress, and a bit red faced. Tina had *strict* instructions *never* to let any unaccompanied bird in, especially if they asked for me. I sat her down next to Sammy who looked her over with some disinterest. I ordered her a Coca-Cola, wasn't getting *her* loaded. Then I did a fast vanish and sat down with a couple of fag songwriters who had the current hot show in town. Idle chat.

172

Then up to greet old time movie star, five feet tall. He looked like a giant on the screen. He was with 'The Twang', fast becoming everybody's date.

'Tonee babee,' she squealed, 'you're going to be so proud of me, I'm signed for two new movies. First "MUD" and then a picture with my gentleman friend here.' She squeezed old time movie star's arm and giggled. Her left tit reached his mouth!

I wondered if she'd still be available for me if I wanted her, or did she only put out for a part in a movie now?

'That's wonderful,' I said, phoney bastard that I am.

'Yes, isn't it though? I'm so thrilled, it's all so wonderful! Have you got a good table for us?'

All of a sudden she was talking to me like a waiter!

'Franco will see to you.' And I went out front, where Tina looked at me shyly. 'Thank you, Mr Blake.'

The poor kid was washed out.

'Why don't you go on home? One of the boys can come out here.'

'Mr Blake, I'm fine—really.'

I felt like taking off early myself.

'Tony!!' A shriek from a deep throaty voice. 'You old sexy bastard. How are you darling? Still the greatest fuck in town, I bet!'

It was Margo Castile, famous sex change ... lady ... I mean *he* was originally a fishmonger or something, but after many operations *she* was a well-known personality around town. Rather exotic, lovely looking, but with this deep butch voice and language like a fishwife. She was with two men, a small beaming Italian and a queer English actor.

'Well, Tony darling. When are you going to show *me* what you keep in those sexy tight pants?' She shrieked with laughter. She was always drunk.

'Yes, Tony,' the English actor lisped excitedly, 'when are you going to show Margo?'

I smiled weakly. I wasn't ready for *this* group tonight. We all went inside.

'I say, let's have an organised fuck!' Margo shouted. 'All those that want to join in, hands up!'

'Oh do shut up, you are awful,' giggled the actor.

I got them seated at a table and warned them to behave. Margo laughed and patted a pretty little blonde girl sitting at the next table. 'You're sweet,' she drawled, 'perfectly sweet! Do you fuck?'

The girl gasped and turned away. Margo roared.

Her language really was too much.

'Look, if you can't behave,' I said, 'I'll just have to throw you out.' I was always threatening her with that, but it never did any good.

'I promise to be a good girl,' she smiled at me, 'promise promise!'

She was a nut, but you couldn't help liking her. Back at my table, Sammy was chatting Madelaine.

' 'Ere, who is she?' He whispered.

I told him all I knew.

'Not much to look at, but I bet she's a lunatic in bed!'

He was welcome.

I suddenly decided the hell with it. I was going home. The place gave me a goddamn pain! I briefed Franco and quietly left.

Who needed it?

THIRTY-FIVE

FONTAINE

The old millionaire bastard can think again if he imagines he can treat *me* like this. Oh no, definitely not. I am not his ugly first wife, ready to be quietly discarded like a little white mouse.

Of course, the whole thing has come as such a surprise, although I should have realised as soon as he came to New York and wasn't ready to leap straight into bed with me, that *some*thing was amiss.

There must be another woman. A scheming money grabbing *bitch*! I go hot and cold with sheer and utter anger. *How dare he.*

And as for that Adamo. I shall see he never works anywhere again. How revolting to think of him watching me in bed. Where on earth was he hiding? And Tony, Allen. Were they in on it? I can't wait to phone my darling friend Vanessa. If there is gossip around, she will know of it.

As it was a Sunday I was forced to wait until at least ten to phone her, and then I got Leonard.

'She's still sleeping, Fontaine. We were out at your club last night. When did you get back?'

'This morning. How was the club? Anyone interesting?' Leonard then started to tell me a boring story about how Margo Castile had done a striptease down to brief bikini panties.

'Fantastic bosom,' he added, 'all there, just like a real woman.'

'Injections, darling, you too could have one like that. Although what you're worrying about bosoms for with your wife's mammoth proportions I don't know.'

He laughed, slightly embarrassed. 'I'll get Vanessa to phone you when she wakes. I'm sure you two have a load of gossip to catch up on.'

Did he know something?

I prowled around my house. My beautiful house that was up for sale. Oh just wait until I get in touch with my solicitor tomorrow.

Vanessa didn't phone until twelve.

'Fontaine, sweetie, how are you? When did you arrive?'

'This morning.'

'Oh, my dear, you must be exhausted!'

'No, I feel wide awake actually. I thought I might pop over and catch up on all the gossip. I'm sure there's lots of it. How are the children?'

'Who? Oh, the children, noisy as ever. I'm still in bed but I'd adore to see you. Come for lunch, Leonard's out golfing.'

'Divine.'

I was depending on Vanessa being able to tell me exactly what was going on.

I was right. She couldn't wait to tell me all about Benjamin and a ghastly scrubber model called Delores.

'Why on earth didn't you phone me in New York?' I demanded. My God, had I known I would have been in a much stronger position.

'I thought you would know,' replied my loyal friend, sloppy in a blue cashmere cardigan with a button missing.

'Apparently he's given her a huge emerald and diamond ring, a car and several fur coats.'

'How nice.' My voice was acid.

'What are you going to do?' Vanessa gushed.

I shook my head slowly. 'Divorce the bastard, and take him for every penny he's got.'

THIRTY-SIX

TONY

I have phoned my lovely Alexandra every day. But each time I get old hawk nose the butler or 'Mummy'. Both tell me Alex is fine, making wonderful progress, but can't come to the phone yet. Charming! Can't even speak to her. Today is the last straw. Phoned as usual and was told Miss Khaled had left to spend Christmas with the Newcombes.

It's Christmas Eve, pissing with rain, and miserable. I have spent a lousy week searching for a spot for the new place. Haven't come up with anything. The club has been a drag, everyone away for Christmas. Even old Sammy hasn't been in.

I miss Alex like mad, in *every* way. It is getting difficult not to take some bird home and bang her purely for physical reasons. Fontaine is back, but I haven't heard from her. On top of everything else I have a lousy cold.

I spent hours trying to find the Newcombes in the phone book. Why hadn't I been nicer to Madelaine? Now she was with my Alex somewhere, and I couldn't even phone. Choked! Mind you, I was a little bit cross with Alex. She should have phoned me or something. But then I remembered she didn't even have my number or address or anything. Oh well, get Christmas over with and then she'd be back, everything was going to be cool.

After Christmas Eve the club shut down for five nights, opening again on the night before New Year's Eve.

I got this horrible dose of flu and sort of collapsed in bed during that time. Ate out of cans and spent a really wonderful Christmas in a cold sweat and fever.

Sadie came over once with a jar of chicken soup and a lecture about how this was all due to too much sex. Too much sex yet!! Ha!! 'You live like a pig,' she said, 'when are you going to settle down, get yourself a decent job. You should see your cousin Leon now, living in a big house at Finchley, a lovely wife, baby on the way. When are you going to find yourself a nice girl that you're not ashamed to bring home to your mother?'

I was too sick to tell her about me and Alex, she'd know

soon enough. I gave her a hug and kiss and told her not to worry. 'I'll have a surprise for you soon,' I said.

Dear old Sadie, her one ambition in life was to see me married off so she could have a few grandchildren to cluck over.

A doctor friend of mine came by, gave me a shot and told a few dirty stories. The next day, I felt better and got up. I had wasted away five days.

Oh well, it got me through the holiday season anyway. What a drag *that* is.

I shaved, dressed and phoned Alex. *Still* no reply at her Chelsea flat.

I phoned Ian Thaine and he was out. I wanted to get hold of that contract. I was sure to find a property this week. I went over to the club and looked through the reservations for New Year's Eve. The place was going to be a mad-house—booked solid.

When the hell was Alex coming back?

THIRTY-SEVEN

ALEXANDRA

'Super to see you,' Maddy said, 'I have absolutely heaps of news.'

It was so good to be out of bed and about again. My ankle felt fine now and I was looking forward to spending Christmas at Maddy's house.

'Is Michael here?' I enquired anxiously.

'Coming down tonight, it's all over between him and that model girl, you'll be glad to know.'

'Oh,' My heart did a lurch. I couldn't *wait* to see him. 'What's it been like in London all alone? How's Jonathan?'

Maddy shrugged. 'All right. I say, Alex, I've met this absolutely awful little man and I'm simply *mad* about him!'

'Who?'

'Well after I got back to London, Tony insisted I went to "Hobo" with him. I think I was next on his list. Then I met this friend of his, quite old, a raging cockney, but *so* funny and frightfully sexy. I just couldn't help myself. I did the most ghastly things with him!'

'Maddy! What about Jonathan? And what do you mean you were next on Tony's list?'

'Oh, I think he just goes to bed with as many girls as he can, and I was to be the next victim. That's what Sammy says anyway. I saw Jonathan one night, but he was so dull. Sammy makes hats and I went to his office one day and he gave me two. Alex, he's Jewish. My mother would have a fit!'

'Maddy, I can't believe it. Have you actually—well you know...'

'Not exactly—everything but, though. I think I shall after Christmas. I promised him I would. He's frightfully pleased I'm a virgin. Oh, and, Alex, I have the most juicy piece of news. Sammy said that Tony and your dearest stepmother are having a violent affair. What do you think of that?'

I felt sick. How could I ever have let him touch me? It was obscene. How awful. He had probably been laughing at me all along. Perhaps he had even told Fontaine all about me. I shuddered.

'Maddy, you're kidding.'

179

'No, brownie's honour, Sammy told me all about it, said it's the only reason Tony is at "Hobo". Ghastly isn't it? I say, Alex, I thought we might pop down to the shops, get a few last-minute things.'

I shook my head numbly. 'You go, Mads, I've got a head-ache.'

THIRTY-EIGHT

FONTAINE

'Mrs Khaled?'

'Yes.'

'My name is Ian Thaine.'

'Yes?'

'Er—you do know who I am?'

'No, Mr Thaine, I do not.'

'About the new club, our new club, I mean Tony Blake has told you it's me that's putting up the money?'

'What new club?'

'The new club, the place that's going to take over from "Hobo". I thought perhaps you and I should meet since we're going to be partners.'

'Mr Thaine, I don't have the slightest idea what you are talking about, but it sounds interesting, perhaps we *should* meet. Tell me, are you anything to do with "Thaine" shops?'

'I am Thaine shops.'

'How nice. Perhaps you would care to come for tea today, about four. Oh, and Mr Thaine, don't mention anything to Tony Blake about our little conversation, let's just sort it out between ourselves first.'

THIRTY-NINE

TONY

New Year's Eve is a drag. They should print little badges with that slogan on and have everyone who feels the same way as me wear one. A poor excuse for a giant booze up, wreck up and fuck up.

The club was festooned with balloons, paper balls, party hats, blowers, the lot.

I got there very early, choked because I had finally got an answer from Alex's Chelsea flat, and Madelaine had informed me that Alex was out and wouldn't be back until late. Out where? She didn't know. Who with? She didn't know. How was she? Fine. Madelaine Newcombe is an up-tight cow. I left the club's number and my home number and told her to have Alex phone me the minute she came in. I was going to get some things sorted out fast. In fact I didn't see any reason why we couldn't get married at once, sort of nip into Caxton Hall or something and keep it a secret until the new club was all set. Great idea—maybe tomorrow—New Year's Day.

Really, thinking about it, it was the best way. Do it, then tell people. That way Fontaine couldn't try and stick her nose in.

Flowers appeared wearing yellow pants and shirt and embroidered sheepskin waistcoat.

'Very smart,' I said, thinking that some of my bread had ended up on his back.

He put on Sergio Mendes and went in the kitchen for some food. Not a bad idea, there was at least another hour until people would start arriving. I hadn't phoned Sammy, Massey, or any of the boys. They were probably at Steve Scott's party. I wouldn't go near the little bastard, although his wife (Ha!) had phoned while I was sick and begged me to come.

I had a steak and a couple of scotches—had to get in some sort of festive mood. Then a sheepish Franklin arrived with Molly Mandy—dressed—though only just.

She was beaming all over her face, and kept on throwing her arms round his neck and kissing him. He smiled politely. I guess he has finally blown his cherry!

Flowers launched into James Brown and the evening was beginning.

On New Year's Eve it all starts much earlier and by eleven the place was getting pretty jammed. Franco and his boys were doing a great job serving chicken in the basket and champagne —standard fare for the special entrance tickets. Ian Thaine had a table booked for ten, even old Sammy had reserved. The thing was to make it before twelve, and by eleven-thirty a stream of faces appeared. 'The Twang', Suki with Massey, three of the 'Must', a couple of film stars, two Members of Parliament, and the whole group of models, photographers, actors, who made up the scene.

Then Fontaine, looking really fabulous in some kind of fantastic coat. I hoped Franco had somewhere for her to sit as I didn't remember her name being down as having booked. Trust her to try and screw up the table plans.

'Funky Broadway' was blasting out, and I laid a smile on my face and went to greet her.

She gave me an ice cold look and brushed past, followed closely by Ian Thaine, then Vanessa, Leonard, and a whole tacky group.

'Hi, Ian,' I put out my hand. He squeezed it limply. 'I've been trying to phone you, you're always out.'

Vanessa edged forward and I kissed her on the cheek. Her face was flushed and she looked uncomfortable.

Where the hell is Franco? Some schmucky waiter is sitting Fontaine down with Ian.

'Get me Franco quickly,' I hissed to another waiter. Franco came running over, sweat streaming down his face.

'What's happening here?' I demanded. 'Get Mrs Khaled her own table.'

He rushed over to where they were all seated and spoke to Fontaine, then he rushed back to me and said, 'Is O.K., Mr Blake. Mrs Khaled is with Mr Thaine's party.'

'What?' I couldn't believe my ears. I stared over at the table and caught Fontaine's eye. She smiled coldly at me and then turned to Ian, beside himself with joy.

I had a funny feeling in the pit of my stomach that I had just blown a deal. Well, screw Ian Thaine and his millions. Who needed him anyway? I could find someone else, there must be lots of people who would be only too delighted to put up some loot for me. Yeah, but who?

Someone was throwing paper balls at me. It was the luscious

Carla Cassini, squeezed into a black dress with lots of bosom popping out.

' 'Ello, Tonee darling,' she purred gaily, sitting safely with her 'Producer' and several other people ' 'appy New Year!!' A whole group from Steve Scott's party came rolling in. I was getting loaded. What the hell.

Then Sammy with Madelaine—what a daily double *that is*! Then Alexandra, my wonderful precious baby had come to see the New Year in with me after all. I lifted her chin in my hand and smiled softly. 'Hello, my lovely.' She looked knockout in something pink and soft.

'Hello, Tony—you remember Michael Newcombe, don't you?'

Michael the schmuck. What the hell was he doing with her? 'Come on,' Maddy shrieked, 'let's sit down before midnight. I say, Tony, has Alex told you the super news, she and Michael are engaged! Can you imagine, we're going to be sisters-in-law!'

There comes a time in life when the bottom drops out. When everything just collapses and you don't care about anything. This was it for me. I stared at my Alex in disbelief, and she looked back at me with her big liquid brown eyes and I felt like I'd been kicked in the stomach by a thousand horses. I made it out to the kitchen and grabbed a bottle of scotch, drank from it until the fire burned through me.

I've never cried in my life. But the kitchen was so goddamned smoky and it gets underneath your eyelids.

Franco came in looking for me. 'Mr Blake, only five minutes to midnight.'

'Yeah, baby.' I was out of my skull. I weaved back inside and grabbed the nearest girl.

'Hey,' she protested as I dragged her up to the stand next to Flowers.

'O.K., everybody,' I yelled, 'make the most of it. Five more glorious minutes—drink up.'

The girl pulled herself away from me. 'My boy-friend will be choked,' she said dashing off.

I got a waiter and told him to get Miss Cassini up here to announce the New Year. Smiling, escorted by two waiters, she was soon beside me, her 'Producer' beside her. Flowers was just finishing 'Land of 1000 dances' and the streamers were flying, balloons popping.

'Here, count down from ten.' I handed Carla the mike and

she started to count—

'Nine, eight, seven.'

Why had Alex done this to me?

'Six, five, four.'

How *could* she do it?

'Three, two, one—'appy New Year everyone!'

'Auld Lang Syne' blared out and everyone was kissing and laughing and shaking hands. I grabbed Carla and forced my mouth down hard on hers. She struggled, and I bit her tongue. Pay the bitch back for that night.

She pushed me away, and her 'Producer' gave her a stream of abuse in Italian. I laughed and wandered into the crowd. Happy New Year. What was so bleedin' happy about it?

' 'Ere, Tony,' Sammy was calling me over, 'come and 'ave a drink with us.'

'Oh yes, do,' Madelaine urged.

Oh sure, sit and watch Alex and Michael gazing into each other's eyes.

'The Twang' appeared and I clung on to her, kissing her fleshy lips and pressing my leg between hers.

'What about you and me later?' I asked.

'Oohee, Tony, I can't. I'm with such an important director, and he says there may be a part for me in his next film.'

'Yeah, but I've got a part for you now.'

She giggled.

'Come on, come down to the office a minute, I've got something for you.'

She hesitated, then thought better of it. 'Another night, Tony, I really can't leave this very important director.'

Screw her then. The room was spinning. Screw everyone. I could give a good one to Fontaine now, I could really wham it at her the way she liked. I went over to her table.

'Happy New Year everyone.'

'Thank you, Tony,' Fontaine replied, twirling her finger in the champagne glass. 'Oh by the way, masses of luck with your new club, Ian has decided to become partners with me here, so count him out, but lots and lots of luck, I'm sure you'll do very well. Oh, and in the circumstances I think it's best that you don't work here any more. I've arranged for you to get two weeks' money, so you really needn't bother turning up after tonight.'

Oh God! Her face weaved and buzzed in front of me, mean cold eyes, thin lips. She ignored me and turned to speak to Ian.

They made a good pair. He didn't even dare look anywhere near me. I caught Vanessa peering at me, looking concerned, so I laughed. Didn't they all realise that the place would fold without me anyway?

The noise, the screaming, the bursting of balloons. People tangled up in streamers of coloured paper. I want my baby, Alex. Where is my darling girl?

I staggered out on to the balcony and shut in the gang bang. The cold air hit me like a punch and my eyes were running and I wished I hadn't drunk so much. I wanted to think clearly, sort things out.

I sat on the ground. It was spitting with rain. Nice. I'd lost my girl, I'd lost my club. What was I going to do? I sat there for a bit and then I thought. So what? There's other girls and there will be other clubs. Life is *great* baby. So I went back inside and drank, danced, shouted, burst balloons, and threw streamers, and drank and drank and drank.

Then Hal appeared with his old dreamboat Mamie.

'Hey, Tony, sweetheart, Mamie and I got married, say congratulations.'

I looked at Hal. The last of the great promoters had finally got caught. Mamie was smiling and clinging to his arm fondly. She could have been his mother.

'We flew in from Rome to sign some papers, I'm taking over the studio you know.'

What studio? 'Great!' I tried to smile.

Mamie beamed. 'Tony dear, this is my dear friend, Delphine Cohen from Miami. This is her first trip to Europe and Hally and I are going to show her the sights.'

Delphine Cohen was a dyed blonde, somewhere in her fifties. I nodded at her. She showed me a lot of teeth back. She was wearing a pale mink coat and lots of what looked like real diamonds.

We all sat down and I ordered champagne. Sammy came hopping over to see what was up. Mamie and Delphine went off to the Ladies room and Hal immediately grabbed a hold of me.

'Listen, Tony, don't be schmuck! I know it's not your scene but Delphine Cohen's old man practically *owned* Miami, and he dropped off with a heart attack six months ago, so she's hot as a pistol, raring to go. What are you going to do, hang around this joint all your life? Smarten up, fellow, look at me, I'm a big man now.'

I looked at Hal. He was so stoned his eyes held a permanent glaze.

Mamie and Delphine came back and we drank more champagne. Franco kept rushing over to me with minor dramas but I told him to stuff 'em. 'Hobo' wasn't my bag any more, let someone else run their ass off.

Delphine had plump arms with freckles on. I suppose she wasn't too bad for an older bird. Oh boy, more champagne. Much much more.

Mamie was saying, 'Tony, why don't you come to Rome with us for a few days. Hally's so busy now and we need a man to protect us on the streets. It's true what they say about the Italian men, poor Delphine's black and blue!'

Poor Delphine laughed and jangled a heavy diamond bracelet in time to the music. She was wearing a black dress cut wide and low to reveal a load of fat. I wondered if I could make it? I wondered if I *should* make it?

She was very suntanned, very lined, very over made-up, and very old-fashioned in her dress.

Hal gave me a wink. 'Yeah, come to Rome, baby, we'll have a great time. What do you say, Delphine?'

'Sure,' she smiled at me, 'wonderful idea. Will you come?'

Her eyes lingered on my face asking their own personal question. I stood up abruptly. 'Yeah, maybe, I'll have to see. Excuse me, got to see what's going on, I'll be back in a minute.' I rushed out to the desk.

'Happy New Year, Mr Blake,' said Tina.

A group of people were coming in, girls dressed up like Christmas trees, an agent and a well-known American actor. Automatically I went into the whole greeting bit. One of the girls was fantastic, long dark hair with pearls in, a white-fringed trouser outfit, staring green eyes. Someone introduced us, she smiled at me and licked full pink lips. I felt a familiar stirring, which I knew I should be keeping for Delphine Cohen. The girl's name was Miranda. I asked her to dance. The agent and the actor had three other girls with them, so nobody minded. Flowers was freaking out on Clarence Carter and I gave him the signal and he switched to Jose Feliciano's 'Light my Fire'. Miranda was tall and soft in my arms. I held on to her tightly. To hell with Delphine Cohen and all her loot, I wasn't getting caught in one of those sick scenes again.

So I'll be busted out. So what? Something will come along, something that I won't have to sell myself for. And if it

187

doesn't? Well, that's life. I can always wash dishes.

The girl in my arms isn't Alex, but she is certainly a beautiful girl. Creamy skin, and bright eyes.

'I wasn't expecting to meet anyone like you tonight,' I whispered, pulling her a little closer.

'Me neither,' she said, laughing softly. 'I only flew in from New York yesterday. I thought Englishmen had this reputation for being all uptight and stuffy.'

'What do you think now?'

She just pushed her body hard against mine. We danced and danced. Hal and his group eventually left. 'Schmuck!' he came up and muttered to me, 'you're blowing a great set-up for another din-a-ling.'

Fontaine swept out after three with her entourage. Ian Thaine thin and smirking at her heel.

I didn't see my Alex go. I didn't want to, I just wanted to forget her.

Miranda and I left at six in the morning. She was trailing a load of balloons and we walked through the deserted streets to my pad.

I loved her face. It was serious and sexy. She had a boy's firm body with lovely small breasts, and I had to push her long dark hair away to kiss them.

'I just got disengaged when I left,' she said as I explored her with my hands, 'my fiancé could only make it in group scenes. Ugh! I hated that. My daddy said I should fly off somewhere and forget about him. He certainly knew what he was talking about. Oh I love *that*!'

'My fiancé just got engaged to someone else.'

'Oh how awful. Oh, oh, oh—do *that* again! You should come to New York to forget.'

'Yeah.' I climbed on top of her. She was a gorgeous girl. 'With what?'

She wriggled around. 'Hey, Tony, you're *fantastic*! That is *too* much!! Listen. I know. You can come and work for my daddy, he's got all sorts of businesses. Oh—wow! Happy New Year! Baby, baby, baby! Do that again. We've got this insane disco in New York called "Picketts" that would be just right for you and, ooh, Tony, that's so beautiful, so *wild*. I love it! I love it! Like yes! Wowee, Tony—you're *such* a stud!'

188

FILMS & TV

0352	Star	
397756	**THE ARNHEM REPORT** Iain Johnstone	60p
396881	**A STAR IS BORN** Alexander Edwards	60p
398256	**CANNON: THE FALLING BLONDE** Paul Denver	50p*
398728	**CANNON: IT'S LONELY ON THE SIDEWALK**	50p*
396687	**CARQUAKE** Michael Avallone	60p
397349	**COLUMBO: ANY OLD PORT IN A STORM** Henry Clement	50p*
398183	**COLUMBO: A CHRISTMAS KILLING** Alfred Lawrence	45p*
300795	**COLUMBO: THE DEAN'S DEATH**	40p*
30006X	**THE CREATION OF KING KONG** Bruce Bahrenburg	60p*
395613	Hazel Adair and Peter Ling **THE CROSSROADS COOKBOOK**	70p
30099X	**DIRTY HARRY** Phillip Roch	60p
396903	**EMMERDALE FARM (No. 1) THE LEGACY** Lee Mackenzie	50p
396296	**EMMERDALE FARM: (No. 2) PRODIGAL'S PROGRESS** Lee Mackenzie	60p
395974	**EMMERDALE FARM: (No. 3) ALL THAT A MAN HAS . . .** Lee Mackenzie	60p
397489	**ESCAPE FROM THE DARK** Rosemary Anne Sisson	50p
395575	**THE GREAT HOUDINIS** Mel Shavelson	60p
398493	**HAWAII 5-0: THE ANGRY BATTALION** Herbert Harris	50p*
300876	**HAWAII 5-0: SERPENTS IN PARADISE**	45p*
397500	**INSERTS** Anton Rimart	60p.

†For sale in Britain and Ireland only.
*Not for sale in Canada.

0352 Star

397438	**KOJAK: GIRL IN THE RIVER** Victor B. Miller	50p*
397357	**KOJAK: GUN BUSINESS**	50p*
397446	**KOJAK: MARKED FOR MURDER**	50p*
398671	**KOJAK: TAKE-OVER**	50p*
398957	**THE MARRIAGE RING ("COUPLES")** Paddy Kitchen & Dulan Barber	60p
397276	**MURDER BY DEATH** H. R. F. Keating	60p
397470	**ODE TO BILLY JOE** Herman Raucher	60p*
301198	**THE QUEST** G. S. Madden	60p
398191	**THE ROCKFORD FILES** Mike Jahn	50p*
398981	**THE SENTINEL** Jeffrey Konvitz	70p*
398442	**THE SIX MILLION DOLLAR MAN 3: THE RESCUE OF ATHENA ONE** Mike Jahn	45p*
398647	**THE SIX MILLION DOLLAR MAN 4: PILOT ERROR** Jay Barbree	50p*
396490	**SIX MILLION DOLLAR MAN 5: THE SECRET OF BIGFOOT** Mike Jahn	60p*
396660	**SPACE 1999 (No. 1) PLANETS OF PERIL** Michael Butterworth	60p
396652	**SPACE 1999: (No. 2) MIND BREAKS OF SPACE**	60p
396075	**SPACE 1999: (No. 5) THE TIME FIGHTERS**	60p

†For sale in Britain and Ireland only.
*Not for sale in Canada.

0426	Tandem	
180240	**AT THE EARTH'S CORE** Edgar Rice Burroughs	50p
180321	**THE LAND THAT TIME FORGOT** Edgar Rice Burroughs	50p
164164	**LENNY** Valerie Kohler Smith	50p*
16184X	**ONEDIN LINE: THE HIGH SEAS** Cyril Abraham	60p*
132661	**ONEDIN LINE: THE IRON SHIPS**	60p*
172671	**ONEDIN LINE: TRADE WINDS**	60p*
168542	**SHAMPOO** Robert Alley	50p*
0426	Target	
11826X	**SINBAD AND THE EYE OF THE TIGER** John Ryder Hall	70p*
0446	Warner/Wyndham	
883662	**THE ENFORCER** Wesley Morgan	60p
765015	**MAGNUM FORCE** Mel Valley	60p
893617	**THE MAKING OF 'THE HERETIC'**	65p

†For sale in Britain and Ireland only.
*Not for sale in Canada.

Wyndham Books are obtainable from many booksellers and newsagents. If you have any difficulty please send purchase price plus postage on the scale below to:

Wyndham Cash Sales
P.O. Box 11
Falmouth
Cornwall
OR
Star Book Service,
G.P.O. Box 29,
Douglas,
Isle of Man,
British Isles.

While every effort is made to keep prices low, it is some-times necessary to increase prices at short notice. Wyndham Books reserve the right to show new retail prices on covers which may differ from those advertised in the text or elsewhere.

Postage and Packing Rate

UK: 22p for the first book, plus 10p per copy for each additional book ordered to a maximum charge of 82p.
BFPO and Eire: 22p for the first book, plus 10p per copy for the next 6 books and thereafter 4p per book. **Overseas:** 30p for the first book and 10p per copy for each additional book.

These charges are subject to Post Office charge fluctuations.